Wight Moon

BY

Elaine Berry

With Best Wishes
Elaine Berry

First Edition
published in Great Britain 2010 by Elaine Berry

The moral right of Elaine Berry to be identified as the author of this work has been asserted.
Email: **wightmoon@onwight.net**

This book is dedicated to the memory of
Alison Sowerby,
A true friend.

*The fairy who reached for the stars
and became an angel.*

And also to
Bill Berry BEM
A loving father-in-law

Acknowledgements

I would like to thank the following people for making this book possible: Keith and Shelly who initially gave me the necessary information, drive and enthusiasm to go for it; Tracey Hook, who had to put up with my constant medical questions; Brian and Kay Marriott, for their fantastic artwork for the cover; Carol Trow, for her hard work correcting all my spelling and grammar mistakes (believe me, I kept her busy); M J Trow, for his help and support to a new author, and for his book review.

My special thanks go to my husband John, who had no idea what I was up to – thank you for not being nosey whilst at the same time supplying me with plenty of sandwiches and coffee. I hope that this didn't come as *too* much of a shock to you.

Thank you also to Michael and company for allowing me to tell some of their story.

CHAPTER ONE

It was a late winter evening when Ann Grayson walked out of the Medical Centre, out into a cold night that was about to change her life forever. She found it ironic that they should build a new Medical Centre right next to a large cemetery; it tended to remind people of their own mortality when they had just been diagnosed with some sort of illness. Fortunately, Ann was only suffering from a chest infection, along with most of the people on the Isle of Wight at the moment.

The car park didn't seem to have a lot of lighting for its size and Ann was having trouble finding her car keys in her bag. 'One of these days I *will* buy myself a smaller bag,' she muttered to herself as she stumbled along the car park. Because there had been a lot of patients in the centre, Ann had had to park right down the slope in the bottom end. 'At last! Why is it that everything you are looking for is always at the bottom?' she cursed, through a coughing fit.

Half way down the slope she suddenly stopped. For a moment, she thought that she had heard what sounded like a child's whimper. Now all she could hear was a slight winter breeze blowing through the trees.

'Now I'm hearing things,' she coughed, 'and talking to myself.'

Ann walked on, nearer to her car looking forward to a nice hot bath and bed. Her chest and back were sore and all she wanted to do was sleep.

All around the car park was a brick wall, which separated her from a small reservoir on one side and the cemetery on the other. She was about to open her car door when she heard laughter coming from the cemetery followed by the cry of a small child, *I did hear it,* she thought.

Nervously she crept forward through a gap in the wall and looked around. If it hadn't been for the small child's cry she wouldn't have gone through of course. Having just moved from a rowdy part of Yorkshire, she knew better. Her parents had assured her that living on the Isle of Wight would be a lot more relaxing. They had moved to the Island some fifteen years previously, after Ann herself had got married. She had spent many happy holidays on the Island, and it was here that she had sought sanctuary, after her divorce.

As she inched her way forward, she could just make out some of the gravestones from the lights in the car park. Then she saw them; there were three figures, in the shadows. From the sound of their voices she could tell they were teenage youths. They were taunting someone, but she couldn't see who.

'You shouldn't be on this Island, you don't belong here,' one of the youths cried angrily as he picked up a large tree branch and broke it over his knee.

Panic set in as she heard the cries again. Before she knew what she was doing, she had crammed her car keys into her coat pocket, picked up a large tree branch of her own and was running across the cemetery towards them. This Zulu like war cry came out of her mouth trying to make herself sound menacing. Fortunately because of the lack of light the youths had no idea what was coming towards them and took off as if the very devil was after them.

She heard movement behind her and spun around, 'Oh my God,' she whispered to herself.

Sitting, curled up against a gravestone was a slim young child of about six years old with long blond hair, shaking like a leaf and crying. She was dressed in a white nightdress, pink dressing gown and slippers. Ann couldn't move at first, trying to decide if the child was shaking from fear or the cold. But the thing that shook her most was the little girl's features, which slowly appeared as her eyes became accustomed to the shadows. The bright red eyes were piercing and the strange ridges across her forehead made her look like she was from outer space. But Ann knew that this child was no alien, but used to be human. She had heard a brief mention about the Island Vampires, from one of the removal men. He had said, 'If you can cope with the ghosts and the vampires, you will love it here.' She had thought he was joking, until now.

Ann took a deep breath and tried to calm herself, 'It's alright', she said, in as calm a voice as she could manage 'I'm not going to hurt you.'

She dropped the tree branch and removed her coat then slowly inched her way towards the shaking child, who was very much alert. 'You must be frozen. Here, put this around your shoulders. My name is Ann, what's yours?'

The little girl didn't answer; she just opened her mouth slightly to reveal her fangs and hissed at her.

'Please' Ann said, 'I only want to help you.' She crouched down low; thinking that this would look less threatening. The result was a throbbing headache and she could hear her own heartbeat, booming through her ears. She started to pray that the child's parents were not close by. Now that would really upset her day.

Slowly the little girl's features returned to normal, to reveal a sweet child with blue eyes. Of course she knew that if all the horror movies were true. This child could turn at any moment and tear her throat out, but Ann tried to remain calm in case she could smell her fear. The little girl slowly reached out her hand and smiled.

'Mary,' she said sweetly, 'my name is Mary,' Ann took Mary by the hand and gently brought her closer towards her; she was frozen. Was this normal for a vampire? The coat was soon placed around Mary's shoulders, and then Ann stood up and felt a little dizzy. She was also feeling the chill of the late evening air now that she was coatless. Then another coughing fit struck her.

'Where do you live?' Ann asked, once she had got her breath back.

'Not far,' came the reply. Then several thoughts struck her all at once.

Am I really planning on taking Mary home and what will I say to her parents? Will I end up being their next meal? Now it was her turn to start shaking. *Please let it be a house, I'm too ill to go into a crypt,* she thought. They both walked through the cemetery. Ann started to formulate a plan in her head. *When we get there I will leave Mary outside, that way I can avoid any confrontation,* she thought. But sometimes even the best-laid plans don't work out the way you expect them to, do they?

Ann let out a sigh of relief as they left the cemetery grounds. *Phew, no crypt, that's one good thing,* she thought to herself.

They crossed the road and began to walk down the street. 'So what were you doing in the cemetery, in your nightdress, Mary?'

'I don't know,' came back the matter of fact reply.

Well so much for that conversation, Ann thought to herself.

They walked hand in hand down the road and passed the mini supermarket until they came to a small stone built cottage, up a side street on the right. It was very close to the road and had a low stone wall around it and to one side there was a gate. Mary held on tight to Ann's hand and pulled her through. There were lots of bare rose bushes about, tightly packed around the path which would make the cottage look delightful in summer.

Before Ann could pull away from Mary and bid her goodnight, she had tried the door and found it locked and was now shouting through the letterbox 'Uncle Michael!' Mary had a tight hold on her hand as if she had just brought the shopping home. All Ann could think was, *I'm going to die!*

After a moment she could hear someone coming towards the door. There was a noise that sounded like someone had just stood on a toy, 'Oh damn it!' said a male voice from the other side, then she heard a key turning in the lock.

'Well, you're okay now, Mary,' she said in a panic. 'Give me back my coat and I will be on my way.' But she had left it too late, the door opened.

Standing in the doorway was the most handsome fair-haired hunk that Ann had ever seen. Standing about six feet tall, he was wearing gray tracksuit bottoms and a tight black tee shirt, which showed off his muscular form. Although slightly overweight, she could tell from his arms that he obviously worked out. He had a round face, which was clean-shaven. Ann immediately fell into his deep blue eyes, and for a second or two, was mesmerised.

'Oh Mary not again. Come on let's get you inside.'

Ann suddenly woke up, hearing his soft voice. 'I found her in the…ceme…tery' her voice trailed off as the handsome hunk led Mary inside and down the hallway, leaving the front door open. 'Well thank you Ann, for bringing Mary home safely, don't mention it,' she grumbled under her breath and started to cough. 'Oh no,' she croaked as a sudden realization hit her. 'Err excuse me my car keys are in my coat pocket,' she called out.

Before she realised, the handsome hunk had returned to the door with her coat over his arm. She couldn't remember him walking back down the hallway towards her; one minute she was looking into an empty hall, the next she was looking into his deep blue eyes. Her heart was threatening to burst through her ribs; she felt dizzy and her knees were beginning to give way. She didn't know if it was those eyes, fear, or her body finally saying, enough is enough, now take me home.

'I'm sorry' he said gently, 'I had to get Mary indoors as soon as possible. She's very shy around strangers, well normally anyway.'

'That's okay,' she dreamily answered. 'May I have my coat back please?'

'Of course you must be frozen. Would you like to come in and warm up for a while first?'

Before she could answer, another coughing fit hit her and she couldn't breathe, Michael went to catch her as her knees finally gave way. *Oh crap,* she thought, as she slumped into his arms and everything went black.

Michael managed to catch her with one arm; he let the coat fall to the floor then scooped his other arm under her legs and lifted her without any effort. He could hear that her heartbeat was slightly on the fast side but steady; her breathing however was slightly laboured. Of course he knew what the problem was straight away.

'Mary,' he shouted,

'What,' came a tiny voice from the kitchen?

'Will you close and lock the front door for me, then bring my bag up to my bedroom please.' Mary let out a can't-be-bothered sigh. She had just been into the fridge and helped herself to a nice cup of blood and retrieved some rusks from the cupboard. She was cold and hungry. But what she didn't know was, Ann, who had helped her, was now fighting a battle of her own, and needed help.

Michael carried Ann up the narrow cottage stairs and into his bedroom with no effort at all. He laid her down onto his bed gently then propped her up slightly with the pillows. Mary followed, a few minutes later, carrying a black bag, which was nearly as big as she was.

She stared wide-eyed at her uncle from the doorway. 'You didn't have to do that,' she yelled. 'There's plenty in the fridge.'

Michael looked round at her disgusted. 'I haven't bitten her,' he said slowly and calmly. 'She collapsed on me. Thank you for bringing my bag up. When you have finished your drink you can go back to bed.'

'How did you know I was raiding the fridge?' she said sheepishly.

'Because, I heard you, it doesn't matter how quietly you do it, I have good hearing remember. And, you always seem to work up an appetite after you've been sleepwalking.

'Oh,' Mary said, as she disappeared from the doorway and went back downstairs.

Michael opened up his bag and took out his stethoscope; he then very gently removed Ann's polo neck jumper, only to find a long sleeved t-shirt on underneath. *Ah well, it is cold outside* he thought. So he

9

set to and removed that as well, only to find another, this time short sleeved t-shirt under that. 'God, this is like playing pass the parcel with Mary,' he muttered to himself.

Finally he got to the bottom of it and reached her bra. Putting the stethoscope to his ears he listened to Ann's breathing. Although he could hear her heartbeat and breathing without a stethoscope, he needed to work out how much fluid she had in her lungs. He could hear that there was quite a lot in there but it wasn't too bad. Next, he removed a thermometer from his bag and placed it under her arm; after what seemed only moments, it bleeped. 'Well that explains why you've passed out on me, you're running a temperature,' he whispered to her. Michael then removed her shoes, thick socks and trousers and covered her with the lightweight duvet to make her more comfortable.

He sat on the bed looking down at her. She was slim, about five foot two with long, wavy, dark brown hair. He had noticed before she had passed out that she had a slight oriental look about her, due to her brown deep set eyes. It suddenly occurred to him that he didn't even know her name. While he was thinking, He heard Mary coming back up the stairs.

'Mary, did this lady tell you her name?'

'Yes, it's Ann.'

'Did I hear her say that she found you in the cemetery?'

'Yes.'

'Which direction did she come from?'

'The hole in the wall that leads to the car park,' she replied. Michael then realised that she had come out of the medical centre. Therefore hopefully she may have some antibiotics with her.

He went back downstairs and picked up her bag which was still laying in the hall, soon he found what he was looking for and returned back upstairs with a glass and bowl full of cold water, collecting a flannel from the bathroom along the way.

Mary joined him in the bedroom and told him what had happened. How she had woken up sat on one of the graves, about the three boys and how a screaming banshee had saved her.

Michael laughed. 'Did she see you change?'

'Yes, she did,' Mary, said worriedly.

'And yet she brought you home safely, knowing what we are, that's one brave girl,' he said. He knew from her accent that she wasn't an Islander so she wouldn't know much about the Island vampires.

There may be trouble when she wakes, he thought, to himself.

Michael took Mary into her small room and tucked her into her coffin for the second time that evening. 'This time I'm not only locking your window I am taking the key with me,' he said.

'No please don't' she cried, what if I have another nightmare?'

'I will hear you. I will only be in the next room with our patient,' he emphasised.

'You didn't hear me last time,' she whined.

'That's because I fell asleep downstairs after a long day at work, and instead of kicking off, you jumped out of the window! Now try and get some sleep I *will* be close by.'

Mary gave him a hug and rolled over as he closed the lid. She was the only vampire on the Island who slept in a coffin; it made her feel secure after the house fire that had killed both her parents.

He returned to his bedroom. Ann was still sleeping, but he knew he would have to wake her to get some antibiotics inside her and plenty of water. 'Well, here goes,' he said to himself, under his breath.

He sat on the bed and started to bathe her face with the cold water, trying to bring her temperature down and bring her around. While he was doing this he started to talk to her gently. He knew that if he could stir her subconscious he could get inside using his powers of suggestion and bring her forward.

'Ann, can you hear me? Come on, concentrate on my voice and latch onto it.' He wet the cloth in the water once more and applied it to her forehead. He did this several times until eventually she started to stir. 'That's it' he said gently. 'It's okay, I'm not going to hurt you, that's it, come back to us.'

Ann slowly opened her eyes. Everything was slightly fuzzy at first and she wanted to go back to sleep, but she could hear a voice trying to wake her. She looked round through sleepy eyes and couldn't work out where she was; she remembered having a strange dream but couldn't remember what it was. As she tried to focus, she became aware that there was a weight on the bed at the side of her.

'*Ahhhhhhhh*,' came the scream. It took Michael by surprise he didn't expect such a strong reaction so quickly. At the same time there was a loud clatter from the next room and he knew Mary was up again.

He placed his hands firmly on each side of Ann's face. 'It's okay, calm down, I'm not going to hurt you.'

The scream had hurt her throat and she started coughing again;

it had also hurt Michael's ears. He sat her up against his chest and started rubbing her back, and then he reached for the glass of water and lifted it to her lips.

'Oh my God! You took my clothes off!' she cried.

'I had to; you're running a high temperature. I needed to bring it down and bring you around, so that I could get some antibiotics inside you.' Ann sat there for a few seconds, staring into his eyes. 'I'm Michael Moon, by the way, I'm a doctor, I didn't get a proper chance to introduce myself.'

'You're a doctor!' She said totally baffled. 'Of what?'

'Medicine. I'm an orthopaedic surgeon at the hospital.'

'What? But... I... thought... that... I... saw,' she said totally confused, pointing to Mary who was now standing in the doorway.

Michael stood up and walked towards the wardrobe, where he took out a large t-shirt, he then put it back, having realised that it was one that his brother had given him as a joke, and didn't think that it was appropriate for her to wear, so he found another. 'Here, put this on, It will make you feel less exposed,' he said kindly. Then he handed her the antibiotics that he had taken from her bag. 'You had better take these, and have a good drink. Mary told me what had happened, whilst you were unconscious. I put two and two together and realised that you had been coming out of the doctors; when you heard Mary's cries. I found those in your bag.' Ann took the tablets from his hand.

'Thank you,' she said, quietly. Then promptly took the tablets and had a good drink.

'Mary please go back to bed or you'll be really tired in the morning when Aunt Sadie comes to pick you up.'

'I can't,' she replied. Her uncle looked at her. 'When Ann screamed, I jumped, and my lid came off.'

'Her what came off?" Ann asked, looking at Michael, rather baffled.

'Nothing. Excuse me. I'll go and tuck her back into bed.'

Ann found herself alone trying to piece together the events of the evening. *Did I imagine what I saw in the cemetery? If I did, why were those youths taunting Mary? A vampire can't be a surgeon can he? This is stupid; vampires don't exist.* She picked up the glass and had another long drink. *I must have been hallucinating all along*, she thought. *What am I doing here? I should be going home, I should be in my own bed. My car is still in the doctor's car park.* All of these things were swimming around in her head as she sat there in someone else's bedroom. *I must go home,* she thought.

She got out of bed and tried to walk towards her clothes. Her legs wouldn't co-operate, but she took a deep breath and pushed herself along. She started coughing again but managed to calm it down. *I really must get dressed and get out of here, before he comes back,* she thought. As she battled against her own body, she knew there was something not quite right about all this.

'Going somewhere,' a voice sounded behind her and made her jump.

Oh crap, she thought, for the second time that evening. She turned round and sat on the chair where her clothes were. 'I really must go home,' she said.

'How?' came the answer. 'You can't possibly walk, I assume your car is still in the car park and I can't take you home in case Mary goes on a walk-about again.'

He began to walk towards her and she shrank back away from him.

'I don't mean you any harm, and I don't believe I have actually thanked you for rescuing Mary.'

'Why were they taunting her?' she asked.

'You don't remember?'

'I think I do, but I must have been mistaken.'

'Let me help you back into bed,' he said, changing the subject, as he held his hand out to her, and smiled.

'Why are you doing this?' she asked.

'You collapsed on me, remember. You can't take yourself home and I can't leave the house, so come back to bed, please.'

She took his hand and allowed him to help her back to bed. 'Don't worry there's a couch downstairs. I won't haunt you all night.'

'Why does Mary sleep walk?' she asked.

Michael looked at her and took a deep breath. 'She was my sister's daughter. There was a house fire; I managed to rescue Mary but my sister, Alice, and her husband David, perished.'

'I'm sorry, I didn't realise,' she said sadly.

'Mary still has nightmares about that night and sleepwalks. After I'd got her to bed this evening, I fell asleep downstairs and didn't hear her leave the house. Which is a rarity. I have good hearing, but I had had a busy day at work. I didn't know she was gone until you brought her back.'

'How did she get out?' Ann asked baffled. 'The door was locked.'

'She lets the latch drop,' Michael answered. He couldn't tell her that she could climb out of the window, without the aid of a tree or a drainpipe. It was so obvious that she wasn't sure what she had seen in the cemetery. He didn't want to frighten her. 'At least allow me to look after you for a while. I'm on call for the next few days, but hopefully, no one will need me. I'll bring you some more water, then I'll leave you to get some sleep.' He then picked up her glass and disappeared downstairs.

Ann sat there stunned; she didn't know what to think. She began to wonder how she had got into this mess.

It wasn't long before Michael returned with her glass of water. 'Thank you,' she said. 'And I'm sorry, I have been a complete ass, first fainting on you and then screaming at you.'

'Believe me, I've had a lot worse. Try and get some sleep,' he said. 'Goodnight,'

'Goodnight,' Ann replied.

CHAPTER TWO

Evie Martin was slim about five feet tall, with long blond hair. She had an oval shaped face with a clear complexion and very unusual green eyes. Evie had just helped the last customer in the shop; she thought that she would never go. First she tried on one dress, then another, then back to the first but in a different size and she couldn't believe it when she came out with the classic one. 'Does my bottom look big in this?' Evie had cast a glance at Clair who worked with her, who by now was trying to stifle a laugh and ended up having to disappear into one of the changing rooms.

When the customer had left empty handed Clair came out of her hiding place and burst into laughter.

'It was alright for you,' Evie said. 'I was the one in here trying to keep a straight face. I wouldn't mind, but she didn't buy anything in the end.'

'Never mind, she'll probably be back tomorrow having thought about it overnight,' Clair joked.

'Oh please, I couldn't cope with her again,' Evie replied with a laugh.

'Did you notice what she was?' Clair asked.

'I couldn't help noticing what she was. Do you know her?' Evie enquired.

'She works for Mr Joshua Ellis at the castle, the guy who owns this place. She refuses to take human form. Lucy, I believe her name is,' Clair said calmly.

'It's the first time that I have knowingly been close to one; it's one thing to grow up on this Island knowing about the vampires, but to see one for the first time in their natural form is another,' Evie said, as she opened the till.

'Are you calling at your Mum's on the way home Evie?'

'Yes, she's making me some tea again.'

'Well you're lucky. I have to set too and make ours, after I've picked the children up from the child minders,' Clair complained. 'I do wish my husband had time to cook.'

Evie counted up the money from the till and filled in the paying in slip. 'Would you mind coming to the bank with me, Clair, to pay this in.'

'Of course I will. I'll just get my coat.'

Evie had been working with Clair now for about six months; they really got on well together. Clair was a good eight years older than Evie. She was the same height but had a slightly heavier build. Her long, straight light brown hair was held back from her round face with a hair slide. She always looked healthy as her cheeks always appeared on the rosy side which made her perfect white teeth stand out all the more. Having set the alarm and locked up the shop, they made their way to the bank. It wasn't too far away, but they always went together for safety. The shop was situated in the Island's capital town of Newport, opposite the bus station. They walked down the road a short distance, and turned right down a side street. After crossing the road they cut through a short narrow alley lined with shops into St Thomas's square. This was a perfect square with the beautiful stone church of St Thomas at its center. As they walked around the church, Clair noticed someone.

'That man over there by the church' Clair whispered, 'I think I saw him earlier watching the shop.'

'Stop spooking me, we've got the day's takings here,' Evie whispered back.

Clair put her hand in her pocket and got hold of her personal alarm. Just in case he were to try anything.

Gary King was tall, of medium build with short dark brown hair. It was going slightly grey in places. He had a round face with a moustache. Dark rings had begun to appear under his eyes, due to the long hours that he worked. He had a few muscles for his age; he tried to keep fit, but he knew he was beginning to get too old for this kind of work. He reached into his coat pocket, pulled out his phone and dialed the number. It rang a few times before it was answered.

'I've found the perfect target,' he said. 'About five foot tall, long blond hair, slim, good looking, best of all she lives alone'

'Are you sure she lives alone,' the voice on the other end asked.

'Definitely. I've been following her for a few days; she doesn't even have a boyfriend, only a mother. Do you want me to take her?'

'Yes.' the disembodied voice answered, 'but no witnesses. If there are any, you're on your own. Understand?'

'Perfectly' Gary replied.

'Alive, she must be alive and no drugs, her blood must be clean,' the voice insisted. Gary knew exactly where to pick her up.

They made their way out of the square and up the road to the bank. Evie put the day's takings into the night safe, without incident. They started walking back towards the shop to pick up their cars.

'He's gone now!' Clair remarked.

'Maybe he wasn't following us after all. You watch too many spy films,' Evie remarked.

'Oy! Don't knock my film choice! One day I may find out that my husband is really a secret agent.'

'Yeah, whatever,' Evie scoffed.

They both made it safely to their cars, which were parked in a car park opposite the shop, next to the bus station. They said their goodbyes. Evie got into the driving seat and didn't give the strange man in the square another thought. As she drove away from the Island's main town towards Wootton she was thinking about her lovely tea.

Gary didn't call for help; he knew that he could take her single-handed. He had worked for his rich boss for several years as one of his bodyguards. During that time he had managed to fend off a lot of crazy people, both men and women. So a slip of a girl would be no problem. Or so he thought.

Evie drove towards the small village of Wootton. Her mother had lived there for many years. It consisted of one main road through, lined with several shops and two small supermarkets. The village spread out on either side of the main road, which dropped down steeply to the bridge at the bottom. A river ran underneath with a lake on one side with sluice gates, used to prevent flooding at high tide. On the other it meandered out to sea. The river was known locally as Wootton Creek and was lined with sailing vessels of all kinds. Evie turned off the main road and parked her car outside her mother's bungalow.

'Hi Mum,' Evie shouted out from the hallway as she came in.

'Hello love, have you had a good day at work?'

'Oh yes, apart from our last customer,' she replied. 'She couldn't make her mind up. I thought she would never leave. All I wanted to do was sit in front of my shepherd's pie.'

'Well it's nearly ready,' her mother replied, as she checked that it was browning, through the glass in oven door.

Gary had driven to Evie's apartment, which was situated in a large cream coloured, Art Nouveau style apartment block, on the promenade at Cowes. *She must be getting a damn good wage to be able to afford this,* he thought to himself.

He looked around, there was no one about, *good,* he thought.

He locked his car and walked across the car park to the front door. Then he looked around once more. The place was really busy in summer, especially during Cowes week. When everyone comes for the yachting. But thankfully for him, in winter it was really quiet.

He pressed the intercoms to several apartments, until eventually someone buzzed him in without question. Gary had been following Evie for days, during which time he had managed to follow her inside, pretending to be another resident. So he already knew her apartment number. Her neighbour was playing loud music. He thought that this should give him some cover.

He was already wearing gloves because of the cold. He dipped his hand into his inside pocket and pulled out a small wallet, in which he kept his lock picks. With very little work he was inside and had relocked the door. He then had a good look around Evie's home, two bedrooms, one still full of boxes, bathroom, kitchen and a lounge. Gary walked over to the window and looked out. The apartment was at the front of the building, it had a panoramic view, over the Solent and across to Southampton. *Great for ship spotting,* he thought. He then found the phone and disconnected it, doing the same in the bedroom.

Whilst he was in the bedroom he looked around for a weapon especially under the bed; women, on their own, tend to keep something there as a weapon, but he found nothing. There were also not many hiding places, but he did find a cupboard in the hall with plenty of room for him. *She shouldn't be too far behind,* he thought.

Margaret was a very homely woman a little shorter than Evie with a fuller figure, with short curly fair hair. She loved to cook for her daughter. She was living on her own now; her husband had died some years before. Evie had moved out six months ago, after living with her for eighteen months, whilst she found herself another job. When she had, it was the job of her dreams. She had become the manageress of a very posh fashion shop called Re-Vamp your style, owned by one of the Island's well known vampires, Mr Joshua Ellis. Evie had always been interested in fashion, so this new job was perfect.

Margaret was very proud of her daughter. Whilst spending some time back home, she had turned herself around, after being made redundant from her previous job. She had not only done well job wise but had found herself a new home. Because the shop owner was a multi - millionaire he could afford to pay good wages so her daughter had not looked back.

She should be walking in any minute now. She was on her way back to her car when I last saw her, Gary thought to himself.

They sat together now with a rather large shepherd's pie between them. Margaret began to serve, as Evie drifted off into a world of her own. She was wondering who that man could be? She had been mocking Clair, but Evie knew that she had learned to become very observant, being married for seven years to a police detective. She was thinking about ringing Mr Ellis in the morning, when her mother interrupted her.

'Is there something wrong, dear?' Margaret asked.

'No, not at all. I was just thinking about our new range that was delivered today, that's all.' She didn't want to worry her mum.

'I wonder if she has called at the shop on her way home? Yes maybe that's it.' Gary said out loud, trying to keep himself company.

'Is it a good range then?' her mum asked.

'Yes, it's all the new spring clothing it looks good.'

'I'll have to pop in, maybe I can choose something for your birthday,' Margaret said smiling.

'Make sure that you take advantage of my discount if you do,'

Evie reminded her mother.

'Oh what rubbish is that guy playing now, has no one these days got any taste in music?' he muttered under his breath. It was beginning to give Gary a headache. Hopefully though it should work to his advantage if he couldn't knock her out with anything.

'This pie's nice, Mum.'
'Good. I miss cooking for you every day. I hope that you're feeding yourself well at home.'
'Of course I am,' Evie answered quickly.
'How's Clair doing?' Margaret asked.
'Fine, I get on really great with her, we make a good team. Yes, she's older than me and has a family, but we do think alike.'

'Now I'm getting cramp, how much longer can she be, I left her nearly two hours ago?' Gary said to himself through clenched teeth, now getting a little agitated, as he stood up to stretch his legs.

'I'm really glad you're happy now dear. I'm so proud of you.'
'Thank you, Mum.'
'Have you met that new boss of yours yet, what's his name again?'
'Mr Ellis,' Evie answered.
'Oh yes that's it. I hear he's very old you know.'
'Mum he's a vampire, they usually are. I haven't met him yet but I hear he's a really nice guy.'
'Would you like some pudding, dear?'
'I would love some mum, what is it?'
'Fresh fruit salad.'

'I need the bathroom now!' Gary mumbled, 'I thought this operation would be easy, where the hell is the woman?' he muttered, as he made his way quickly to the bathroom.

'Mum that was wonderful as usual, thank you.'

'You're welcome dear. Would you like a coffee, or must you be getting off now?'

'No a coffee would be fine.' Evie and her mum moved to the couch with their coffee and carried on their conversation a little bit longer.

There was now no sound at all from the cupboard.

'Well I really must be going now mum, my bed is calling me.'

'You're welcome to stay the night if you wish, it will save you going all that way home,' Margaret said hopefully.

'No, it's alright, mum, I'll be fine. I'll see you tomorrow.' Evie put on her coat and kissed her mum goodbye.

On the way home she thought about ringing Mr Ellis straight away. She had been given his number when she got the job. Apparently he liked to make sure that all his human staff was safe and happy. If they had any problems or they were worried about anything. He liked them to know that they could talk to him. He didn't like the idea any human thinking that all vampires were monsters. If they looked after his interests he would look after them she'd been told, and apparently he was very protective. *Had it been their imagination?* She didn't want to disturb him. *Were all the Island vampires out during the day?* She knew that Lucy was. *Do they stay up all night? Would he be mad at her if she were wrong?*

All these thoughts spun around and around in her head; before she knew it she was home and felt safe. But very soon she would wish that she had made that phone call.

Evie parked her car and went to her apartment. She unlocked the door and put the light on in the hall. Leaving her bag and coat on a chair, she went through to the bathroom and brushed her teeth.

'Snooorrre.'

What was that noise? She hadn't heard properly as she was brushing her teeth at the time. *Must be next door,* she thought. Then she noticed something, the toilet seat was up, *I never leave the toilet seat up, that's strange,* she thought as she lowered the seat back down again. After brushing her teeth Evie moved into the kitchen to get her breakfast things together for the following morning.

'Snooorrre.'

What is that noise? It sounded like a snore but she had never

21

heard her neighbour snore like that before.

Luckily for Gary, he woke himself up on the second snore and noticed a light seeping through under the door. *At last!* he thought, *she's back.* He slowly inched the cupboard door open and he could just see her in the kitchen, it was then that he noticed her bag on the chair. *Mobile phone,* he thought to himself.

Evie was busy with her head in a cupboard, so he took the opportunity and sneaked out. Reaching into her bag, he removed her mobile phone, and then disappeared back into his hiding place. He turned her phone off and put it in his pocket. Then he suddenly realised that it had gone quiet, the music had stopped next door; his cover had gone, he would have to act fast.

Evie had got everything together for the following morning's breakfast. It was a habit that she had had for a long time; it made it easier when getting up in the morning when she was still half asleep.

Gary knew that he wouldn't fall asleep again as adrenalin was now coursing through him. He would now wait until she had gone to bed and was asleep. That way he could use the bedclothes, to help subdue her. Then she wouldn't be able to kick him, while he handled the top half. He decided to wait half an hour.

Evie walked into the bedroom, got undressed and put on her nightdress, then she set the alarm and got into bed. She settled down, reached out and turned the bedside lamp off.

Gary pressed a button at the side of his watch face, it lit up to tell him the time. Half passed ten. He would wait until eleven. He stood up carefully inside his little cupboard to exercise his legs. The last thing he wanted was to be too stiff or get cramp whilst he was grappling with her, it could go wrong. He passed the time and calmed his nerves by playing games on his mobile phone. It was during one of these games, that his phone vibrated in his hand and made him jump.

The caller I.D said Andrew. *What does he want?* Gary thought. He pressed the green button on his phone. 'Hello, what's up?' he whispered.

'The boss rang me, thought you may need some help.'

'It's a good job my phone is on vibrate, I'm hiding in her apartment.'

'You always have it on vibrate! The boss got worried, he hadn't heard from you for a while. I take it you haven't got her yet?'

'No,' he whispered into the phone. 'She's only just come home.'

'Where's she been?'

'How the hell do I know? I'll ask her shall I, before I kidnap her.' Gary was beginning to get a bit annoyed at all this; it was supposed to be such a simple little job.

'Where are you?' Andrew asked.

'In a cupboard,' Gary replied.

'No! The address?'

'Shhhhhh! Don't shout down the phone, you'll wake her.' Gary gave Andrew the address. 'I'm moving in at eleven,' he said.

'I'll be there.'

Gary went back to playing games on his mobile, to pass the time.

'Eleven o'clock, I'm going in,' he muttered. He took out his black balaclava and put it on. Then he slowly opened the cupboard door and sneaked out, crept down the hall and put his hand on the bedroom door handle. Taking a deep breath he slowly pushed the handle down and opened the door. Evie was sleeping soundly on her side with her back to him. He inched forward taking out a pair of handcuffs as he went. He wanted them ready so he could have his hands free as quickly as possible. *I don't want to risk her screams as I put these on,* he thought to himself. It wasn't an ideal situation; it would have been easier earlier on, when the neighbour was playing loud music. It was now that he wished Andrew had arrived.

He was at the side of her bed now, noting where her arms were, one was on the pillow, the other one, part way under the quilt. He quickly cuffed the wrist he could see whilst putting his other hand over her mouth. Evie suddenly woke up in shock and tried to scream but she couldn't.

'Don't scream! I'm not here to rape or kill you,' he said. He removed his hand from her mouth whilst he quickly felt for the other hand. Suddenly Evie's hand came out from the duvet of its own accord, *Whack! A baseball bat where the hell did that come from?* He thought, as he saw stars and fell back onto the floor.

Evie dived out of bed and ran into the hall, heading for the phone. She picked up the receiver with the handcuffs dangling from one wrist. 'No dial tone, oh my God, he's disconnected the phone,' she said to herself in a panic. *Mobile,* she thought.

She grabbed her bag and tipped the contents out onto the floor. Gary took a while to recover and go after her. As he got out into the hall she was knelt on the floor looking for her mobile with her back to him. He came up behind her fast, putting his hand over her mouth again and lifting her up at the same time.

He took her phone out of his pocket. 'Looking for this?' he said, bragging. It was then that she noticed a small tattoo on his wrist, two A's close together. The central V formed between them, was slightly higher than the top of the two A's.

Before he knew it, she had lifted her legs up against the wall and pushed with all her might. With all the adrenalin now in her system, she had found a strength that she didn't know she had. As his back hit a small table behind, they both heard something in the lock.

Gary was winded but still held onto her. She tried to bite his hand but he was holding her too tight. The front door opened, Gary breathed a sigh of relief, as Andrew appeared. He was of similar build to Gary, only a lot younger with some martial arts training behind him. He was also wearing his black balaclava and gloves so Evie couldn't make out his features. She was horrified.

'Need some help there?' he asked calmly. Gary didn't answer.

Andrew walked up to Evie and got hold of the wrist with the handcuff dangling from it; he knew from experience that if he could hold her gaze and talk calmly to her, this would go a lot easier for all concerned. 'Now calm down and relax,' he said to her.

Is this guy for real? She thought, as he managed to get her arm behind her. Gary had eased off a little to allow Andrew to cuff Evie behind her back.

'My coat pocket,' Gary indicated with a nod.

Andrew found a roll of tape, and tore a piece off. He held Evie's gaze with his eyes, and put his finger to his lips although she couldn't see them. 'Shhhhh,' he said.

Gary let go and Andrew quickly applied the tape to her lips before she could scream. They then pulled her down to the floor with Andrew holding onto her legs. Evie tried to kick him away but he held on tight and taped her ankles together. She then noticed that the second kidnapper also had the same tattoo on his wrist.

'I'll see if I can find a blanket to wrap her up in, we don't want her to freeze to death its cold out there,' Andrew said, as he walked down the hall.

'Well you got me there, girl. A baseball bat?' Gary said, in disbelief. 'I didn't see that one coming. I give you ten out of ten for initiative.' He then produced a blindfold and put it over her eyes.

Andrew returned with a throw from the couch in the living room and between them they managed to wrap her up. They then removed their balaclavas. Andrew was a handsome looking guy with wavy, black, shoulder length hair. Slim face with large brown eyes. Gary picked her up and put her over his shoulder. He made his way out of the apartment, whilst Andrew closed the door, and then went out in front of Gary to make sure that no one was about outside.

All was quiet. They walked out into the car park. Evie was in a panic now. Who were these guys and what did they want with her? Were they going to kill her? Evie tried to think fast, *I have to try and get free or at least attract attention.* She tried to thrash about as much as possible, in the hope that she could delay them from getting her into the car, hoping someone would see them.

Andrew approached from behind and lifted Evie's head slightly. 'Stop struggling. All you're going to do is hurt yourself, you can't get free.'

They laid Evie down in the back seat of Gary's car. Her heart was pounding and she was terrified. 'I'll follow you in my car, just in case you can't cope,' Andrew said.

'Very funny.' Gary had known Andrew now for long enough and knew when he was joking; they worked well together as a team. It's just that this time he didn't think that he would have any problems. He jumped into the driver's seat and started the engine. When he saw that Andrew was also ready, they set off together. He didn't say a word to Evie all through the journey. She began to shake but it wasn't from the cold.

They drove for a little while before the car slowed down and stopped. Hearing her kidnapper get out of the car then open the back door, she drew her knees up to her chest so that he couldn't get to her. But the other door opened by her head.

'Come on let's get you inside,' she heard Andrew say. He pulled her out of the car and she tried to scream. 'No one will hear you out here, it's very secluded,' he said, 'so save your breath.' He carried her into what Evie thought sounded like a caravan but, she had no idea where. He then laid her down onto the bed. 'I'm going to take this tape off now. You can scream all you like; there is no one about for miles. This blindfold stays on, you understand,' he said. Evie nodded.

He took the tape off very quickly and it stung her lips. 'What do you want from me?' Evie whimpered.

'We're only following orders. Our boss wants you, for some reason.'

'And you just follow orders just like that? What if he wants you to kill me? Would you do that?'

'Yes, but if he wanted that, we would have done it by now.' It made Evie's blood run cold as she took those words in.

'Do you want a drink of water or anything?' Andrew asked.

'No, I want you to let me go, please.'

'Sorry, no can do, but I can make you a bit more comfortable. If you promise to behave and not remove your blindfold, I will bring your arms around to the front.'

Evie thought that this was a start. Maybe this guy was softening a little. 'Okay, I promise,' she said. Andrew leaned her forward against his chest and unlocked one handcuff, then gently pushing her back up to sitting position, he brought her arms around to the front and relocked them. 'You should get some rest. You may be here for a while,' he said, as he left the room.

Evie broke her promise; knowing that she should get out of there. She removed her blindfold. Looking around once her eyes had begun to focus, she saw that she was indeed inside a caravan. There were two beds, built in wardrobes and a chest of drawers. Evie realised that she was probably on a caravan site; and there would be no one there at this time of year.

She got to work on the tape around her ankles. She knew that no one would know that she was missing until morning, when she didn't show up for work. And when she didn't answer her home phone or her mobile, they would get in touch with her mum. Then she remembered Mr Ellis. The vampires, she had heard, they were good at tracking; surely they would find her, if she couldn't escape herself. Evie went to the fire escape window, and putting her hand on the latch she prayed, 'please open.'

Andrew walked into the lounge area of the caravan; Gary was on the phone, reporting back to the boss. 'Yes, I'm sorry about that,' he was saying. 'It took longer than I anticipated. Well she didn't come straight home; I had to wait for hours'.

Andrew sat down as he listened to this one sided conversation.

'Yes, Andrew got in touch, he's here now. Okay. He wants to

speak to you.' Gary said, as he handed over the phone.

Evie had to use both hands because of the handcuffs, the latch didn't move, 'Oh God,' she whispered, nearly in tears now.

Trying again she found that the latch had actually been stuck; it gave way and the window opened. Returning to the bed she picked up the blanket, went back to the window and climbed out as carefully as she could but the handcuffs didn't make it easy. She held the blanket in front of her then flipped it over her head leaning forward at the same time to get it around her shoulders; it was freezing and she was barefoot.

Andrew took the phone from Gary. 'It went well once she came home.' There was a slight pause. 'No we haven't used any drugs.' Another pause. 'We've left her alone to calm down.'

Gary disappeared outside to fetch the beer in from the car boot.

Evie crept around the caravan and saw their car. She looked around to find something to poke into the pressure valves of the car tyres. Finding some small twigs she started to let the tyres down. Then she stopped suddenly as she heard one of the kidnappers come out of the caravan and head towards the boot. She crouched down at the side of the car as he took something from the boot and went back inside.

'Okay, we will wait for your call.' Andrew disconnected them.

'I think we have earned this,' Gary said, as he handed Andrew a beer.

'Thanks,' he said, taking the bottle from his hand. They sat together and clinked their beer bottles,

'Cheers,' they said in unison.

Evie decided that it was too much of a close call; she should get out of there, now! She made it over the grass to the road. It was a quiet country lane. One way was dark but she could see streetlights a little further along the lane in the other direction. She only had one way to go.

Half running, half walking she made her way along, not knowing when they would discover her missing. If she heard a car behind, she could dive into the bushes. Evie began to see the streetlights of the main road getting closer. Once she got to the main road, she could get help.

'Want to watch something on T.V?' Gary asked.

'Yeah, you see what's on while I go and check on our guest.' Andrew disappeared into the bedroom, as Gary switched on the TV.

Suddenly Andrew burst out of the bedroom, shouting. 'She's gone out of the window.'

'What?' Gary couldn't believe how his day was going.

'Come on, we'll use my car, put your headgear on, she can't have got very far.' They both raced out to Andrew's car and jumped in. They knew that she would head for the road. They drove slowly along so that they wouldn't shoot passed her.

The main road was getting nearer now, but the trouble was, the hedges were very dense. If they came now she wouldn't be able to hide.

'No!' Evie could hear a car engine. Was it coming from the main road? She stood for a few seconds to listen. It was behind her! There was nowhere to hide.

'There!' Gary cried, as he saw a figure up ahead.

Andrew drove closer; when he got along side he stopped the car and noticed that she was stood there like a frozen rabbit caught in a cars headlights. 'Take the wheel,' he called out, as he opened the door.

Gary slid across behind the wheel. 'Good luck mate,' he said.

Andrew approached her slowly but she didn't move. He held her by the shoulders, but she was looking straight through him as if he wasn't there. 'You're shaking, you must be frozen, come on, let's get you back and warmed up,' he said gently. He was beginning to feel sorry for this girl and that worried him.

They got her back to the caravan with no problems. By this time she had switched off, and Andrew knew that she had resigned herself to her fate, whatever that may be. It was a sort of defence mechanism that some people went through, because of the fear and shock. People either fought like crazy or they pretended that it wasn't happening to them, like they were seeing everything through someone else's eyes.

They took it in turns all night to sit with her while she slept, although restlessly. She wasn't going to get away from them again, although Andrew sensed that she wouldn't try. Which would make his job a hell of a lot easier. During one of Gary's watches, Andrew sneaked out for some fresh air.

CHAPTER THREE

Michael was woken up by the alarm on his mobile phone. He reached out but couldn't find it on the table. Cursing he sat up and found it on the floor. 'Oh God, it can't be morning already,' he grumbled.

He climbed the stairs and got into the shower, allowing the hot water to run over his face to wake him. He wondered how his patient was feeling. He turned off the shower and stepped out into the bathroom and started to rub himself down with a large towel. He knew now that she didn't believe what she had seen last night. He also knew that he would have to come clean with her. But she wasn't an Islander; she was going to have a fit when he told her that she just spent the night with two vampires.

He put the jogging bottoms on that he had been wearing the night before. Then he made his way towards his bedroom. Opening the door very carefully, he crept inside. Ann was sleeping soundly. He approached the bed and listened to her heartbeat and breathing. The lungs were rattling just as much as they had done the night before. She had only taken one antibiotic so far. In a couple of days she would be feeling well enough to go home. Michael sneaked into his wardrobe for some fresh clothes then left again, closing the door quietly as he did so.

When Michael lifted Mary's coffin lid she was still in a deep sleep. 'Come on sleepy head, your uncle Richard and aunt Sadie will be here in an hour to pick you up.'

'Err,' was the only reply he got, while she reached up with her hand, got hold of the toggle that was attached to the lid and pulled it closed.

'I thought you wanted to go to Joshua's birthday party,' he said through the lid.

'I'm tired, can't I go a bit later.'

'No. I'm on call remember.' He lifted the lid once more and picked her up.

'Breakfast first, then you can get washed and changed.'

'How's Ann?' Mary asked, sleepily whilst rubbing her eyes.

'She's still sleeping at the moment,' he replied, whilst carrying her down the stairs.

'Did you manage to sleep for her coughing?' Mary asked.

'Yes, fine, I slept downstairs.'

Mary gave him a puzzled look 'Why?' she said, as she sat down at the table.

'Difficult questions first eh,' he muttered, as he put his head in the fridge, smiling. 'It's an adult thing,' he replied, whilst coming out of the fridge with a fresh bottle of red stuff.

He poured out two cups and handed one to Mary along with a packet of rusk biscuits.

Mary had a drink, 'O,' she said, with a curled up nose.

'What do you mean oh, is it off?' Michael said as he sniffed his drink.

'No I said O.'

'Yes I know you said oh, but it's not off, I just checked.'

'No I said O, I don't like O, I prefer AB.'

'Oh, I forgot, sorry,' he said going back to the fridge; 'I'm still asleep myself. Here, give me that one and I'll pour you another.' Michael got Mary another drink and set it down on the table. After downing one cup of blood he turned to Mary and said, 'I'm going up to see if Ann is awake yet.'

'Richard! I've poured you your breakfast out, are you going to be much longer in that bathroom? You're worse than any woman,' Sadie shouted up the stairs.

'I'm nearly ready, leave it in the kitchen,' he shouted back, whilst thinking at the same time, how he could get her back for that comment.

Sadie was a little over five foot, slim with short, dark brown hair cut in a bob. This framed her round face and deep brown eyes. She had been married to Richard, Michael's brother, for 16 years now. She met him after she had fallen overboard whilst sailing on a yacht with friends.

Richard was sailing nearby on Joshua's luxury cruiser at the time and just dived in without any thought at all. He had managed to get her back to her yacht safely. Then he quickly disappeared again, before she could thank him.

It was only later on dry land when she bumped into him again that she discovered what he was. Sadie found him very laid back and calm. He had fair hair and blue eyes, just like Michael but slighter in build and not quite as tall. His calm nature helped him in his work as an anaesthetist at the same hospital as Michael.

After being together for two years, Richard had finally managed to ask her to marry him. Of course she took a while to say yes because of the rather large difference between them. Besides the obvious, she knew that he could never give her children, but in the end she realised that she loved him too much to care. As for the other problem of growing old while he stayed young, she would have to face that later.

They had settled in the picturesque village of Shalfleet. A lovely little place with narrow roads, thatched cottages and a small stone church opposite the local pub. Richard and Sadie lived on the outskirts of the village, a short distance up an unmade road. As soon as Sadie had seen the cottage she had fallen in love. Richard had had to buy it for her. It was double fronted, stone built with a thatch. Someone had painted over it in the past in a cream colour, it really set it off, especially in summer when the sun reflected off the walls. The only problem was the low ceilings inside. This was all right for Sadie, but in the beginning Richard was always hitting his head on the beams until he got used to it. This resulted in Sadie having to live with a vampire with a permanent headache.

'Bathroom's free,' he shouted after a while.

'About time as well,' Sadie said as she pushed past him in the doorway.

Richard put his arms around her from behind and whispered into her ear, 'You just called me a woman. Are you going to apologise.'

'Or else,' she replied. Turning into vampire form he put his mouth to her neck, she could feel his fangs digging in. Sadie loved the sense of danger when he turned, even though she knew that she was safe. It wasn't long after their first date that Sadie had first seen him turn. Richard knew that if their relationship were to last, she would have to get used to him. The last thing that he wanted was for her to be frightened of him. He wanted her to know that she could trust him. So, early on in their relationship he started to turn on a regular basis and he soon discovered just how much she liked it. Somehow it made both of them more passionate.

Sadie reached around with one arm and hit him on the head, laughing. 'We don't have time for that now, stop messing about,' she said. Richard let go and by the time she had turned around to kiss him, he had turned back again, into human form.

Sadie busied herself in the bathroom whilst Richard got ready in the bedroom; it wasn't long before she joined him. 'No! You can't wear that sweatshirt.'

'Why not?' He replied smirking.

'You're just trying to wind me up now because I called you a woman.' She said as she picked up another shirt for him to wear.

'No I wouldn't do that,' he answered sarcastically.

'Please put this shirt on.' She pleaded.

'No I'm getting my own back.'

'But that's embarrassing.'

'Serves you right then, doesn't it,' he said playfully.

'Please Richard, I don't think that wearing a sweatshirt saying *My Blood Sport Sucks* on the front of it is appropriate for a posh party do you?'

'Only if you make it up to me later,' he replied.

'I might,' she said, lifting her eyebrows at him.

When they were both ready, they left the house and got into the car. They didn't notice the figure of a man over the road, watching them from behind the trees and making notes.

Michael went into his bedroom to see Ann. She was awake but drowsy. 'How are you feeling?' he asked as he put his hand on her forehead.

'Hot and I can't stay awake.' She started coughing again and he helped her to sit up.

'Here, you need to take another antibiotic,' he said as he handed her a glass of water. He pushed the tablet out of its bubble.

Ann took the tablet then asked, 'Have you put something in my water?'

'To make you sleepy you mean?' He said with raised eyebrows.

'Yes,' she replied a little groggy.

'The answer is no! It's your own body shutting you down so that it can heal. I wouldn't do that to you. You must be hungry by now. What would you like?' he asked.

'Have you eaten?' Ann asked.

'Yes!'

'Then I will have whatever you have had. I don't want to put you out.'

'Mmmm,' he said, 'you definitely don't want what I have had.'
'Why?'
Sounds like Mary he thought, 'I had... err... cold left over pizza,' he lied.

'Oh, in that case I'll have bacon, eggs, mushrooms, beans, tomatoes and sausage with two slices of bread and butter and a cup of tea,' she said, trying to laugh without coughing.

'Not much then.' He was glad this girl wasn't a vampire, there wouldn't be enough blood on the Island to feed the rest of them.

'Toast with marmalade, will be fine, thank you.'

'Okay, no problem, I just need to sort Mary out first, she's being picked up shortly, by my brother and his wife. I won't be long,' he said, as he left the room.

'Have you finished your breakfast yet Mary?'

'Yes,'

'Come on then, let's get you ready for that party.' Michael took Mary to her room and helped her to get ready. Dark blue tights under a red and blue tartan skirt, white blouse with a frill around the neck covered by a dark blue jumper. They finished off the whole look with a red bow in her blond hair. 'Absolutely perfect,' he said, 'give me a twirl,' Mary twirled around for him, giggling.

They both heard Richard and Sadie arrive. When Michael opened the front door, Richard had Sadie pinned up against the wall, kissing her passionately.

'Am I interrupting something here?' he asked.

Richard stopped kissing Sadie, 'No. I was just feeling a little peckish.'

Mary ran to them both as they came in, she had woken up now and was exited. 'Oh, look at you. Is this a new outfit?' Sadie asked.

'Yes, do you like it?' Mary said, giving Sadie a twirl.

'You look lovely,' She replied.

Michael smiled at Sadie, 'Would you both mind just doing me a quick favour before you go?' he asked,

'Sure, what is it,' Richard asked curiously.

'Would you mind just hanging on here while I call at the shop, I need some things.'

'Of course,' Richard replied.

Suddenly a little voice piped up 'Uncle Michael has had a lady in his bed all night.' Richard and Sadie looked at each other stunned.

Michael didn't know where to put his face.

'It's not what it sounds like. She brought Mary home last night from one of her sleepwalks and she collapsed into my arms.'

'Oh you certainly know how to attract a woman. What did you use, vampire sleep?' Richard joked.

'She has a bad chest infection and she passed out. I need to go and get her some breakfast.'

'Of course you do. We'll wait,' Sadie replied.

'Thanks, I won't be long.' He picked up his wallet and disappeared out of the door.

'Well! What's gone on here then overnight?' Richard asked, turning to Mary.

'I think he likes her,' Mary said with a big grin across her face.

They heard coughing from upstairs, Richard moved but Sadie stood in front of him. 'Don't be nosey,' she said. 'Leave her alone.'

'I only want to introduce myself.'

'Yes and see what she's like,' Sadie finished for him.

'Well, she's obviously human,' he said.

'And what's wrong with that?' Sadie said, whilst grabbing hold of the front of his shirt.

'Nothing dear,' he said smiling 'You're creasing my shirt.'

Michael soon returned with a loaf of bread, butter, marmalade, tea bags and milk. Richard followed him into the kitchen, and watched him start breakfast. 'Do you like her?' he asked.

'I only met her last night,' Michael said, as he put the kettle on.

'Is she an Islander?' Richard asked, beginning to tease him now.

'No!' Michael replied, as he was trying to work out how to use the grill on his built in cooker. This was the first time he had ever had the chance to use it.

'Does she know?' Richard asked with curiosity and mischief in his voice.

'What is this, an interrogation?' Michael replied, a little annoyed at his brothers nosiness.

'You're the one that's good at that Michael, not me!' Richard said, a little more strongly than he meant to. 'I'm sorry,' he went on.

'She saw Mary change, but she thinks that she was hallucinating because of the state she's in,' Michael replied thoughtfully.

'Mmmm, so you haven't told her yet?'

'I'm working on it,' Michael said, trying to sound convincing.

'Come on, I think that we should be off. Leave this to Michael he knows what he's doing. He doesn't need you breathing down his neck,' Sadie interrupted. 'You go and get Mary into the car, I won't be long.'

Richard took Mary by the hand and led her out of the kitchen.

'Have a good day at the party!' Michael shouted after her.

'I will and good luck upstairs,' Mary said, throwing him a wink as she left.

This made Michael smile. Both he and Richard missed their sister but Mary kept them going. It was because of her in the first place that peace now reigned between humans and vampires on the Island.

'If you need me to talk to her for you I will. She might feel better talking to a human, especially one that has spent the best part of 18 years with a vampire,' Sadie offered.

Michael gave Sadie a hug. 'Thank you, I may have to hold you to that one,' he said to her softly.

'Well they're waiting in the car for me, so I'll see you later. Good luck.'

'Bye.' Michael let her go and watched as she left the cottage and closed the door.

He placed the breakfast on a tray and climbed the stairs.

Richard drove into Newport and then out of the other side towards Wootton. They were both very quiet whilst Mary sat there humming to herself in the back seat. As they arrived at Wootton, Richard couldn't stand the silence anymore.

'What did you say to him?' Richard enquired as he turned off the main road and drove towards Joshua's.

'I offered to talk to her for him that's all.'

'I thought you might,' he said smiling. 'I guess it would be good for you to find a friend who would have the same worries as you.'

'What's that supposed to mean!' she shouted at him.

'Whoa, don't think that I haven't noticed the torment you're going through, as you get nearer to my age.' Richard drove the car down the long unmade road that eventually led to two large wrought iron gates, which were always kept closed. He stopped the car, opened the window, looked up at the security camera and waved. The gates then began to open.

He turned to Sadie and took her hand in his. 'You know that it's

36

entirely your decision whether you want to join the nest or not. And I will love you no matter what you decide,' he said to her softly. Sadie couldn't say anything; she knew that he meant it. He turned back to his driving and steered the car down the long gravel drive towards the Castle.

Michael sat there, as Ann ate her breakfast. It took her a while in between having coughing fits and trying to get her breath back. 'Is there something wrong,' she asked. 'I can go home, I already feel that I've outstayed my welcome.'

'You're not going anywhere until you are well enough,' he said, a lot stronger than he meant it. 'I'm sorry, I didn't mean to come on strong there, I just have a lot on my mind at the moment, and I'm trying to work out the best course of action.'

'Does it have something to do with me?' she asked.

'Yes, I'm afraid it does.' The reply made her a little nervous but she didn't know why.

Andrew was on the last shift watching Evie, as the morning got brighter. She was laid on the bed her breathing steady; he knew she was asleep even with her blindfold on.

The smell of coffee came into the bedroom; she stirred and began to sit up. 'Don't remove your blindfold,' he said to her, making her jump. 'Do you want some coffee?' She answered with a nod.

'Milk and sugar?' he asked.

'Yes please,' He left the room and joined Gary in the kitchen area.

'She awake?' he asked.

'Yes, she wants a coffee, milk and sugar.'

'You don't think that she'll try another stunt like last night do you?' Gary asked.

'No, she won't.'

'How can you be so sure?' Gary asked.

'Because I can tell, trust me.'

Andrew took a coffee in to her, wearing his balaclava. Removing her blindfold he handed her the cup. She began to drink; it tasted good but all she wanted to do was cry.

'Have you heard from your boss yet?' she asked.

'No. Drink that coffee, he will ring soon.'

'I need the bathroom,' she said, he knew she was telling the truth; he was good at reading people.

'Okay,' he said walking towards her. He unlocked one handcuff, and led her by the arm towards the toilet cubicle. 'You will find that the window isn't big enough in there, and I can unlock the door from this side if necessary.'

She just nodded as she went in.

Andrew strolled into the lounge area to see Gary. He was eating some toast. 'Want some?' he asked.

'No, thanks.'

'What do you think he wants with her?' Andrew asked.

'We'll get to know soon enough. You're not getting worried, are you?'

'No, just curious.'

He left Gary and headed towards the back of the caravan as he heard Evie unlock the door. She was led back into the bedroom and re-handcuffed, just as they heard a phone ring.

'Yes, I have that. What do you want me to do with it?… What?… No I don't have a problem.… Where?… Yes, I have that. Okay we'll get on with it.' Gary hung up. He turned around to see Andrew stood behind him. He hadn't heard him come back in.

'So what are our instructions?' asked Andrew.

'He sent me this a few days ago,' Gary said as he put his hand in his bag and fished out a small package, and opened it.

Gary held up what looked like a small garden fork with only two prongs, it looked really sharp. When Andrew saw it he began to get worried.

'What does he want us to do with that?' he asked.

'He wants us to drive to Wootton, use this instrument to puncture the girl's neck, let her bleed a bit then leave her outside the Ellis residence.'

Now Andrew realised what his boss was planning and why he wanted her blood clean. A vampire wouldn't need drugs to subdue its prey. They use vampire sleep. 'I'll do it,' Andrew said.

'Are you sure you can?' asked his partner.

'Yes, no problem.'

The castle was actually a manor house; it just looked like a castle.

Locally it was affectionately known as Dracula's castle because of its famous resident, Mr Joshua Ellis. The manor was a large building built of stone in the early sixteenth century.

It was three storeys high, a flat fronted building apart from two rather large bay windows at either side of a grand entrance, an arched door under a stone canopy, which was held up by two stone pillars. The place had turrets along its roofline; this gave the manor its look of a castle.

The whole place was set in its own grounds which rolled slightly downhill giving a magnificent view of the sea and the entrance to Wootton creek.

Just anchored off shore where he could see her, was Joshua's 10 bed-roomed luxury yacht *Die Fledermaus*. This was besides his private jet, which he kept at Bembridge Airport.

Joshua Ellis had made his money from owning several successful businesses including a fashion chain. When you live forever, your money has more of a chance to grow. So he had built up quite an empire. He had never married, having never met the right girl; it was difficult for him to find someone who loved him, rather than his money. He had short black hair, slightly wavy. His muscular build was due to having his own gym at home. He didn't want to be totally reliant on his bodyguard, Eric. Unfortunately he was only about five foot two tall; the other vampires were always having him on about his height.

Mary jumped out of the car, 'Joshua!' she cried, 'Happy Birthday.'

'Thank you Mary,' he said as he scooped her up into his arms. They entered the hall of the castle followed by Sadie and Richard. 'It's a shame your uncle Michael couldn't join us,' he said to her. Before Richard could say anything, Mary spoke up.

'He's busy with a lady at home.'

'Really!'

'Yes, she spent the night in his bed.'

'Now tell him the rest, Mary. Michael spent the night on the couch, he is looking after a damsel in distress,' Sadie put in.

'A human?' Joshua asked, raising his eyebrows.

'Oh yes,' Richard replied. 'I just hope that he realises just what he's letting himself in for,' Richard said, as he smiled at Sadie.

They passed the highly polished coffin that was kept in the entrance hall, Joshua's idea of a joke because of what the locals called his home. They moved on through to the back of the castle, passing the grand staircase as they went and into the now modernised kitchen. Joshua had had a large window removed and a conservatory put in, which had opened out the kitchen into a large social area where a lot of his guests were gathering.

'Can I get you guys a drink each?' Joshua asked them.

'AB please,' Mary piped up.

'I'll have the same please,' asked Richard.

'Is yours a white wine Sadie?' Joshua asked.

'Yes please.'

Joshua gave them their drinks but as he turned to Sadie he said, 'You're not going to get drunk again this year are you? And try to climb inside my coffin in the entrance hall.'

'It was holding me up at the time, I was leaning on it, and I was curious as to what you kept in there,' she said under her breath, a little embarrassed.

'I believe you. Thousands wouldn't,' Joshua joked.

Sadie disappeared to find Mary; she found her talking to Lucy who worked for Joshua as his housekeeper. She was slim with long straight red hair. A really nice girl of twenty-five if you could get used to her being in vampire form all the time. So her piercing red eyes matched her hair. The Island vampires had no reason to hide from the humans so Lucy's attitude was 'why should I?'

'So tell me all about this girl that Michael's kidnapped,' Joshua pleaded, as he took Richard to one side.

'I haven't met her yet, but Mary thinks that he likes her. From what I hear she rescued Mary and then collapsed on him, apparently a chest infection.'

'Is that it?' Joshua exclaimed.

'That's all I know.'

'What's her name?' Joshua enquired.

'You know, I never got around to asking, but Mary will know. Where is she?' he said walking away looking for the two women in his afterlife. Richard found Sadie talking to Lucy, but couldn't see Mary.

'I must have been in the shop a good hour,' he heard Lucy say as he approached. 'Even then I couldn't decide which one to choose, so I went with my old faithful.'

'Do you know where Mary's gone?' Richard asked as he approached.

'Try the front lounge, she loves to play computer games on the large screen T.V,' Lucy answered.

'Thanks.'

Richard disappeared into the hall, passed the staircase and headed back towards the front door. Just before he came to the coffin he turned left through a large wooden arched door into the front lounge.

The room was large with a bay window which looked out over the front lawn and out to sea, letting in plenty of light. The stone fireplace housed an open fire, which wasn't lit due to the central heating that Joshua had turned on for his human guests. Vampires liked a little warmth but they didn't feel the cold like humans did.

Over the fireplace hung a large oil painting of a gentleman from the chest up. His nose and chin were long with a wide moustache. His long dark hair was covered by a red cone shaped hat decorated around the bottom edge by several rows of pearls. There was a large gold star at the front with a square ruby at its center. He looked to be wearing a red tunic underneath a brown fur cape.

The room had a large blue and cream patterned carpet in the centre, over dark wooden floorboards. There were large comfortable deep blue couches all around the room with cream cushions on them, all facing the 50 inch T.V. screen. Mary was sitting on the floor with the controls to a computer game in her hand and was concentrating hard.

Richard approached, and sat on the floor behind her with his legs at either side of her small body. 'Good game?' he asked.

'No. I can't get past level five,' she replied.

'That shouldn't be a problem with your fast reflexes,' he said, trying to encourage her along.

'So what do you want to know?' Mary asked.

'What? How do you know that I'm going to ask you something?' Richard asked.

'Because I know that you wanted to ask me more about Ann, but aunt Sadie stopped you.'

'So her name is Ann, is it?' Richard replied.

Evie felt her stomach lurch and she felt sick as Andrew returned to the bedroom. 'We have our instructions,' he said, as he tore off a strip of tape and applied it across her mouth. 'It will soon be all over.'

He got hold of her chin and tilted her head up so she could look straight into his eyes through the small gap in his balaclava. The whisper that she heard was barely audible, but it seemed to calm her, even though she hadn't heard what he had said, having now switched off and gone into a trance, to try and escape her ordeal.

Evie was bundled up and blindfolded once again in the back seat of Gary's car. They drove for what seemed to be about fifteen minutes before arriving into Wootton and turning down the unmade lane, which led down to the Castle. They drove past the gates a little way and reversed back into the entrance of a field.

Covering his face once more, Andrew opened the back door and dragged Evie out. He then forced her to the ground into the long grass.

'Now,' he said, 'I need you to keep absolutely still, Do you understand?' Evie nodded. She knew she should be terrified, but a strange calm had come over her. Perhaps this was the strange calm that comes over you when you are about to die.

He didn't want her to see the forked instrument so he left the blindfold on for now. Andrew then turned Evie's face to the left, exposing the right hand side of her neck and held her head firmly with his hand.

He hesitated, he really didn't want to do this to her. Then changed his mind turning her head the other way. Gary got out of the car.

'What are you waiting for,' he asked.

'I need to get this absolutely right. Now, stop breathing down my neck, get back into the car and drive back down the lane.' Gary did as he was told, he jumped back into the car, started the engine and left them alone.

Evie felt the sting as the two-pronged fork burst through her skin. Even though it was sharp she still felt the pain, followed by a steady stream of what she knew was her own blood, flowing down her neck.

He stayed where he was for a little while. Allowing her to bleed a little, not too much he had to time this right. Andrew picked her up and put her over his shoulder. He then poured a bottle of water over the area to swill away the blood in the grass. He then carried her the short distance to the wrought iron gates.

Without looking up towards the camera despite having his features covered. He removed her blindfold, gag, and handcuffs. Evie watch him walk away down the lane as her vision began to go fuzzy.

Eric Sharp was in his office as usual watching the security cameras closely. He had extremely short black hair and was built like a tank with a large rounded face. He always wore a suit and looked smart. Taking great pride in his appearance, as he had been so used to wearing a uniform. He hadn't been out of the Special Forces for long when Joshua had employed him for the security of his estate. Eric thought that it would be another normal birthday party for his boss until he saw someone dump something at the gates.

He ran out of his office and down the drive in a blur, getting there in seconds. Evie was barely conscious as she saw the gates open and saw a face looking down at her. He quickly checked her pulse then picked her up and brought her into the grounds, pressing the button to close the gates again as he did.

Joshua was having a laugh with one of his guests when Eric ran in with Evie in his arms and laid her down on the kitchen floor. Everyone looked around in shock at the girl covered in blood.

'What the…?' Joshua started to say as he dashed towards Eric.

'Someone just dumped her at the gates and disappeared,' he said.

Lucy grabbed some tea towels and pressed them to the wound. 'There's two puncture marks,' she said as she leaned forward to smell the wounds. 'I can't smell any vampire saliva,' she said puzzled. Lucy realised at the same time that she had seen this girl before. 'She works for you in Re-Vamp,' she said, turning to Joshua, who suddenly disappeared.

Richard had heard the commotion from the lounge where he had just been playing computer games with Mary and losing. As he entered the kitchen he saw that everyone was gathering around something on the floor. As he got near, he could hear Sadie on the phone calling for an ambulance. He pushed his way through and couldn't believe what he was looking at.

'I was just about to shout for you,' Lucy said, as she moved aside to let him in. Richard took hold of the tea towels and moved them so that he could assess her wounds.

There were two puncture wounds on the left side of her neck, the bleeding had slowed down and had nearly stopped completely. Richard was totally baffled and it showed on his face.

'I can't smell vampire saliva on her,' Lucy said. Richard bent down over the wounds to smell them for himself.

'The ambulance is on its way. How is she?' Sadie asked as she looked over Richard's shoulder.

'Her heart beat is strong. I don't think she's lost that much blood.' Richard told her in a trance.

'Have we got a rogue vampire on the loose?' Sadie asked.

'No we haven't!' Richard replied quickly.

'Please, don't tell me it's one of our own,' Sadie said backing away from the crowd. Joshua appeared with a blanket and handed it to Richard. As he covered the girl he noticed that Sadie had moved away from everyone, upset.

He barely heard Joshua as he said, 'I've just been on the computer, her name is Evie Martin, she has a mother who lives in Wootton. I'll give her a ring.' As he was dialling the number on his mobile, he turned to Eric, 'You had better go and wait for the ambulance by the front gate.'

Lucy was trying to console Sadie but she was having none of it; she was determined that none of them were coming anywhere near her.

Richard moved towards her but Sadie tried to push him off, it didn't work of course. He held her tightly against his chest. 'It wasn't a vampire that did this,' he whispered gently in her ear.

'How do you know that?'

'We know, trust me. None of this fits, we'll find out when she comes around.'

Sadie had begun to calm down as he held her tight. 'Has anyone rung Michael?' she asked.

'Oh God no. Are you alright now?' Richard asked her as he gave her hand a squeeze.

'Yes sorry, I shouldn't have reacted like that. I've known you all for long enough.' Lucy turned up with a brandy and handed it to Sadie smiling, 'I'm really sorry, Lucy.'

'I know, no offence taken.' They could both hear Michael's phone ringing at the other end as Richard rang him.

CHAPTER FOUR

Ann finished her breakfast in silence; Michael had moved over to the window and was staring out, deep in contemplation.

'Please come to the point, you're scaring me.'

He knew this, but he didn't know how to explain things, without terrifying her.

Michael moved back to the bed and took her breakfast tray away, then sat down by her side. 'How long have you been on the Island?' he asked.

'Just over a year, why?'

Michael held both her hands and gently rubbed the back of them with his thumbs. 'First of all, I need you to know, that you are not in any danger, you can trust me. I would never hurt you.' He paused slightly before continuing. 'What do you think you saw in the cemetery?'

Ann looked down, watching his thumbs. She couldn't look at him, feeling embarrassed about what she was about to say, 'You will think that I'm stupid really.' She coughed. 'It might be the state I'm in. It was quite dark, but I thought at first that Mary,' she paused uncertain, 'was a vampire.' She gave a nervous laugh as Michael let go of one of her hands and reached up for her chin. He lifted her face up, to look at him.

'You didn't imagine it. Mary *is* a vampire.' He waited for a reaction. There wasn't one, just stunned silence.

'While you've been here, has anyone told you about the Island vampires?' Michael waited, but still there was no reaction, not at first. Ann just stared blankly right through him.

'Vampires don't exist,' she suddenly said, coming out of her trance.

'Ann, you saw Mary with your own eyes, she told me you did. It's okay, there's no need to be afraid of me.'

She stared at him, while his words sank in. 'Are you...?' she started to say, but couldn't finish it.

'Yes,' he finished for her, and then he saw the panic in her eyes. Ann started to move away from him but was stopped by the headboard behind her. He held her hands again but he wasn't forceful. 'We live openly on the Island. We don't hide and we haven't taken a human life for over a hundred years now.'

Ann sat there and shook her head, trying to work all this out. 'But you said that you were a surgeon.'

'I am.'

'How can you be?' she yelled, beginning to cough once more.

'Why not? It's not as if I can't stand the sight of blood, is it?' he said, with a slight laugh, trying to make her feel a little more at ease. But the joke went over her head. 'The people on this Island embalm their dead, the embalming fluid chases out the blood. We simply get what they would normally throw away; they give us the cream off the top as it were. There are several pints before the embalming fluid starts to come through. We also have a few human volunteer donors. In return we don't take human life. We have no need; the Islanders keep us well fed. We also take an active role in helping the community. How fast do you think my brother and I can diagnose a patient's problem, with one small sample of blood? One small sample and we can tell you not only what blood group they are, but what's wrong with them as well. It takes a lot longer in a laboratory and delays could mean lives.'

'Your brother, are you trying to tell me, that your brother works at the hospital as well?' Ann's voice was becoming higher in pitch.

'Yes, he's an anaesthetist. We have other talents that he uses as part of his work.'

'Oh! This just gets even better!' she yelled, trying to take all this in. 'No! I don't believe you, this is your idea of a sick joke, I'm going home, you're crazy.' Ann leapt out of bed, Michael didn't stop her, she immediately started with another coughing fit but before he could help her, his mobile phone rang.

Michael looked at his phone and read the front display 'Richard', he said to himself as he pressed the green button to answer, he moved across to Ann to hold her up. 'Now isn't the best time Richard, I'm having problems here.'

'Let go of me!' Ann screamed. Then began to cough once more.

'Are you playing with your dinner?' Richard asked.

Michael ignored the joke. 'Whoa!' he said, putting his hands in the air. 'Calm down. I will leave the room, you can get dressed and you can go home if that is what you want. But I will drive you home.'

'I don't think so. I don't want you knowing where I live.'

'Your address is on your antibiotics and you are not fit to drive. That is the deal. You either stay here or I drive you home.' Michael said sternly.

Ann stood for a while thinking this through. 'Okay!' she yelled, 'but I am not inviting you in.' This started another coughing fit. 'I appreciate what you have done for me, but I cannot cope with this.'

'Fair enough. I understand,' he replied as he left the room.

Richard, Sadie and Lucy had all heard what was going on at the other end of the phone. 'Okay I'm back, what can I do for you, Bro?'

'We have a problem. Someone has just dumped a young girl outside Joshua's front gates, unconscious with puncture holes in her neck.'

'What?' Michael couldn't believe what he was hearing. Richard moved away from Sadie and Lucy, and then went to check on Evie once again.

'Lucy recognised her; she works for Joshua in Re-Vamp, her name is Evie Martin. The good news is, it's not a vampire bite, but it looks like someone is trying to set us up.'

Michael could hear Ann in the background trying to get dressed in-between coughing fits. He moved further away from the bedroom door. 'Is she alright,' Michael asked?

'Yes, she hasn't lost that much blood but she has passed out. We're just waiting for the ambulance and no doubt the police will be here shortly as well. The puncture wounds have completely missed the jugular vein and the carotid artery. It also clotted fairly quickly.'

At that moment Ann emerged from the bedroom holding on to the doorframe exhausted.

'I will go and meet up with the ambulance at the hospital and see what I can find out; hopefully they will let me speak to her when she comes around. You will probably have to sit tight while the police make their enquiries. There is just something that I need to do here first.'

'Good luck with that one,' Richard replied. 'I take that you've broken the news to her then.'

'Yes, and it didn't go very well,' he said as he hung up.

'Come on; let's get you home. Is there anyone I can ring for you? You shouldn't be on your own,' Michael said, as he approached her.

'There's mum and dad but they will only make a fuss. I just want to be left alone.' He picked her up and she began to protest with what little strength she had. By the time he had carried her down the stairs, she had given up, realizing that she wasn't getting anywhere.

Clair had turned up for work as usual at 9am. The shop was still locked up and there was no sign of Evie. Thinking that she may have slept in, she decided to give her a little longer. She stood on the doorstep and watched as all the other shops began to open up. After about twenty minutes, Clair took out her mobile phone and rang Evie's number; only to discover that it was switched off. Beginning to get a little worried, she then tried her home number. Again she couldn't get through and by now she was beginning to get very cold.

After nearly an hour, Clair went back to her car and headed for Evie's apartment. Managing to get one of the neighbours to buzz her in, she made her way up the stairs and knocked on the door. There was no answer. Then she started banging really hard, which brought one of her neighbours out.

'What are you doing?' a middle-aged man asked.

'I'm really sorry, but have you seen Evie this morning? She hasn't turned up for work and I'm beginning to get worried,' she asked.

'I haven't seen her this morning, but I think she came home a little drunk last night, she was knocking a lot of furniture about.'

'What! Evie wouldn't get drunk like that. Did you ring the police; there might be something wrong?' Clair couldn't believe how stupid this guy was.

'I'm sorry, but I tend to mind my own business,' he said apologetically, then went back inside.

Clair took her phone out of her bag once again and rang Tony, her husband. She couldn't help thinking about the man she and Evie had seen the night before.

The sound of sirens began to fill the air, as they got nearer. An ambulance, 3 police cars and a forensics van turned up outside the front door. 'Talk about overkill,' Joshua said under his breath. 'I thought these people trusted us.' He led the paramedics and the forensics team through to the kitchen, where Richard gave them an update on the girl's condition.

Joshua heard someone shouting orders to the Police out in the hall. 'I want those gates closed as soon as the ambulance leaves. Every vampire here stays here, until I've spoken to them all and had an update from the hospital.' Joshua walked up to the person who seemed to be in charge and introduced himself.

'Ah, Mr Ellis, I've heard so much about you, I'm Detective Tony Peters. Pleased to meet you at last.'

Joshua shook his hand. 'You seem to be a little young to be a detective, or am I getting too old,' Joshua joked.

'I don't know. How old are you exactly Mr Ellis?'

'I have been 28 since 1897 which I believe makes me the young age of 141,' he said with a broad grin.

'Well I hope that I'll look that good at your age' the detective said sarcastically. Detective Peters was in fact in his early 40's with a closely cropped head of black hair. He had a very slim build; which made him look even taller than he actually was, but Joshua was still forced to look up at him. But then again Joshua had to look up to everyone, except of course Mary. Joshua thought that he needed building up a bit, but his broad shoulders made him look top heavy or was it the suit he was wearing? Joshua was trying to work this out, then said, 'So tell me who's been talking about me then?'

'Oh my wife, she works for you at Re-Vamp. Mrs Clair Peters.'

'I see. I do hope that she doesn't speak ill of me. I don't often get to meet all my employees. I have other people that do all the interviews for me. Maybe I should make the effort.' Joshua said a little embarrassed. 'Talking of which, our young victim's name is Evie Martin; she also works at Re-Vamp so your wife will know her. As her employer I've already informed her mother of the situation and she's on her way to the hospital.'

As Tony Peters and Joshua were talking in the hall, the two paramedics came past them, with Evie sat in a chair. She was still unconscious.

'How is she?' the detective asked, 'She hasn't lost a lot of blood, judging from her colour. I think she has passed out from the shock but the doctors at the hospital will be able to tell you more when they've seen her.' One of the paramedics gave Joshua a worried glance as he walked away; obviously he couldn't get out fast enough.

'It isn't a vampire bite you know. Someone is trying to set us up,' Joshua informed the detective.

'Really, well please forgive me for saying this, but you would say that wouldn't you.'

Joshua didn't take any notice of him, but continued. 'The wounds had completely missed the carotid artery and the jugular vein.

A vampire would not have made this mistake. Our saliva also contains an anticoagulant. These wounds clotted fairly quickly and there isn't any vampire saliva on her or we would be able to smell it.'

'I will take into account what you have told me, Mr Ellis. But I will also wait for the report from the hospital and the forensics team. Now tell me, where was she found?'

'Eric saw her being dumped by the front gate; he was in the office watching our security cameras.'

'Good, I will need to see the recording and speak to Eric. Is there an office I can use?'

'This way,' Joshua said, as he led him into the office, which was opposite the front lounge.

The office was a slightly smaller room. It had the large bay window, which mirrored the one on the other side to take in that sea view. Near the far wall was a long desk. Tony could see the back of the entire camera monitors arranged along its length.

Opposite this there was another desk, slightly smaller but antique looking in dark wood. This had a computer on it and various other office paraphernalia, (*Joshua's probably*, the detective thought.) In the middle of the room, in between the two desks and facing the bay window was a large comfy couch to take advantage of the sea view. This had what looked like a very expensive dark oak coffee table in front of it. Just as he walked in, the detective's phone rang.

'Tony it's me; Evie's missing! There's something wrong, I can't find her. Her neighbour says that he heard a lot of furniture being kicked about last night.' Clair was in a panic by now and Tony couldn't get a word in at first.

'It's okay, I know. We've found her, she's all right,' he said quickly, before she could get herself even more flustered.

'What! Where?' she exclaimed.

'I can't talk right now, go home, calm yourself down and I will speak to you later.'

But before he could hang up she said, 'We saw a man hanging about last night after work. I'm worried that it might have something to do with him.'

Joshua watched the detective move further into the office, but this didn't stop him from hearing both sides of the conversation.

'What man, where?' he asked.

'I thought I saw someone watching the shop yesterday, then I

50

saw him again by St Thomas's church in the square, as we were going to the night safe,'

Tony couldn't believe that his wife may be a witness to all of this. 'What did he look like?' he asked her.

'He was tall, medium build with short dark brown hair. He was wearing black trousers, black polo neck jumper and a black coat and leather gloves.'

'Well done, I *have* taught you well. Why didn't you mention this last night?' he asked her.

'I don't know. I guess I thought that I may have imagined it.'

'Okay, go home,' he said to her calmly.

'I'll ring Mr Ellis up and let him know what's happened and that his shop won't be opening today,' she said, trying to think straight.

'You don't have to, I'm with Mr Ellis now, he knows what's going on.'

'What! But... what's going on, Tony?'

'Go home. I'll speak to you soon, bye.' Tony hung up. When he turned around he noticed that Joshua was still standing in the doorway.

'Is there a problem?' Joshua asked.

'Nothing for you to worry about. Now, where is this recording, and Eric?'

Joshua showed the detective around the other side of the large desk and sat him down opposite the bank of monitors. 'I'll go and get Eric for you,' he said, as he left the room.

When the paramedics had taken Evie away, the forensics team started to get to work. They were all over the kitchen, taking swabs of this, that and the other and plenty of photographs. Joshua noticed that they were also searching through the knives and other sharp kitchen implements, obviously looking for a weapon.

Some of them had also taken the vampires over to one side and were swabbing for DNA. Sadie was giving one of them what for, trying to convince them that she wasn't a vampire. Joshua found this slightly amusing. Richard was trying his best to control his wife. 'Calm down and let them do their job. We have nothing to hide and they will want everyone's DNA.'

One of the team members noticed Mary clinging onto Sadie's leg, 'Well little one, will you allow me to take a sample from you? It won't hurt.'

'You're joking aren't you, she's only a child!' Sadie protested.

51

'She's still a vampire Sadie, don't forget that,' Richard reminded her. The guy turned around to get his swab and when he looked back again, Mary had turned and was smiling sweetly at him showing off her fangs, and staring at him with her red eyes. He jumped and nearly dropped the swab, which made Mary giggle. Richard and Sadie couldn't help smiling and had to turn away.

Joshua found Eric having a drink of the red stuff, 'I don't think that's wise at the moment,' he reminded him.

'Why not? They know we have to feed; at least it isn't from them,' he said, slightly annoyed.

'Eric, calm down. We know that we are innocent, and soon they will find that out for themselves, then we can hopefully piece this thing together. Detective Peters wants to see you in my office so you can have a look at the surveillance recordings with him.' Eric handed over the glass to Joshua, who dutifully finished it off, then Eric left the kitchen and headed for the office.

Joshua stood in the corner of the dining area away from everyone and was watching everything that was going on. He could see Richard on the other side of the room with Sadie and Mary. Very quietly he called out to Richard across the room; only the vampires would be able to hear him. He knew that there weren't any among the police. Not any of them that were there, anyway. 'Richard, can you hear me?' Richard hugged Sadie tight to him, to hide his face.

'Yes I can hear you, what is it?'

'Who are you talking to?' Sadie asked.

'Shhh. Joshua,' he answered.

'Why, what's the problem?' Joshua asked.

'No, not you, Sadie.'

'Oh, right, apparently there may be a witness, Detective Peter's wife, would you believe?' Joshua then told Richard everything that he had heard in the office.

'Hopefully they will have the culprit on CCTV, then,' Richard whispered. Then he remembered something. 'Don't we have someone in the council, working in that department?'

'Yes, Lucy used to date him. Mark Elliot. I'll get his number from her.'

'Luckily, I still have it,' Lucy whispered back.

Michael had taken Ann home. From here he would go straight to the hospital. Fortunately Ann only lived a little further down the road, in a large Victorian semi-detached house, with off street parking to the front. Michael thought that it was rather big for one person and wondered how she could afford to live there. But he didn't have time to ask her about it, so he filed the question away for later.

'When I've finished at the hospital, I'll bring your car down to you,' he said, as she was unlocking her front door and coughing again. 'Please give your mum a ring; you're too weak to be on your own. It's either that or I'll kidnap you again,' he said with a smile.

'Okay, I promise. You make me too nervous.'

'You shouldn't be nervous. I'm a pussycat really.'

'Yes, with big teeth,' she replied.

This made Michael smile. 'At least you can make jokes about me,' he said.

The hospital was a large modern grey building, situated just on the outskirts of Newport. The car park stretched all along the front and up the left hand side of the building, lined with trees, giving the place a nice open feel. The Emergency department was situated on the right of the building. Around the corner was a large ornamental pond, with a variety of wildlife. In spring and summer, ducks and other birds could be seen wandering around the grounds.

Michael arrived at the hospital and parked in his designated spot, then walked the short distance to the front entrance. He passed through the double doors and turned right, walking past the reception area into the emergency department itself and spotted Dr Angela Carter, short and plump with short light brown hair, going slightly grey in places. She had a kind round face and dark grey eyes. He knew her very well and had worked with her for a long time.

'Angela,' Michael called, to get her attention.

'I didn't think it would be long before you showed up. Where's your brother?' she asked.

'He's stuck at the castle with everyone else. I was the only one not at Joshua's party.'

'I take it from your tone that you know what's going on, then,' she asked.

'Yes, Richard rang me. What do you know?'

'I've just examined her. The wounds are superficial. She passed out from shock and she also has slight hypothermia but I don't think it will be long before she'll be coming around. Then she can give a statement to the police.'

'Good, then she can clear all this up. I don't like any distrust between humans and us. Can I see her?' he whispered.

'She has a police guard, and her mum is with her, so I don't think it will be possible, and anyway there's no way on earth that they will allow a vampire anywhere near her,' she informed him crisply.

'Okay, no problem. I'll be in the staff lounge. Please let me know when she comes around.'

'What are you up to?' she asked.

'That would be telling wouldn't it. Trust me. I won't get you into trouble, I promise,' he said, blowing her a kiss as he walked away.

'I've heard that one before, from both the Moon brothers,' she chuntered under her breathe. She hadn't forgotten the stunt they had pulled on her when she had first qualified.

Ann poured herself a drink, took her antibiotics and paracetamol then rang her mother. She knew that it was a bad idea but she didn't want Michael plaguing her any more. If her mother were there when he brought her car back, he would leave her alone. If truth were known though, she quite liked him; she just didn't know if she could trust him. 'Hi, Mum,' she said, then started coughing.

'Oh dear, you don't sound too good. Have you seen a doctor?'

Have I seen a Doctor? If she only knew, she thought. 'Yes I saw a doctor yesterday. I have some antibiotics.'

'Oh good,' her mother said. 'I tried to ring you last night but you weren't in. I hope that you were well wrapped up.'

'You could say that,' she said, almost to herself.

'What was that dear? I didn't quite hear you.'

'Yes, I was wrapped up, Mum.'

'You sound really tired, do you want me to come round and cook you something?'

'Oh Mum, that would be really nice, thank you.'

'See you soon, dear.'

Ann sat down in her pyjamas and waited for her mother to arrive, trying to think of a way to ask her what she knew about the Island vampires.

Eric showed Detective Peters the dvd recording. The camera was focused on the outside of the gates. First, they saw the side edge of a dark car going past. After less than 10 minutes it drove past again in the other direction. Then a figure appeared, all in black. He knew that the camera was there, as he never looked up, even though his face was covered with what looked like a balaclava.

He laid Evie gently down on the ground and disappeared. In less than a minute the gate opened, and Eric appeared, checked for a pulse, picked her up and went back down the drive, the gates closing behind him.

'Did you see anyone when you went out to pick her up?' Tony Peters asked Eric, who had just sat down on the large couch.

'As you can see from the recording, detective, I didn't exactly look, but I did hear a car driving away. My main concern was to get her inside; she was extremely cold, bleeding and unconscious.'

Tony thought for a while. 'Are there any more cameras around this place, Eric?'

'Of course, both inside and out, at each entrance and all around the perimeter.'

'I would like to see all the recordings for around the perimeter and this front entrance.'

'Of course,' Eric replied, 'no problem.' He stood up and walked back to the desk with all the monitors and started to show the detective how to use all the controls, so that he could view any of the recordings he wanted.

'Were you watching these monitors all the time during the party, Eric?' Tony said, without looking up.

'Of course. I take my responsibility as head of security here very seriously.'

'Did you see anyone leave the castle at all?'

'No. I watched everyone arrive and they all went through to the kitchen area. Only two people came back out. One was little Mary, who went into the lounge; she likes to play the games on the large screen television in there. Richard Moon followed her in there after about five minutes.'

Tony paused for a while, watching the monitors. He saw Mary and Richard enter the room opposite, just as Eric had explained. 'Is there any possibility at all that someone could leave these premises without you knowing?'

Eric stood up; he didn't like being questioned about his

responsibilities in this way, and became a little agitated. 'This place was built in the 1500's with fortification in mind; that is why Joshua bought this place, initially to protect us, before we came to an agreement with the Islanders. Not only is the castle itself secure, but it also has an 8-foot high stonewall around the grounds. The only gap there is is where we meet the sea, and the tide never goes out far enough for you to walk out. The only way out that way, is either by boat, swimming or scuba-diving. Bearing in mind the strong currents out there in the Solent, the best way would be by boat and once again, there is a camera hidden on the jetty.' Eric took a deep breath and sat down again.

'I'm sorry if I offended you there. I'm only trying to rule out the possibility that someone may have left the party, then sneaked back in through the gate behind you when you brought Evie in. Could a vampire scale those walls?'

'Yes, but the perimeter cameras are situated where their fields of vision overlap; there aren't any blind spots.'

'I'm impressed!'

'Thank you,' Eric replied.

'Thank you for your help and co-operation Eric. I will need to take copies of these recordings with me of course.'

'Sure.' Eric made a copy for the detective, and then handed it over. He then followed him out of the office.

When they returned to the kitchen, the forensic team had finished all their work and the police officers had taken statements from everyone. The detective approached the forensics team and although he spoke quietly, Richard and Joshua still heard him informing them about the surveillance tapes and asked them to move up the road and see what they could find up there. The car had obviously turned around somewhere up there and hopefully they would find tyre tracks.

Then the detective walked over to Joshua.

'Have you got everything you need, detective?' the vampire asked.

'Yes, thanks. Eric was very helpful. I have a copy of your security recordings for today. They will be returned, of course, if everything checks out. As Evie's employer, I gather that you will have her address.' Tony knew that he could get this from his wife, but he didn't want to cause her any more stress.

Joshua smiled. 'Of course. I have it ready for you,' he said, as he handed a piece of paper over. Tony was impressed with the foresight.

'Thanks. Just one more thing though, out of all the vampires that you invited, are there any unaccounted for?'

'Just one,' Joshua answered 'Richard's brother, Mr Michael Moon.'

'Any idea why he isn't here?'

Joshua was trying to hide his annoyance. How dare he think that Michael might have something to do with this? 'Yes, he's on call at the hospital.'

'Right, thank you. I'm on my way there now. I'll talk to him.'

'He may be at home. Just because he's on call doesn't mean that he's at the hospital.' Joshua gave him the address. Tony Peters walked away and took out his mobile and Joshua heard him making arrangements for another forensics team to go to Evie's address.

As soon as the police had left, Joshua obtained Mark's number from Lucy. After a few rings Mark answered. 'Hello?'

'Hi, is this Mark?' Joshua enquired.

'Yes.'

'Hi, it's Joshua Ellis.'

'Hello, what can I do for you? Is Lucy okay?' There was a slight panic in his voice. Lucy had heard this and raised her eyebrows at Joshua.

'Yes she's fine. I need a favour from you, if possible.'

'What's that?' Mark sounded cagey.

'The police will be coming to your department shortly. Asking about CCTV footage for the market place, near St Thomas's church in Newport, for late teatime yesterday. There may be two women on the tape at the same time, going to the night safe at the bank. Can you get me a copy?'

'May I ask what this is about? I could get the sack if I'm caught.'

'Someone is trying to set us up, faking vampire bites. We think the culprit may be on that tape.'

'Consider it done.'

'Thanks and don't worry if you get the sack. I'll find something for you.' Joshua hung up and found Lucy staring at him. 'Don't worry, it won't be here.'

Ann was now settled down with a large bowl of home made soup courtesy of her mum. She felt more relaxed now that she was in her own home with the door locked. Sylvia was slightly taller than her daughter with a fuller figure. Her face was framed with soft dark brown permed hair.

'So what's his name, then?' her mum asked.

'What makes you think that there's a man in my life?'

'Because you didn't come home last night, and while I've been here you haven't heard a word I've said, plus you're dreamy.'

'It's not what you think. I rescued a little girl last night when I came out of the doctors, she was being harassed by some young lads so I took her home.'

'And?' her mother pressed.

'She lives with her uncle. When I got there, I passed out on him.'

'You what!'

'It's okay, Mum, calm down; it turned out that he's a doctor.'

'Well, he would say that, wouldn't he? And you stayed there all night?'

'Yes. I wasn't in a fit state to leave.'

'Why didn't you call me?'

'I was barely conscious.'

'Did he drug you?'

'No!' Ann started coughing again, then calmed down. 'Mum, it wasn't like that; he was really nice.'

'There's something you're not telling me isn't there. What's his name?'

'Mr Michael Moon, he's a'…

'I know who he is!' her mum interrupted, 'He gave me my new knees.'

'What!' Ann went into another coughing fit and her mum had to give her a drink. 'You know him!'

'Yes, and you're right, he's a really nice person, despite what he is. You do know, don't you?' Her mum looked at her, concerned.

'Yes, he told me; it made me a bit nervous, but I can't get him out of my mind.' Ann started to drift off again into her dream world and smiled.

'Oh dear,' her mum said.

'Half of me likes him, but the other half can't get past what he is.'

'Do you think that he likes you?' her mum asked curiously.

'I don't know. He certainly had a lot of concern about me last night and he wasn't keen on me coming home today. He made me promise that I would ring you. He said that I shouldn't be alone.'

'Well there you are then, if he had an ulterior motive he would have made sure that you stayed with him, or that you were alone here,' her mum said, trying to cheer her up.

'I guess you're right.'

'Where is he now?' her mum asked with a curious look on her face.

'I think he got an urgent call from the hospital. Wait a minute! You knew he was a vampire and yet you agreed to let him operate on you?'

'Yes of course I did. You have a lot to learn about our vampires. Your father and I found out about them when we first moved down here. It did worry us in the beginning, but we soon got used to them. After a while you tend to forget that they are on the Island at all.'

'So they are safe, then?' Ann asked.

'Well, we've never come across a vampire attack whilst we've been on the Island. Plus, if a surgeon who is a vampire can manage to get through an operation without having a taste, then I am sure we're safe.'

'It's still a bit weird though, don't you think?' Ann asked, unsure.

'The Islanders keep them well fed and they are quite proud of them.' Her mum answered.

Michael's phone rang, while he was waiting in the staff room. It was Richard. 'Thought I would give you an update,' he said. 'They have taken DNA samples and statements from everyone but they may be looking for you.'

'Why?' Michael asked.

'Because you were invited to the party but didn't show up, of course. Joshua told them that you were on call.'

'Thanks. As it happens, I have an alibi anyway. I was with Ann all night. The only trouble is, she was unconscious.'

'Ah, slight problem there, then, I have a feeling that they don't really believe us. Have you managed to see Evie yet?'

'No, Angela knows that I'm here; I'm just waiting for her to come and get me. She's under police guard, so I may have to improvise somehow,' Michael said thoughtfully.

'Well you had better make it quick. Detective Peters is on his way to you now, but of course he won't be able to talk to her either, if she's still unconscious.'

'Well, maybe I can keep out of his way and hopefully get in to see her before he does,' Michael said, trying to sound hopeful. Then Richard remembered something else.

'Before I forget. Joshua overheard a conversation between the detective and his wife; apparently she works with Evie and last night they thought that someone was following them. Joshua is trying to get a copy of the CCTV footage.'

'Good, I'll work on trying to get in to see Evie.'

Richard moved across the kitchen to talk to Sadie. 'I'm going to join Michael at the hospital, I want you to stay here, *don't* go home.'

'Why?'

'Sadie, think about it. We don't know if this is a one off. For all we know she was chosen because of her connection to Joshua. You're safe here; no one can get to you, plus we have the added problem of Mary. I don't want you alone with her if she falls asleep,'

Sadie knew that he was right. Mary still had nightmares and quite often she would turn in her sleep and when she did, she didn't know what she was doing. 'Okay, I'll stay,'

He gave her a long lingering kiss then left, leaving Joshua and Eric to look after her. 'Make sure that she doesn't leave,' he said to them on his way out. He knew how sneaky his wife could be.

Mark Elliot made it in to work very quickly and managed to beat the police. It was his day off, but he knew how important this information was to them. He went into one of the side offices only to find that there was someone working in there. This technician was a new employee so he had never seen him before.

'Can I help you?' he asked.

'Yes, you can help me, if you don't mind,' Mark replied.

'What with?' he asked. Mark turned and looked him straight in the eyes, holding him with his gaze.

'You can sleep,' he said, and with that the technician fell unconscious.

Mark was of average height and build, with shoulder length blond hair, which he held back in a ponytail; he had a long narrow face and blue eyes. Over the long years as a vampire he took great pride in keeping up with technology. This had turned him into quite a computer geek. He soon got to work and managed to break through all the security codes and found the recording he was looking for.

He saw someone dressed in dark clothing hanging about around the church; he noted the time on the tape. He played with the computer a little longer and found another recording from another camera and found the two girls visiting the night safe at the same time. He knew then that he had the right person; he inserted his memory stick and recorded both cameras quickly.

Then he had a thought and went back to the first recording. He watched as the person in question made a phone call and then walk off. Mark then switched to other cameras and followed him right to the car park. Unfortunately his car was parked at such an angle that the camera couldn't get a good look at it.

He set to work once more and recorded everything. When he had finished he turned to the young man asleep in the chair. 'Can you hear me?' he asked.

'Yes I can hear you.'

'When you wake, you will not remember me, do you understand?'

'Yes.'

Mark removed the memory stick from the computer and then returned the screen back to what the technician was working on when he came in. He then pushed the chair, complete with the sleeping employee, back to the desk, and then walked to the door. There was no-one around and from the doorway he said, 'One, two, three, wake!' He saw him stir, open his eyes and look at his computer. Mark quietly closed the door, knowing that he would think that he had just nodded off.

As Mark was leaving the building through the reception area he saw someone enter wearing a dark grey suit. 'Detective Tony Peters. I believe that I am expected by the supervisor of the CCTV department.' Mark heard him say as he walked out of the building.

Mark smiled to himself, *that's one to us,* he thought. Once he was outside he called Joshua on his mobile. 'I have the recordings,' he said, with a smile.

CHAPTER FIVE

Andrew had walked further up the lane to where Gary had parked the car; he jumped in, taking off his balaclava. Gary drove off, 'Did it go according to plan?' Gary asked.

'Of course it did, easier than I thought it would.' Andrew used some wet wipes in the car to clean the two-pronged fork, and then placed it into a plastic bag. He then took out his mobile phone.

'Hi, boss, all went well, do you want us to dump the weapon?'

'No, you're going to need it again. Keep it safe.'

Andrew didn't like the sound of that, but he knew that he would have to follow orders. 'I don't like keeping weapons on me afterwards. They're evidence.'

'Sorry about that but you will need it again. I want you to stay on the Island and find another victim. It doesn't have to be someone close to them, I want to make them sweat for a bit. Ring me when you're ready to make another move.'

'Okay, I'll let Gary know.' Andrew hung up and put the phone back in his pocket. 'He wants us to stay on the Island and seek out another victim. You had better drop me off, at my car. I need to move it, just in case the police find out about the caravan.' Gary drove out of Wootton and headed towards Whippingham.

'Why do you think he hates the Island vampires so much?' Andrew asked.

'I don't know, but all vampires should be wiped of the face of the earth, right. Well it's not natural is it? I mean they're not in the natural order of things, we are the ones that are supposed to be at the top of the food chain. If it's the boss's goal to wipe them out, we can't be left with the Island vampires.'

Andrew thought for a while. 'I must say it's a good plan. Discredit the Island vampires, and then let the Islanders do our work for us. It certainly saves us trying to fight them and losing more men,' he said, with a smile.

'Yes and we get to do the easy part, unless they all have baseball bats hidden,' Gary said, with a laugh.

Gary drove to Whippingham then turned down a narrow lane, which led down to a caravan park and eventually down to the River Medina which separated Cowes from East Cowes.

They both arrived at the caravan site and put gloves on, then they went into the caravan to make sure that they hadn't left any evidence behind; they wiped everything down and removed their beer bottles. 'We had both better find separate hotels, use false names and cash, remember, no credit cards,' Andrew said.

'I know! I do know how to do my job, you know.' Gary was beginning to get annoyed. This was supposed to be his project, but even he had to admit that he had been relieved when Andrew had turned up.

Edmond Parr sat at his desk, smiling; everything was going to plan; he just had to keep it up. Soon the Islanders would turn, and the friendly vampires would be a thing of the past.

Edmond was in his fifties. A rather large man with a chubby face. He had inherited his father's shipping business in Southampton, ten years ago; it had made him a very rich man. He was a very strict boss, a large man who liked to push his weight around. Having the responsibility of a large shipping company thrust upon him so suddenly, after his father had been involved in a fatal car accident, had made him go grey overnight; this was soon followed by his divorce, as the strain of the new responsibility had destroyed his marriage.

But he had pulled himself together, got on with things and was proud of what he had achieved. He also enjoyed the power he felt, coordinating the downfall of all vampires in the country. It was his little hobby as he called it, helping the community. His daughter and family lived on the Island; he wanted to keep them safe, as his grandson would one day inherit the business from him.

'Everything okay?' he heard a voice ask him from the couch. Edmond looked round; his girlfriend of 3 years, Stella, was sitting there doing her nails. She was only thirty five. A slim, long-haired brunette who looked fantastic – arm-candy was the term. He felt young again with her on his arm. She could have entered Miss World.

'Everything is going really well,' he said cheerfully. 'Gary and Andrew are doing exactly what they are supposed to do.'

'I know that vampires need to be destroyed, but aren't the Island ones supposed to be friendly?' she asked, but as she said it, she knew that she shouldn't have.

'Are you questioning me?' he shouted, and shot up from his chair. Stella drew her legs up in front of her and put her head down, waiting for the blow.

'No, I'm not. I was just thinking about your family; they live on the Island. It might cause a blood bath and if the vampires find out about them they could be in danger,' she said, trying to avoid his anger.

'I know exactly what I'm doing, so don't question me!' he shouted, as he stormed out of the room.

Stella sat there shaking but thankful that he hadn't hit her this time, wondering if she would ever learn how to keep her mouth shut. They lived in a large double-fronted three storey Georgian manor, which Edmond had also inherited from his father. It was built of red brick with large white sash windows, which had been triple glazed against the noise from the aircraft overhead, as they were not too far from Southampton airport. Two plain half columns set against the wall framed the large front door. Three wide stone steps led down to the long gravel drive and the perfectly manicured lawns.

When his father died, he had sold off the office space near to the docks preferring instead to use part of the manor. There were only two of them living there, with a few staff members, so there was plenty of space unused and he had thought that this was a waste.

Stella left the office and went up to the bedroom. She had heard him go into the kitchen and order the maid to make him a sandwich. In the bedroom she felt she was out of his way. Sitting on the large window seat overlooking the grounds, she started thinking. Stella knew that for her own safety she would have to leave him but was too scared to do so. He had a lot of men willing to do his dirty work for him and she knew that she would be dead within a week if she did. All she could do was sit tight and hope that an opportunity would show itself.

Edmond entered the bedroom. 'What are you doing up here?' he asked.

'I thought that you might want me out of your way,' she said nervously. 'I was only thinking of your family, you know. I know they mean a lot to you,' she said, trying to sound sincere.

'I know. Well, maybe you can help me celebrate my first victory against the Island blood suckers,' he said, grabbing her by the back of her hair.

He threw her onto the bed and sat on her, pinning her down by her wrists. He then leaned forward and began to kiss her hard and slobber all over her. Stella could feel the pulse in her wrists throbbing. Her fingers began to go numb he was holding her so tight; she knew that she would have bruises the next day.

Edmond then transferred both her wrists into one hand; Stella winced with the pain as the bones in her wrists were forced together, but she didn't show it too much, otherwise he would have hurt her even more. He didn't even bother to unbutton her blouse but used his free hand to rip the front open. Stella was trying to switch off but the pain was too much. Edmond then ripped the front of her bra then started to bite her breasts hard. The more she tried to push him off, the harder he bit her.

The phone began to ring at the side of the bed. Edmond ignored it, then he let go of Stella's wrists, and got hold of her forearms beginning to kiss her hard on the lips again.

The phone carried on ringing, '*Ahhh!*' he yelled frustrated. He picked up the phone, '*What?*'

It was his secretary. 'Mr Weston is on the phone, he wants to speak to you about another shipment from Varna.' Edmond released Stella and she disappeared into the bathroom.

'Hello, Mr Weston. How many crates will your client be wanting to ship this time?' Stella could hear Edmond from the bathroom; she locked the door and got into the shower, trying to wash away his smell. Her wrists ached and she couldn't stop crying. 'Yes that will be no problem, Mr Weston. I'll make the necessary arrangements, goodbye.' He replaced the phone, 'I'm going back down to do some work,' he shouted through the door, he then left her in peace.

Stella felt relieved when he left; she dressed in fresh clothes and returned to the bedroom. She locked the bedroom door then removed the bottom drawer from the bedside table, removing her laptop she sat on the bed.

Gary and Andrew had found themselves their own hotels. Gary was feeling really pleased with himself, that everything had gone according to plan. He was hoping that the next one would go equally well. He liked Andrew but he just wished that he didn't try to take over so much. Even Gary had to admit to himself, though, that he was glad that Andrew had volunteered to do the actual deed to Evie; he didn't think that he would have the stomach for it himself.

Andrew showered then settled himself down on the bed and tried to think of a reason why his boss had taken it upon himself to rid the country of vampires. He had worked for him for several years now, working as his bodyguard and doing various errands for him.

This was something new; why the sudden change? 'I need some air,' he said to himself. He got up put his coat on and made his way to the reception to hand in his key.

'Will you be dining with us this evening Sir,' the receptionist asked.

'No, thanks, I have other plans,' he said as he left.

Stella thought for a while. She had heard Edmond mention someone called Ellis, *Joshua* Ellis, that was it. Joshua Ellis, Isle of Wight, she typed into the laptop. Within seconds several websites came up for her to read.

CHAPTER SIX

Richard found Michael in the staff room. 'Have you seen her yet?' Richard asked eagerly.

'No, but I have an idea. Come on, let's find Angela.' They both went out into the hospital and walked down several corridors until they found her, talking to someone.

'Oh no!' Richard exclaimed, pulling Michael back around the corner.

'What's wrong, who is it?' Michael asked.

'That's the detective, Tony Peters.' They both peered round the corner and saw the policeman take a seat.

'Come on,' Michael said.

'Where are we going?'

'In here,' Michael said as he pulled Richard into a storeroom full of linen.

'What are we doing in here? I do hope that you're not planning to get me dressed up as a female auxiliary, to go and change her bed,' Richard said in a panic, knowing his brother all too well.

'*Sssh*,' Michael said, as he waved one hand at Richard and looked out through the slightly open door. 'Get ready, Angela's coming this way.'

'What!'

As Angela was walking past, Michael jumped out of the storeroom, put his hand over her mouth and dragged her back in. Richard grabbed her legs to prevent her from kicking down all the linen shelves. '*Sssh*, it's us,' Michael whispered to her from behind. At the same time she saw Richard and stopped struggling.

Michael took his hand away, she turned towards him, eyes blazing. 'What do you...?' she started to shout, but Michael put one hand back over her mouth and the other at the back of her head.

'Will you be quiet? Please?' he asked, removing his hand for the second time. 'We need you to do us a favour.'

'You must be joking,' she said. 'I'm not getting into trouble over you two again.'

'What do you mean again?' they both said at the same time.

'In case you two have forgotten, I haven't forgiven you for having to do my first consultations with a purple face.' They both tried to stifle a laugh, but Angela wasn't amused.

'That was your fault for struggling; we only wanted to paint your nose. It was your right of initiation, remember, you had just qualified!' Michael exclaimed.

'You didn't have to use Gentian Violet, it took a week to wear off,' her voice got louder.

'Ssssh.' Michael looked at Richard for help but he had a pillowcase in his mouth and was crying. 'Angela, please this is important.'

'What's it worth?' she asked.

'Whatever you want,' Michael said, smiling at her.

'I'll think of something,' she said. 'Now what do you want?'

'First of all...'

'Wait a minute, what do you mean first of all? Exactly how many favours do you need?' she said, cutting Michael short.

He took a deep breath then repeated himself. 'First of all, take our keys, go to our offices, get our white coats and bring them back here,'

'Why can't you do that yourself?' she said, puzzled.

'Because it means passing detective Peters. He knows Richard and although he doesn't know me yet, I don't want him being able to place me in this area later, by memory.'

Michael and Richard gave Angela their keys; she then sneaked out of the door, chuntering to herself. Michael watched her, as she disappeared down the corridor and around the corner.

'So what's the plan then?' Richard asked.

'We get Angela to get rid of the detective for us, then one us gives our friendly police officer a rest, before we go into the room.'

'What about her mum?' said Richard.

'I don't think that she will be a problem.'

'You don't!'

'No, I'm sure that both of us can be charming.'

'Charming!' Richard exclaimed, as there was a quiet knock at the door.

Angela came back into the linen store with their white coats and returned their keys. They both slipped them on.

'Right, one more favour,' Richard said. 'We need you to get the detective out of the way.'

'Excuse me? Please tell me how I'm supposed to do that?'

68

Richard looked at Michael for help. 'Tell him that you wish to discuss Evie's condition in private, and take him away somewhere.' Michael answered.

'Right,' she said, unsure.

Michael put his hands on each side of her face, then gave her a big kiss on the lips. 'You can do this, we know you can,' he said with confidence.

'But wait, Evie's still unconscious. How are you going to question her?' Angela suddenly remembered.

'She shouldn't be that deeply unconscious. I should be able to use my talents to bring her around,' Michael informed her.

'Oh, right,' was the only reply he got. Angela left the linen store chuntering to herself once more. 'Why do I put up with the Moon brothers?'

Michael watched as Angela approached the detective. She said something to him and he dutifully followed her. 'Coast is clear, come on,' Michael said, but Richard stopped him.

'Wait! Which one of us is going to handle the police officer?'

'You are of course, you're the anaesthetist.'

'I will have to change to do it and there are witnesses out there,' Richard said worriedly.

'Not at the moment, it's gone quiet.'

Richard looked out passed Michael, 'Oh yeah.' They both exited the linen store and headed down the corridor. The police officer looked up as they approached and stood up.

Richard quickly changed and before the officer could do anything, Richard was staring into his eyes. He couldn't move. 'Sleep,' was all Richard had to say.

The officer's knees suddenly buckled, both of them caught him and quickly propped him up in his chair. 'I hope he doesn't get into trouble, for falling asleep on duty,' Richard said, as they both entered Evie's room.

The room was only small; there was only one bed inside. Evie was laid asleep with a dressing on the left side of her neck. Her mother was sitting at her side, holding her hand, and had her head down on the bed.

Michael approached and put his hand on her shoulder; she sat up and looked at him. 'Mrs Martin?' he asked.

'Yes.'

'My name is Michael Moon and this is my brother Richard, we are both doctors here at the hospital and we want to help.'

Margaret looked at her daughter and said, 'She won't wake up.'

'Yes, we know, I'm going to work on that now, that is if you will allow me to,' he said.

Margaret nodded and turned back to look up at him. 'What are you going to try?' she asked a little baffled. Michael looked across at Richard as if to say, *well here goes*, then looked back to Margaret.

Richard stayed by the door in case someone came in. Michael sat on the edge of the bed and took Margaret's hand in his. 'I don't want you to be alarmed, but we are both vampires.'

'Oh my God,' she whispered.

'It's okay, I'm the leader of the Island Vampires, You're not in any danger. I know what this looks like, but I can assure you that this is not a vampire bite. Your daughter was attacked by someone else and we want to find out who.'

'The police wouldn't have allowed you in. What have you done with the officer outside?' she asked in a panic, snatching her hands away from his.

'He's fine, we haven't done anything to hurt him. Please, we can help each other here. You're an Islander, you know us, have you ever known any of us attack or kill a human?'

'No, I must admit that I haven't, but could it be one from the mainland?' she said thoughtfully.

'No. A vampire would not have missed the artery, believe me. Will you allow me to wake Evie up? I won't hurt her, I promise.'

Margaret didn't answer him; she just nodded, then started to cry. Michael briefly put his hand on her shoulder then moved around to the other side of the bed.

Michael sat down and put his hand on the side of Evie's face. Her mum watched him closely. Leaning forward he began to speak to her, 'Evie can you hear me? My name is Michael, your mum is here.' He heard a little sob from Margaret, so he reached across the bed and squeezed her hand. 'Evie come on, I know you can hear me, latch onto my voice and follow it.'

Margaret felt her daughter's hand twitch and Michael saw it too.

'Come on, follow my voice,' Evie's eyelids began to flutter.

Her mum stood up and joined in and Michael didn't stop her. 'Come on darling, it's me, Mum, come on, wake up.'

70

Evie's eyes opened and focused on both of them.

'Where am I?' she asked, as she felt at her neck.

'You're in hospital, but you're going to be alright,' her mum informed her.

Evie looked across to Michael, 'Was it you I could hear?'

'Yes,' he said, smiling. 'I'm Michael, and this is my brother Richard,' he indicated towards the door.

'Welcome back,' Richard said.

'Thank you,' she said quietly.

'Can you remember what happened to you?' Michael asked.

She thought for a little while then brought her hands up to her face and started to cry, 'Oh, Mum, it was awful. I thought that they were going to kill me.'

Michael allowed her to calm down before he asked her again.

Evie began to tell them about her kidnapping. Stopping every now and again as if in a dream, re-living every moment.

'Did you see their faces?' Richard asked from the door.

'No they were both wearing black balaclavas.'

'Have you any idea where they took you?' Michael asked.

Evie explained about the caravan and her attempt to escape, whilst holding on tightly to her mother's hand. It wasn't long before her mum also began to cry. Michael and Richard didn't say anything for a while, allowing them both to calm down once more.

'It's okay, you're doing really well,' Richard said kindly.

They both listened as Evie told them about the kidnapper who seemed to care. There seemed to be something about him, that they couldn't quite put their finger on.

Evie finally began to describe the end of her ordeal. 'He turned my head to one side.' She said thoughtfully, trying to remember, raising her hand to her neck at the same time. 'To the left,' she said. Then he seemed to change his mind, and turned my head to the right. I felt two sharp points digging into my neck and I felt my blood running down my neck.' Evie began to sob and her mum squeezed her hand.

'It sounds as though this guy hesitated for some reason,' Richard said, looking at Michael.

'You said that you felt two sharp points, did you feel his mouth?' Michael asked.

'Oh no, this guy wasn't a vampire, he had some sort of instrument, because I felt him pushing with his hand.'

'Are you sure about that?' asked Richard.

'Yes definitely. After about 5 minutes he picked me up and carried me down the road. He leaned me against a wall and I vaguely remember him removing my handcuffs and blindfold. Then he walked away to leave me to die.' At this point she reached out for her mum. 'There were large gates! I remember large iron gates,' she exclaimed as she turned towards Michael. 'They opened and someone picked me up, that's the last I remember.'

Both Michael and Richard were impressed with all the detail that Evie could remember.

'Mum you had better ring Mr Ellis and Clair, let them know what has happened. They will be wondering where I am,' she said in a sudden panic.

Before she could say anything, Michael interrupted her, 'It's alright, Mr Ellis already knows. I have no doubt that he'll be here shortly himself. That is when the police decide to let him near you.'

Evie began to shake.

'What's wrong?' asked Richard.

'The only vampire that I have knowingly met is Lucy.'

'You were left outside Mr Ellis's gates and were carried inside by the head of his security team. It was Lucy who recognised you,' Richard informed her with a smile. 'As to Lucy being the only vampire that you've met, you've just met us.'

Evie's eyes widened in disbelief but they both just smiled back at her. 'How did you get in here? Surely they wouldn't allow you to come near me,' she said.

'We both work here,' Richard answered.

'So those white coats are genuine then?' she asked.

'Of course they are,' Michael replied.

'Is there anything else that you can remember?' Richard asked.

Evie thought, and then looked up. 'They both had tattoos on their wrists!' she exclaimed. Evie then went on to describe the tattoos. They both looked at each other baffled.

'Well I can guess what the 'V' stands for,' Richard announced, looking at his brother.

'We had better go,' Michael informed them, 'but do us a favour.'

'Anything,' Margaret replied.

'You haven't seen us.'

'I think that we can manage that,' Margaret said. 'After all, you have helped my daughter so it's the least we can do.'

'Thank you for that and your help,' Richard replied.

They both left the room after making sure that the coast was clear. Richard bent down over the police officer outside the door, while Michael kept watch. 'Can you hear me?'

'Yes,' the officer said.

'When you wake, you won't remember us. Is that clear.'

'Yes, that's clear,' he answered.

Michael began to walk away towards their offices.

'One, two, three, wake,' Richard said then quickly followed after Michael, briefly looking back to make sure that the officer was indeed waking up.

They both ended up in Michael's office, where they removed their white coats. Michael picked the phone up, and had Angela paged, and then put the receiver back down. 'What do think?' Richard asked.

Michael sat down and leaned forward onto his desk. 'She's a good witness and is certain that it wasn't a vampire, which backs up what we already know,' Michael said. 'But who is it and why?' he went on to say.

'None of us have taken a human life for over a hundred years, so it can't be revenge against one of us,' Richard added, as he sat on the edge of the desk.

Michael's phone rang; it was Angela. 'The coast is clear and she's awake,' he said into the phone.

'Well it's about time, what took you so long? I had to buy him lunch in the canteen to try and stall him for longer. You two owe me big style.'

'Yeah, sorry about that but she had quite a tale to tell. Thanks for what you did, and yes, we know we owe you one.' Michael put the phone down.

'We'll have to make it good, you know, to pay her back, otherwise we won't hear the last of it,' Richard said joking.

'Come on,' Michael said so suddenly that he made Richard jump.

'What! Where are we going now?'

'Well you're going back to the castle to give your wife a hug, while I run a small errand. Then I'll join you there, and we'll look at the evidence and make a plan of action.'

CHAPTER SEVEN

Lucy was making cup cakes with Mary, trying to keep her occupied. This was a rather strange hobby for a vampire to have, but Lucy loved cooking and baking.

Sadie was walking up and down the kitchen floor getting more and more restless. Joshua got hold of her by the shoulders, 'Will you please sit down, you're making me dizzy.'

'I'm sorry, I just want to know what's going on, who's doing this to us?' Sadie said, worried.

'Us!' Joshua remarked.

'Yes, us. Why, what's wrong?' she asked.

'Doesn't that tell you something, that you regard yourself as one of us,' Joshua said, with a smile.

Sadie looked round and saw that Lucy and Mary were also smiling. 'I hadn't thought of that, I've known you all for so long. I feel like one of the family,' she said thoughtfully, looking Joshua in the eyes.

'You are one of the family, but could you actually bring yourself to become one of us? Because I think that your subconscious has just answered that question for you, without you realizing it.' Joshua gave her a hug. 'In answer to your question,' he said, changing the subject, 'we don't know yet, but we will find out, okay.'

Sadie nodded.

'Do you want a drink to calm your nerves?' he asked her.

'Yes please.'

Joshua poured her a brandy and sat her down in the conservatory area, just off the kitchen.

Eric came in to see Joshua, 'Mark's here with the CCTV footage,' he said.

'Excellent, hopefully this will give us some kind of a clue.' Joshua smiled at Lucy. 'When you have a minute, would you mind bringing three drinks into the front office please?'

Lucy looked at him, with a worried look on her face. Sadie noticed and stood up, 'I'll bring them,' she said.

'Are you sure?'

'Yes! I've been looking after Richard all these years, I'm hardly squeamish am I.'

'Okay,' Joshua said, as he left the kitchen with Eric.

As Sadie was pouring the drinks, she heard Richard come back from the Hospital and go straight into the office.

She poured an extra drink and put them onto a tray. 'Mary would you mind coming with me to open the office door,' she asked. Mary walked in front of her with the wooden spoon in her hand, licking at the cup cake mixture.

Mary knocked on the door first and waited for an answer. 'Come in, Sadie,' Joshua called. Mary opened the door for her; she walked in and gave the drinks out.

'Where's Michael?' she asked Richard.

'He said that he had a small errand to run, but he won't be long. Thanks for the drink,' he said, giving her a kiss and a hug.

'Did you both manage to see Evie?' she asked him.

'Yes, and there's no need to worry. I'll tell you all about it as soon as I've seen this footage. Okay?'

Sadie nodded.

'Why don't you stay here and watch it with us?' he asked.

'What! Are you sure?' she said baffled.

'Of course. You're obviously worried about all this. You never know, you might spot something that we miss.'

They all moved to the front of the monitors and Mark put the memory stick into one of the computers. They all watched the screen; they saw a man standing by the church wearing dark clothing. He made a phone call, and then walked away. 'How do we know that this is the right person,' Joshua asked Mark.

'You see that camera opposite,' Mark replied.

'Yes,' they all answered.

'Well that one recorded this, at the same time,' he said whilst clicking on a few icons on the screen. The camera angle changed on the screen and they saw the two girls walking along and depositing the takings into the night safe.

'Is this all we have of him?' Richard asked.

'No, wait a minute,' Mark replied. He once again clicked on a few icons and was able to follow him to the car park, by showing the recordings taken from different cameras. 'Well done, Mark, thank you for your efforts. Can we clean any of this up, for a better view of him?' Joshua asked, looking at both Mark and Eric.

'No, I'm afraid not, the council cameras don't have too much definition,' Mark answered.

'We can't even do anything with our equipment here, except maybe try and blow up the image of him,' Eric put in.

'See what you two can do between you. Blow the car up as well, maybe we can get something from that,' Joshua ordered.

'Well we can rule one thing out,' a voice suddenly said. It was Sadie. Everyone looked round.

'What?' Richard asked.

'Well, at least we know that the man following them wasn't a vampire!' They all looked baffled.

'How do you know that?' Joshua asked.

'Because, as the cameras were following him through town, he had a reflection in the shop windows.'

'Well bugger me!' Mark exclaimed, 'Why didn't we notice that?'

'I knew there was a reason for letting you watch this as well,' Richard remarked.

Ann had woken up about teatime to the sound of voices downstairs. She had gone to bed after her soup, to get some rest whilst her mum was downstairs.

Mum's got the television on a bit loud, she thought. She got out of bed and put on her dressing gown. As Ann got half way down the stairs she heard, 'My knees feel absolutely fantastic now thank you.'

'Oh no!' she said, under her breath, 'please don't tell me she's let him in?' Ann walked down the hall and into the lounge, where she found Michael sat there as large as life.

'Yes, your mum did let me in, for a cup of coffee, would you believe?' he said, with a little amusement in his voice.

'Ah, you heard me. Sorry,' she said a little embarrassed.

'That's okay, maybe one day you will learn to trust me.'

'Coffee! You're drinking coffee!' she said as she suddenly realised what he had said.

'Yes, why not? We don't only drink the red stuff you know. That's our food; we drink other beverages as well.'

'Mr Moon was kind enough to bring your car back, dear. The least you can do is to be civil to him. Especially after he looked after you last night,' her mum put in.

'I'm sorry, I feel as though everyone is ganging up on me, over all this.' Ann said, beginning to cough again as she sat down.

'I think that someone has been watching too many horror movies,' her mother replied.

Michael seemed to find this comment amusing and started laughing. 'Maybe you can make it up to me when you're well and take me out for a drink. Of alcohol, I mean,' he said, raising his eyebrows at her.

She picked a cushion up and threw it at him.

'That's more like it,' he said.

'Did you sort out what you needed to at the hospital?' Ann asked.

'Yes, thank you, I did, eventually.' But it was obvious that he wasn't going to say too much about the subject. Why should he? It was probably a patient and therefore confidential.

Michael stood up. 'Well, I'm afraid that I'll have to love you and leave you. I have things that I really must be getting on with.'

'Thank you once again, Mr Moon, for looking after my ungrateful daughter. I do hope that I will see you again sometime.' Ann's mum shook Michael's hand then turned towards Ann, 'Would you like a sandwich now? I know that you tend to eat a lot when you're ill? She asked.

'Yes please Mum, I am hungry again,' Ann answered. Her mum disappeared back into the kitchen with the cups.

Ann looked back at Michael he was smiling at her. 'What's wrong?' she asked.

'I just can't get over your size and how much you seem to eat,' he said.

'Now wait a minute, I only *asked* for a big breakfast this morning, I didn't eat one,' she defended herself. 'I've always had quite a large appetite, especially when I'm ill.'

'Do you have your mobile phone handy?' Michael asked her, changing the subject.

Ann found her bag lying in a chair and retrieved her mobile. 'Why, have you forgotten yours?' she asked, as she handed her phone to him.

'No! I'm giving you my number. Please think about giving me a ring when you're well enough. You do owe me that drink,' he said smiling. 'And I don't care how many horror movies you've seen, there are some of us that you can trust, honest,' he said, handing the phone back to her.

Michael walked out of the door and they said their goodbyes.

As Michael left he didn't notice a figure over the road, peering from behind the flats opposite taking photographs.

Ann's mum returned from the kitchen with her sandwich. 'You're not sure, are you?' she said.

'No Mum, I'm not. I would think that it's a totally different world; I would have a lot to learn. What if we did get on? I would get old and he won't,' she said sadly.

'It's obvious that you like each other, why not give it time and see what fate has in store? It's no use worrying about things in the future, when they may not happen. You may find that you're not right for each other anyway,' her mum said kindly.

Ann couldn't tell her mum that she already knew, deep down inside, that she had feelings for him. That's why she was pushing him away, because she didn't think that she could handle it.

'You go back to bed dear, take your sandwich with you. I'm going to ring your dad and tell him that I'll be staying here for the night. That's if he isn't in his workshop playing with a plank of wood as usual,' her mum said, as she walked towards the phone. 'I wonder how Mr Moon feels about dating an older woman?' her mother said, under her breath.

'Mum!' Ann exclaimed, and then started coughing again.

'Sorry dear.'

It was now early evening and Ann was feeling wide awake. She picked up her book and tried to read, but she soon found her mind wandering, going over everything that had happened in the last twenty four hours. She was sitting there in bed, holding her book, when her mum dashed into the room. 'I think that you had better put your radio on,' she said.

The news was on, on the local radio station and Ann couldn't believe what she was hearing.

'A young woman was found earlier today, outside the residence of Mr Joshua Ellis. The woman in question is believed to have suffered a vampire bite and was found unconscious. Mr Ellis is a well-known business man on the Island, owning several businesses, including a chain of fashion shops. It is believed that Mr Ellis, a vampire himself, was hosting a birthday party at the time. The Police are looking into the possibility that the young woman was at the party, and that this was an isolated incident. They emphasise that there is no need for concern

78

and the general public are not in any danger.'

Ann sat there stunned, 'Mum, do you think that Michael may have been involved?'

'I don't know, but he was with you all night and most of this morning.' Her mum said, trying to reassure her, sat on the edge of her daughter's bed. 'It can't have anything to do with Mr Moon; He's a respected surgeon and so charming. Besides, they did say that it had happened at Mr Ellis's place.'

'Mum, I was asleep all night. He could have gone anywhere' Ann said tearfully. 'We don't even know if this girl was attacked last night or this morning. Mum I was in his house, it could have been me,' she panicked, then suddenly remembered something.

'This morning he had a phone call from someone. He told them to sit tight and wait for the police while he went to the hospital to find out what was happening. I bet that is what it was about.' She said thoughtfully.

'There you are then, it doesn't sound to me as though he had anything to do with it,' her mum said, trying to sound cheerful.

'But Mum, they're his own kind, he might be trying to protect them.'

'I think that we should wait and see what the police enquiry turns up first, before we start throwing around any accusations, don't you?' her mum said.

Ann couldn't answer, all she wanted to do was ring him and ask him directly. But she was too afraid to do so.

Michael walked into Joshua's office as Richard was filling everyone in on the details of Evie's abduction. He went over to Mark to thank him for risking his job for them.

'No problem,' he said. 'This could end the peace for all of us remember.'

'That's what I am trying to avoid,' Michael said.

'Well at least we know now that Evie is on our side and she knows that it wasn't one of us,' Eric said, with relief.

'And when the forensics have finished, that will be confirmed,' Sadie added.

'We still have some kidnappers to catch though, so does anyone have any ideas?' Michael asked.

'I think we should make some enquiries about those tattoos and see where that leads us,' Joshua said, 'I'll make a list of tattoo parlours on the Island and give them a ring in the morning.'

'Did we get much from the CCTV footage,' Michael asked.

'Not a lot really, we can't even clean the image up. The only thing that we have discovered is that the kidnapper was human,' Richard said.

'How did you come to that conclusion?' Michael asked.

Richard went on to explain Sadie's observations. 'Really?' Michael said, turning towards her.

'Oh thank you, brother in law,' she said storming off out of the office, with Michael hot on her heels. 'What's wrong? Is it because I'm female or the fact that I'm human, that makes you so surprised that I have made such an observation?' Sadie said, disgustedly.

Michael got hold of her from behind, wrapping his arms around her. 'Hey! Calm down, we've got a big enough problem here, without us fighting amongst ourselves.'

'I'm sorry, I just want to try and help. There's been so many times that I have felt useless. I'm supposed to be part of this family, but because I'm human. I'm often left out of the loop,' she said, sadly.

Michael turned her around to face him. 'That's because we love you, and we want to keep you safe. You can help, but nothing dangerous, okay. Your husband would kill me!' he said jokingly.

Michael went back into the office while Sadie went back into the kitchen. 'You did that well, there's normally something flying towards me by now,' Richard said, impressed, as Michael came back in. 'She also has other issues on her mind right now,' Richard went on.

'I know. But that is a decision only she can make. If you like I can arrange for her to talk to someone,' Michael offered. But before Richard could answer, Mark interrupted them.

'Damn it!' Mark said, from behind the desk.

'What's wrong,' Joshua asked.

'I'm trying to work those tattoos out. I put A.V.A into the search engine and came up with nothing. So I tried A.A.V, and unless it has something to do with a virus or an Assault Vehicle, we're screwed,' he said.

'Do you think Evie trusts you?' Eric said, looking at Michael and Richard.

'I think so, why?' Richard asked.

'Well we do have other talents. She gave you a good statement, but what if there is something locked away in her memory that needs to come out.'

'Are you suggesting that we go back to the hospital and hypnotise her?' Richard said thoughtfully. 'It might be worth thinking about. But I'm not going back in there until they drop that police guard.'

Mary was really tired. Lucy had laid her down on a couch in the lounge, covering her with a throw. She then made her way into the office to join the boys, at the same time as Sadie.

'What about the caravan?' Lucy asked. 'We could find clues there, that the police might miss.'

'We can't walk all over that caravan until the police have been. Otherwise we will leave our DNA behind and that will put us at the crime scene. We'll go there if we feel that we need to, but later,' Michael answered.

'What about up the lane?' Sadie said, 'surely the police would have finished up there by now.'

'They have. There was no one there when I came back. Besides, it's got too dark to search now. I know we can see in the dark, but we might just miss something.' Michael said. He was beginning to feel frustrated at not being able to do anything, to restore the reputation of his nest.

Detective Peters eventually managed to return home later that evening. Clair had been waiting a long time to hear what had happened to Evie, and she was onto Tony as soon as he walked through the door. 'Is Evie alright?' she asked.

'Yes she's fine, a little shaken, but she'll be fine,' Tony answered.

'I heard the news on the local radio about the vampire bite, is it true?' she asked.

Tony sat on the arm of the couch and pulled his wife towards him. 'She was found with puncture wounds to her neck. They looked like vampire bites but I have taken Evie's statement since. According to her, two men in balaclavas abducted her, and they were not vampires. They used some sort of instrument to puncture her neck.'

'Is someone trying to set them up?' she asked.

'We don't know if someone is trying to set them all up or just Mr Ellis,' Tony answered. 'I'm hoping that forensics will come up with something. There wasn't a lot on the security tapes at the castle or on the CCTV footage in Newport. We know that there were two of them and that he used his phone while he was watching you two. What we don't know is, was he ringing his partner or is there a third person involved? How are the children?' Tony suddenly asked, changing the subject. He didn't see enough of them.

'They haven't been in bed long; they wanted to see you first. But eventually they were too tired. Go in and see them if you want,' she said.

Tony went upstairs quietly and disappeared into one of the bedrooms. His 6-year-old son, Luke, was sleeping soundly. Cuddled up to his teddy bear. He kissed him gently then left the room.

Tony then entered the next bedroom, his 5-year-old daughter, Sarah, was also sleeping, she was on her front with her bottom in the air, uncovered as usual. Tony smiled then slowly pulled the blankets over her and tucked her back in. He kissed her goodnight and left the room. Clair had made him a sandwich and a drink when he came back downstairs.

'They're both fast asleep,' he said, taking his supper from Clair.

'They were both tired when I picked them up from the child minders,' she answered. 'I'm so relieved that it wasn't one of our vampires, it would have caused a riot. I would have also been worried about the children.' Clair said, as she followed her husband into the front room.

'I think that was probably the intention,' Tony replied.

'But why? You only have to think about all the children. Why would someone do that? Unless they know something we don't?' she said with a worried look on her face.

'I know that has been going through my mind as well. Until we catch them, we won't know, will we? In the mean time, we have to hope that it doesn't escalate,' he said, and then dived into his sandwich.

Gary gave Andrew a ring on his mobile. 'We have to get together and discuss our next move. Where are you?' he asked.

'Watching nature.'

'*What!* Where did you find a strip club?' Gary asked, surprised.

'What are you on about? I'm in Firestone Copse in Wootton, watching nature.'

Gary was baffled, what on earth was Andrew doing in Firestone Copse in the late evening? 'Is there a lot of nature in the winter?' Gary asked, wondering what answer he was going to get.

'I like to go for late evening walks, okay. It helps me to focus. I have been thinking about our next job,' Andrew said, as he walked down the dark path back towards his car.

'Ah good, have you got any ideas yet?' Gary asked him, hopefully.

'Yes, I have a rough idea. How about you?' Andrew asked. But just then he heard a twig break behind him in the bushes. 'I'll meet you tomorrow to discuss plans,' he said, in a whisper.

Before Gary could ask what was wrong, Andrew had hung up and disappeared into the trees.

CHAPTER EIGHT

Tony got out of bed early the following morning. He wanted to get into the shower before his family woke up and turned the house into chaos. The water was nice and hot as he stood underneath its torrent. This however was short-lived when he noticed that all his shower gel had gone.

The bottle was empty; he had only bought it two days before. 'Oh, Luke, what have you done with daddy's shower gel this time?' he said to himself under his breath. Looking around, all he could find was a bottle of Little Angel, no tears shower gel. 'I do hope the guys at the station never hear about this,' he said to himself.

He emerged from the shower smelling sweetly, dried himself, and then went to the bedroom to dress. 'Good morning, dear,' a voice said from under the duvet.

'Morning. Bathroom's free. Do you know where my shower gel has gone?' he asked the duvet cover.

The cover moved before answering, 'Ah, sorry, I caught Luke giving his big teddy a shower. It'll take me days of rinsing to get all that soap out.'

'Right, so Luke now has a teddy that smells all masculine. While I have to go to work smelling like a florist's.'

Tony turned around to see the duvet twitching up and down. He moved across to the bed and pulled back the cover, to reveal Clair laughing. 'I think we had better get the children up and ready, don't you?' he said with a smile.

Tony disappeared downstairs. As he turned the kettle on, he heard movement from above. The sound soon made its way downstairs and into the kitchen. Whilst his daughter Sarah was quiet, her brother Luke made up for it.

Clair made herself busy sitting them down and getting their breakfasts. 'Are you going into work today?' he asked her.

'Yes, Evie's alright so I thought that I would look after the shop for Mr Ellis while she's recovering, why?'

'I would rather you didn't, until I know for sure that he isn't involved with all of this.' He said, worried.

'But you said last night that Evie had cleared them,' she said baffled.

'I know I did, I just worry about you that's all.'

'Everything will be all right. All this will blow over when you catch them,' Clair gave him a kiss. 'Now go to work and stop worrying.'

When Tony Peters arrived at work, he found a forensics report on his desk. He sat down and began to read. It seemed that the vampires were telling the truth; they had nothing to do with the kidnapping.

Vampire saliva hadn't been found on the wound. They had however found DNA from two unknown males, in the caravan, the apartment, and on Evie.

Tyre tracks had been found, both at the caravan and in the lane near Joshua's place. But not enough to identify the make of car, the ground was too hard. He sat there thinking for a while; *hopefully we'll get a lead on those tattoos*. In the meantime he needed to give Mr Ellis the good news.

Joshua was at home co-coordinating the tattoo shop investigation with his staff. The Moon family had spent the night at the castle, and had now returned to their respective homes for a change of clothes. They were all busy in the office when Richard and Michael returned.

George Berry and David Campbell had joined them to help with the search. George was an ex Air Force Pilot. He now worked for Joshua, flying his Private Jet, which was housed at Bembridge Airport. George was tall, medium build but muscular, with closely cropped dark brown hair and deep brown eyes. George had been joining in with the VE day celebrations on the 8th May 1945, when the young woman he was celebrating with, gave him a lot more than he bargained for. 'Let's just say that she got a bit amorous with her teeth' he would say.

David Campbell was ex-Navy and now had the wonderful job as Captain on 'Die Fledermaus,' Joshua's luxury yacht. David wasn't as tall as George but was of a similar build with a very round jolly looking face. He also had a bald head, which he often joked about, saying that it helped him swim a lot faster, which was really helpful, as three ships had sunk underneath him during WW2.

Lucy supplied everyone with drinks. She was feeling a little easier now that Mark wasn't there. He had spent a long time with Eric trying to blow up the picture of the kidnapper. But they couldn't get it any clearer. After that he had gone to work and was keeping his eyes and ears open for any further developments on the CCTV front. As they had a rough idea of what one of the guys looked like, he was watching as many cameras as he possibly could to see if he could spot him somewhere on the Island.

Eric had put a list together of all the tattoo shops on the Island. They then split into three groups. Michael partnered Richard, George was with David and Lucy with Eric. Their plan was to spread out around the Island and find out what they could about the tattoo.

Joshua was going to try and see Evie, if the police would allow him to. She was one of his employees and so he felt responsible for her safety.

They were all about to set off when they heard the buzzer go for the front gates. Eric went to the monitors to investigate. 'It's that detective, Peters,' he said as he looked up from the screen.

'Let him in,' replied Joshua.

'I hope this is good news and they have better leads than us,' Lucy said hopefully.

After about a minute the Detective pulled up outside of the front door. 'Mr Peters, hello. We hope that you're here with some good news,' Joshua said, as he escorted him into the Castle.

'Mr Ellis, you'll be glad to hear that I have. Although I also have some bad news as well.' None of them liked the sound of that.

Tony was shown into the office and was left feeling slightly nervous. Standing in a room surrounded by seven vampires would tend to make anyone a little apprehensive.

'First of all, you'll all be glad to know that you are no longer suspects. I've spoken to Evie and she's certain that the men who kidnapped her were not vampires. The forensic results also back this up. As you said; there was no vampire saliva on her wounds. We have however found DNA from two unknown males at the caravan that she was held captive in, and in her apartment.'

They all breathed a sigh of relief.

'Have you got any further with your enquiries?' Michael asked.

'No, that's the bad news; we only have one lead. We are following that up at the moment,' Tony informed them.

Michael walked towards the Detective, 'May I ask what that is, and can we help in anyway?'

The policeman pondered for a while. 'I'm sorry; I know that you are genuinely concerned, and that you want to help. But I cannot discuss this with you. However if I feel that I need your help at any time, I will ask.'

'Thank you for letting us know that we are no longer on your hit list. Does this mean that I may visit Evie now?' Joshua asked.

'Of course you may, provided that she'll see you.'

'Of course. May I see you out?' Joshua said, as Michael moved to one side.

Joshua saw him out, and then returned to the office. Eric sat at the monitors and opened the gates for him as he left.

'Do you think that he has the same lead as us?' George asked.

'I don't know. We'll just have to be careful that's all, and make sure that none of us bumps into any officers. Come on, let's get this over with.' Michael made for the door and they all followed.

'Did anyone else think that he smelt funny?' David asked. They all turned round and stared at him, 'Well I only asked!'

Joshua found a parking spot outside of the Hospital and made his way inside. On his way through he spotted Angela. 'Hi Angela,' he said cheerfully as he approached her.

She looked up from the paperwork she was doing, 'Oh no, not you as well! Before you ask, no I'm not doing you a favour.'

Angela had got to know Joshua over several years, through Michael and Richard. The three of them always seemed to be together, he had the same sense of humour as them. But he was also known for his generosity towards hospital causes.

'What do you mean?' Joshua asked. 'I only want to know which room Evie Martin is in.'

'There's a police officer outside her door,' she pointed out.

'I know, but we now have permission to see her. They know now that none of us had anything to do with it,' Joshua said with a smile.

'That's different then. I'll go and see if she'll see you.'

Joshua followed Angela down the corridor and around the corner. He waited outside the private room while Angela went in. Joshua looked at the officer at the door and smiled, he couldn't help noticing that he had a plaster on one of his fingers. 'You're bleeding,' he said, 'I can smell it.'

The officer stood up suddenly in a panic, 'What!' he said

flustered.

Just then Angela came back out, 'Evie will see you.' She said. Joshua made a move to pass her, but Angela saw the look on the officer's face. 'What have you said to him?' she asked.

'Nothing,' he said with a grin.

'I know you lot, did you just change?' she asked.

'Would I?' he replied, as he winked at her and went inside.

Evie was sat in a chair at the side of her bed, 'Hello young lady. Let me introduce myself, Joshua Ellis. I'm pleased to meet you last,' he said kissing the back of her hand.

'Hello,' she said, with a little tremor in her voice.

'It's okay, I have eaten this morning,' he said jokingly, with a grin on his face, trying to make her feel a little more at ease.

She smiled at him.

'How are you feeling?' he asked.

Evie started to play with a tissue in her hand, 'Not too bad. I keep going over things in my mind. I thought they were going to kill me. What did they want? Why me?' Evie looked up at him with tears in her eyes.

'We're trying to work that one out. Either someone is trying to set me up or all of us.' Joshua sat on the bed; he could sense her upset and her fear. He held out his hand and indicated with his head for her come and sit with him. 'Come here, trust me,' he said gently. Evie took his hand and sat on the bed.

'I know that this is wrong, I'm your employer. But I think that right now you need a shoulder to cry on,' Evie burst into tears and sobbed. Joshua pulled her to him and held her close. 'Let it out Evie, don't hold it back,' he whispered.

When she had calmed down, she pulled away from him and wiped her eyes. 'Thank you, for that. I didn't know that vampires could be so gentle.'

'The Islanders have been good to us, for over a hundred years. If it weren't for you we wouldn't be leading normal free lives. We owe you a lot. Over the years it has made us gentle, but we are also very protective towards you. Would it make you feel better if you and your mum were to come and stay at the castle for a while? Until we have caught them. Believe me, no-one will be able to get to you there.'

'Do you think that they'll try again?' she asked.

'No, not with you anyway, they wouldn't dare,' he said

reassuringly.

'Thank you, but I think that I'll be alright.' Evie said softly, as she looked down at the bedcovers.

'Are you sure?' he said whilst lifting her face up gently.

'Yes.'

'I want you to stay off work for as long as you need. I've made arrangements for someone to help Clair. If you need anything, anything at all, just call me, okay.'

'Yes.'

'Do you have my number?' he asked.

'I did but one of the kidnappers stole my phone.'

'Yes, of course, Michael told me. He also said that you thought that one of them was trying to help you.'

'He seemed to care, I can't put my finger on it,' she said thoughtfully.

Joshua put his hand in his pocket and took out one of his cards. 'This is my office number, but this is my personal number,' he said as he wrote it down on the back of the card. 'If I don't answer it, then Eric, my security guard will. You can trust him.'

Evie nodded.

'One last thing, did you tell the police about the tattoos?'

'Yes of course, why?' she asked, with a curious look on her face.

'It's just that he said that they had a lead. That's the only thing we can think of, and our team is out there following the same one. So I'll give them a ring and warn them, so that they don't bump into the police. Because of course they don't know that we have already spoken to you.' Joshua stood up to leave. 'Keep that number close. I'll buy you a new phone,' he said gently. 'Is your mum coming to see you today?'

'Yes, she's coming to pick me up. They're allowing me to go home today,' she said trying to smile.

'Good, I'll make arrangements for your new phone to be delivered there then, okay.'

Evie nodded, 'Thank you,' she said.

They said their goodbyes, and then Joshua left the room. The policeman shot up off his chair. Joshua put his hand up, 'It's all right, I was only pulling your leg, relax. Just keep this young lady safe.'

The officer nodded without saying a word, then watched as he walked away down the corridor.

When Joshua emerged from the hospital, he took out his mobile to let Michael know that the police would be at the tattoo parlours.

Andrew had rung Gary earlier that morning. They had arranged to meet on the seafront at Egypt Point, situated just a short distance around the corner from Cowes. They sat on a wooden bench where the wide seafront path widened into a half circle out over the beach, with the old lighthouse just behind them. They both looked out to sea, where they could see the mouth of the river leading into Southampton. 'So what's your idea then,' Andrew asked.

'We need to target somewhere quiet and at night. We want to avoid any witnesses,' Gary said, as he watched a ferry coming into the harbour.

'I would have thought that was obvious. Where are you suggesting?' Andrew asked.

'The hospital, when the late evening shift come off. Or the college, they have a few students there on an evening. Or we could choose a quiet country lane and pretend that our car has broken down.'

'And wait for the first female to come along.' Andrew finished for him.

'Yes, that's it,' Gary answered.

Andrew thought for a while. 'The hospital will be too busy; there will also be visitors about. The college idea isn't bad. We would have to target a female, daft enough to park her car in a dark corner of the car park. As for the country lane theory, we would be more likely to get a male stopping to help, rather than a female.'

'The college then,' Gary said.

'Yes. The college. We can go there this evening and take a look around. Look for security cameras and plot our route out. If we get the opportunity though, we'll pick someone up tonight,' Andrew said, thoughtfully.

'There's the dual carriageway nearby, that will give us a fast exit,' Gary added.

'We may need to find somewhere to keep her overnight. You can break into another caravan site. I'll ring the Boss and find out where he wants us to leave this victim,' Andrew said. 'Meanwhile we need to check out of our hotels. It may raise suspicion if we don't return tonight. I'll meet you at about 6.00pm in the car park at Firestone Copse. We'll leave one car there and take one to the college,' Andrew suggested.

'I'll see you there, then. In the meantime, I'll try and get us a caravan,' Gary said.

Joshua was the first to return back to the castle. His mind was racing. What had happened in the hospital? He had never comforted anyone like that before. Yes, he had been understanding and given someone support, like the day before when he had given Sadie a hug. But this was different; a loving, protective instinct had come over of him. Was it fatherly love, did he feel sorry for her or was it something deeper? Had two of them fallen for a human in the same week? It's strange what stress can do.

He went to the fridge and poured himself a drink, then went to sit down in the conservatory. The castle had never sounded so quiet after all the recent activity. He wanted to take advantage of it while it lasted. They had no idea how long their peaceful existence would last now. They may be proven innocent, but the suspicions will last for a long time to come. He was staring out over the grounds, when he heard the front door go.

Eric and Lucy were the first to return. Lucy was getting them both a drink when she noticed Joshua sat in the conservatory with a worried look on his face. 'Joshua are you alright?'

'Yes, sorry, I was miles away. How did you two get on?' he asked, as he woke up from his daydream.

'Not good, I'm afraid. None of the tattooists that we spoke to had ever seen such a design,' Lucy said as she handed Eric a drink. 'How did you get on at the hospital?' she asked.

'She's in a bit of a state obviously. The good thing is that she not only agreed to see me but she actually trusted me. I even managed to give her a shoulder to cry on.'

'After what she's been through, and she trusts a vampire to give her a cuddle. It says a lot for us; maybe there's hope for us after all,' Lucy said.

This brought a smile to Joshua's face, 'I hadn't thought of it like that, maybe we haven't lost everyone's trust after all,' he said.

'But have we lost trust in the humans?' Eric added.

It wasn't long afterwards that George and David were back. They were a little more cheerful. 'All the artists that we spoke to had no idea,' David said, as they came in.

'But we did have one breakthrough,' George put in cheerfully.

91

'One of the shops had a new apprentice; he has only been over here a few weeks. But he says that he's seen the tattoo over on the mainland, and would make some enquiries for us.'

'At last! A small glimmer of light,' Joshua exclaimed.

Michael and Richard were the last to return. They had the same news as Eric and Lucy, but the news that David and George had returned with gave them some hope.

Later that day Evie was released from hospital. She couldn't face going back to her apartment, so she went home with her mum. 'I had a visitor earlier on mum, Mr Ellis came to see me,' Evie said thoughtfully.

'That was nice of him, what's he like then?' her mother asked.

'Totally different from what I expected,' she said dreamily.

Her mum thought that there was something wrong, 'What do you mean,' she said.

'Well he was like the other two we met, Michael and Richard. He was really nice. He asked me how I was, listened to me, even gave me a shoulder to cry on.'

'Wait a minute! You allowed him to hold you?' her mum said.

'Mum, he was caring; I didn't feel in danger or anything. He was a real comfort to me. I found him soothing, strangely enough, I felt safe. He doesn't want me back at work yet and has offered all the support I need. It seems I'm also getting a new mobile phone.'

'Well he certainly has you wrapped around his little finger. But we must be careful, you're all I have left, and I've nearly lost you once,' she said kissing her daughter on the forehead.

'I know you would like him if you met him.' Evie commented.

'I don't know. I've known about them for a long time. But to have your daughter get close to one. *Well* it just makes me shiver. Let's get you something to eat.' Her mum had changed the subject and disappeared into the kitchen, leaving her alone to think about things.

After a while Evie rang Clair at work.

'Hi, how are you?' Clair asked,

'Okay at the moment, although I've no idea what I'll be like when I go back to my apartment,' Evie answered,

'Give yourself plenty of time, Evie; you went through quite an ordeal. It must have been awful.'

'It was. But now it just feels as though it was all a dream. As if I had detached myself from it,' Evie said thoughtfully.

'That will be your mind trying to protect itself. I don't know how I would have coped if it had been me,' Clair answered.

'How have you been getting on at the shop without me?' Evie asked.

'Not too bad. Mr Ellis managed to get a temp in to help. But I miss our banter,' she said, sadly. 'This girl has no sense of humour at all,' Clair whispered and then gave a slight laugh.

'Has your husband got any further yet with the investigation?' Evie asked, curiously.

'No, I don't think so. He's been looking into something but I don't know what, he's not allowed to tell me. I don't think that he's come up with anything yet,' Clair said, thoughtfully.

Evie's mum came in with something to eat. 'I'll have to go now, we are just about to eat, I'll speak to you soon, okay, Bye.'

'Bye, and take your time,' Clair said, as she hung up.

CHAPTER NINE

Edmond Parr was sat in his favourite leather chair, listening to light music on the radio, with a brandy in his hand. Stella was sat on the couch nearby. She was too scared to even look at him; his mood could change at any moment.

Her wrists were covered in bruises and she had bite marks all over her breasts. Stella knew that she couldn't go on like this much longer. She had to do something, but what? If she left, he would either have her killed or tortured. He was violent before, but since he had started his family tree he'd become obsessional about vampires. *Maybe that was it; she needed to get a look at his family tree.* While Stella was daydreaming the news came on.

'The woman, who was found yesterday with puncture marks in her neck, outside the home of the Isle of Wight millionaire, Mr Joshua Ellis, was not attacked by vampires. The police have issued a statement saying that according to forensic evidence the wounds were not consistent with a vampire bite. The girl in question is recovering from her ordeal and is helping police with their enquiries.'

Edmond flew into a rage, 'what?'

Stella curled herself up on the couch and wrapped her arms over her head.

'Those idiots!' he raged, as he threw his drink into the fireplace, smashing the crystal glass into pieces. 'Can't they get anything right. She wasn't supposed to live. It was supposed to look like a vampire bite,' he shouted. He started to pace the floor, thinking. Stella was too afraid to move or say anything. 'I can't believe that they could botch up such an easy task,' he raged on. 'They had better do it right next time. What is taking them so long anyway, to find their next victim?' he shouted, as he swept his hand across the mantelpiece, knocking everything flying.

Stella moved slowly, she had to get out of the room and leave him alone to calm down. She uncurled herself slowly and stood up. Edmond had his back to her, his face in his hands, his elbows leaning on the mantle shelf, trying to calm down and think. Stella had made it half way to the door when Edmond looked up. He saw her shadow on the wall in front of him.

'What are you doing, sneaking around behind me?' he said, in a low, nasty tone.

'I thought I would leave you alone to think,' she said shakily.

The next thing she knew Edmond had crossed the room in a few strides. He grabbed a handful of hair at the back of her head. 'More like remove my punch bag, you mean,' he said, staring into her eyes. Edmond threw her back onto the couch. He was about to take his rage out on her when his mobile phone rang. Taking it out of his pocket he saw the name on the screen, Andrew.

'This had better be good,' he said, seething.

'Have I caught you at a bad moment?' Andrew asked.

'Have you heard the news? How can you have made such a mess of it like that? She's alive for God's sake!' Edmond could feel his blood boiling as he spoke.

'I let her bleed for a while, and I didn't think that she would be found quickly enough,' Andrew answered.

'Well I just hope that you make a better job of it next time!' he said in a nasty tone of voice.

While Edmond was on the phone, Stella made a break for it again but he caught her by the hair and pulled her back onto the couch. Andrew heard her scream over the phone and he winced. He knew that he couldn't do anything for her. His only hope was that he could calm Edmond down.

'We have another victim in mind,' he said. 'We plan to move in this evening. Where do you want her left? he asked calmly.

'Anywhere. Where are you targeting?'

'The college, we should be able to pick up a student from one of the evening classes,' Andrew said, trying to sound confident.

'The college, you'll have to be careful with that one. Make sure you're not seen, you'll have to find a dark corner of the car park. And make sure that you make the bite look a bit more convincing this time,' he said with a threatening voice. 'Good luck with this evening and remember, no mistakes this time.' he said then hung up.

Edmond looked round at Stella cowering on the couch. 'I've lost my appetite,' he said in a nasty voice, then walked out of the room.

Stella lay there for a while, crying into a cushion so that he couldn't hear her. She knew that she would have to get away from him somehow. Otherwise he would end up killing her anyway.

There were six agitated vampires pacing the kitchen floor, waiting for that one breakthrough. 'Of course, this could also mean that the police have the same lead,' Michael said.

'I don't think they have, because he didn't say that the police had already been in asking questions,' George answered.

'It was also a small tattoo shop up a back alley. We only found it by accident, it wasn't on our list,' David added.

Just then George's phone rang. They all jumped and looked at George in anticipation. 'Hello,' George said. Then put his phone on speaker so that everyone could hear the conversation more clearly.

'Is that George I'm speaking to?' the male voice asked.

'It is.'

'Hi, it's Alex, from the tattoo parlour. I've made those enquiries for you. But first I must ask you a question, because since I've found out about the tattoos, I'm curious,' he said.

'Go ahead, what do you want to know?' George asked with a frown on his face.

'Are you a vampire?'

'What makes you ask that?' George asked.

'Because if you are, you're not going to like the information I'm giving you,' Alex replied.

They all looked at each other, with worry on their faces. 'But you're going to tell me anyway, aren't you,' George said sternly.

'Okay, I get the picture.'

George and the others smiled at each other.

'I spoke to a few of my friends on the mainland, and they recognised the description of the tattoo. It's something that has only recently appeared in Southampton. Only a few weeks they think.'

'Go on,' George said.

'No one seems to know who has done the tattoos, but rumour has it that it belongs to a new gang of some sort. Those letters stand for: Action Against Vampires.' There was silence from them all as the words sank in.

'Hello, are you still there?'

'What did you just say?' George asked.

'Action Against Vampires,' Alex repeated.

'And you say that no one knows who's responsible for these tattoos or who their ring leader is,' George said.

'No, sorry.'

'Thanks, you have been extremely helpful.' George was about to hang up.

'Wait!' Alex said. 'You didn't answer my question. It's the least you owe me. Are you one of the Island vampires?' he asked.

George looked at Michael, who gave him a nod of his head. 'Yes, I am, does that bother you?'

'*Cool!* Are you kidding me, I think its ace. I was listening to the local radio station in the shop and I heard the news. I guess, that it has something to do with that? I wish you all luck catching this idiot. If there is anything more I can help you with, please let me know,' he said enthusiastically.

They all looked at each other baffled, Michael moved forward. 'This is Michael, sorry, we haven't met. You said news.'

'Hi, Michael, Yes. You haven't heard the news this morning?'

'No, we have been kind of busy,' he replied.

'You've been cleared! They know it wasn't a vampire bite,' Alex said cheerfully.

'Excellent, we knew that we had been cleared. But we didn't know that it had been announced. Thank you for letting us know.'

'You're welcome.' They said goodbye and George hung up.

Michael looked round at everyone, they were all smiling.

'Well at least the public knows now. Alex sounded cheerful over it. There may be hope for us yet,' Richard said, as he slapped Michael on the back. 'And we know now that we need to be in Southampton.'

Michael thought for a while. 'No, we're not going to Southampton. We let the police know, and let them go. It sounds as though we are dealing with a gang. If there are a couple of them on this Island, there will be a lot more of them over there, if that's their base. I won't put any of my nest in danger for some enquiries, at least not yet. Let them do that for us. We stay on the Island. I think that there's more to come over here.'

Just then both Michael and Richards's phones bleeped at the same time. They both knew before they looked. The text message was from Angela at the hospital. She always called for them together, when she thought that they may be needed for an emergency.

They both left for the hospital, leaving Joshua to make an anonymous phone call to the police.

CHAPTER TEN

Mark hadn't had any luck at work trying to spot the culprit on camera. But there were a lot of them to watch, and that was a big test even for a vampire.

He travelled home, trying to organise his computer class in his head for that evening at the college. Because he had become such a computer whizz, the college had set him on teaching an evening class. He really enjoyed passing on his knowledge.

All his students were at different levels, so he insisted on having small classes, so that he could give them all individual attention.

He got home and poured himself a cup of red stuff before sitting down. His mind soon filled up with Lucy. He had missed her and now seeing her once more had brought back many memories. At the time she had said that she wasn't ready to commit to a relationship. That had been eleven years ago. He really did miss her and he hoped that she had missed him. Would she be willing to give him another try? His mind suddenly came back to the present, when he realised that he really should be going to the college.

The college was a large brick built building, situated behind a large popular DIY store at the side of the Islands only bit of dual carriageway, which led into Newport. They were separated by trees, on the college's side of the fence, and a wide grass verge with a path, at the side of the road. The large car park wound its way around the building.

When he arrived, most of his students were already there. 'Hi everyone,' he called out as he entered the classroom.

'Hello, Mr Elliot,' they all replied in unison.

His knowledgeable students were busy logging on to their computers. Mark set too and helped his newcomers log on.

Sally was slightly late to class and was in a rush. Her children were home late from school as they had both been doing a project in the library. She had managed to get them both some tea before rushing out to her class. Having two children with computer knowledge had made her feel slightly left out. They had both been helping her a little but she wanted to learn more. A friend of hers had recommended the classes with Mark Elliot, so she thought that she might give it a go. This was her third class and she was really enjoying it.

The car park was busy when she arrived as some of the students had chosen to stay late in the library. She drove around a few times but had to settle for a spot near the far side of the car park. As she was in such a rush to get in, she hadn't noticed a large black car parked a few spaces further up with two men inside.

Michael and Richard couldn't risk leaving Mary with Sadie alone, in case she turned in her sleep during one of her nightmares. So they dropped her off with Lucy at the castle, then headed for the hospital.

They arrived at the hospital to be told they were needed in A&E. They entered the cubicle to meet their patient and smiled. They didn't know if Angela had deliberately called them in or not. Laid on the bed was a young girl in fancy dress. Wearing a black wig, a long red velvet dress, red contact lenses and a pair of false fangs.

The young girl was obviously in a lot of pain. The nursing staff were trying to cut the dress away to get to her leg as they walked in, but she was having none of it. Angela was there, trying to calm her down.

'Is this your way of getting back at us then?' Michael asked.

Angela looked at them both and smiled. 'No, I didn't know that she was dressed like this until she came in a minute ago. I sent you a message knowing that you may be needed. This is Cate, she was supposed to be on a hen night with friends but has fallen off the coach and broken her leg.

Richard moved to the top of the bed, 'Hi Cate, I'm Dr Richard Moon, the anaesthetist.'

'Hello,' she said with clenched teeth.

'I think that the first thing we need to do is to remove your fangs,' he said with a smile. 'Before you choke yourself,' he went on, as he put his hand to her mouth and she spat them out.

Richard looked down at Michael who was now examining her leg. Then turned back to Cate as she let out a cry. 'Have you had any alcohol this evening Cate,' he asked, as the nurse was helping her to remove the red contact lenses.

'No, I got my foot caught in my dress and fell down the steps, I haven't had chance for a drink yet,' she said breathlessly, trying to fight the pain.

'Are you telling me the truth? I need to know so that I can give you something to kill the pain.'

'Yes,' she said, with a strained voice.

'Okay, what about drugs, prescribed or otherwise?' Richard asked.

'None! Please I'm in agony here,' she shouted at him.

'I've nearly finished, are you allergic to anything, such as antibiotics?' he asked calmly, trying to calm her down.

'No,' she said, nearly in tears.

'When did you last eat anything?'

'I had a sandwich about two hours ago,' She said crying through the pain.

'I have all her details here, Dr Moon,' Angela said, as she handed him a clipboard. 'She has signed the consent form for anaesthesia, just in case.'

As Richard was reading, Michael was ordering an X-ray. 'I have a feeling that I may have to set this in theatre,' he said to Richard.

Richard went to the drugs cabinet and came back with some morphine. Not enough to knock her out, but enough to make her drowsy. He could tell by her accent that she was an Islander. Normally he would have just changed into his vampire form and used vampire sleep straight away. But because she had turned up dressed as one of them, he didn't want to embarrass her. He would turn and put her to sleep once she was drowsy. 'Just relax, this will kick in soon,' he said while he gave her the injection. 'If you were a real vampire, you wouldn't need this,' he said with a grin. 'What made you choose a vampire costume anyway?' he asked her, trying to take her mind off things a little.

'They're sexy and mysterious,' Cate said, now with a slightly slurred voice as the morphine began to kick in.

'They are?' Richard asked, smiling.

'Yes, don't you think so? And our vampires seem to be having a hard time at the moment. I feel sorry for them,' Cate said, rather relaxed now.

'A pain in the nether regions if you ask me,' Angela said, under her breath.

Michael looked at her. 'Now who would keep you entertained if it wasn't for us?' he whispered.

Once she was drowsy enough, Richard changed. Cate didn't really know what she was looking at, as Richard leaned over her and began to whisper gently to her. Within seconds she was completely unconscious.

Angela was busy helping Michael, so she hadn't seen Richard turn. 'She is so going to be so disappointed when she comes around' Angela said.

'What do you mean?' Michael asked.

'Well she called you two sexy and mysterious, ha!' she said, then grinned at them both.

Richard had turned back into human form by now, but he wished that he hadn't.

Stella was pacing up and down the bedroom floor. She had her mobile phone in one hand and Mr Ellis's number in the other. She would have to ring anonymously, so Edmond couldn't find out. It would have to be her mobile, not the landline otherwise Edmond would see the number on the bill. But using her mobile would give Mr Ellis her number. 'Oh God what shall I do, I can't let him pick on another girl?' she said, to herself. Plus she had Andrew to think about; if they caught him, it would blow his cover before he could find out exactly what was going on. In the end her conscience got the better of her and she dialled the number.

Joshua was busy at his desk; he had made the phone call to the police and had organised for a new phone to be sent to Evie's address. There was nothing else that he could do at the moment. He hoped that the police would find a lead in Southampton.

His phone began to ring, 'Do you want me to get that? It's not a number I recognise,' Eric said.

'No it's okay, I've got it,' Joshua said, as he picked up the phone. 'Hello, Joshua Ellis speaking,' he said. There was no answer. He gave Eric a puzzled look and indicated that he should pick up the other phone.

'Hello,' he said once again.

'You don't know me but I have information on the kidnapping,' the female voice said. Eric immediately hit the record button on his phone.

'Who is this? What's your name?' Joshua asked.

'I can't tell you, if he finds out that I've helped you, he'll kill me,' she said.

'I can offer you protection,' Joshua offered calmly.

Stella ignored his offer, 'They are planning to take another

101

woman, tonight.'

Joshua could hear that her voice was trembling. She was obviously frightened. 'Do you know who and where they're going to pick her up from?' he asked.

'They're watching the college, but I don't know who their victim is. I don't think that they know themselves. They're just going to go for an easy target.'

'Can you give me the name of who's doing this to us?' Joshua asked.

'No, I've already told you, he'll kill me.'

Joshua and Eric could hear the fear in her voice. 'Please, let us help you. You can trust us. What's your name?'

Stella went quiet,

'At least give me your first name,' he asked.

'Stella.'

'Thank you, Stella. You're obviously in danger, tell me where I can pick you up.'

'No! Just get to the college.' she said quickly, then hung up.

Stella disappeared downstairs and entered Edmonds office. He had gone to London to meet Mr Weston. They had business to discuss about some shipments from abroad. This would give her plenty of time to have a really good search.

She started going through his filing cabinets, looking for his family tree. Stella searched everywhere but couldn't find it. Then she went to the safe; luckily she had seen Edmond go into the safe so often that she knew the combination. Looking inside she found a green file marked *Family History*. Stella took it over to the desk and sat down.

Sally was really pleased with what she had achieved during her lesson. Her confidence was increasing and now she felt more able to help her children with their homework. They would still know more about computers than she did, but at least she could show a little knowledge.

'Are you feeling a bit more confident now with computers, Sally?' Mark asked her as he watched her shut down and switch off.

'I am, at least now I can switch on and find my way around. I used to be terrified off them, in case I did something wrong. Now I'm getting into the habit of saving everything, so if I do go wrong, I can retrieve it,' she said as she got her things together.

'Can I take it then that I'll see you again next week?' he asked as he picked up his car keys.

'Of course you will, hopefully on time as well.'

They were the last two to leave the classroom. Mark locked up and escorted Sally down the corridor.

'So how long have you been playing with computers then?' she asked.

'For a very long time. I have used them in lots of various jobs and it's my hobby. I like to keep up to date with new technology all the time,' Mark said as they approached the exit. 'Where are you parked, can I see you to your car?' he asked.

'No thank you, I'll be fine. I had to park around the corner, nearly at the far side of the car park. It's a good job that I like walking,' Sally said with a smile.

'Are you sure? It's no problem,' Mark offered.

'Yes, I'll see you next week, bye,' she called as she began to walk away.

'Bye,' he shouted back. Mark watched Sally, until she disappeared around the corner of the building.

As he made his way over to his car, he switched his mobile phone back on. He didn't like to have it switched on while he was in class; he liked to give his students his full attention. Mark's mobile rang nearly as soon as he had switched it on. He looked at the display as he was opening his car door, 'Joshua! I wonder what he wants?' he said to himself puzzled. He pressed the button on his mobile to answer.

'Mark! At last! I've been ringing you constantly for the last fifteen minutes,' Joshua said.

'Where's the fire?' Mark asked, after hearing the urgency in Joshua's voice.

'We've just received a phone call. They're going to target the college tonight. Are you still there?'

'Yes, I was just about to leave. It's all quiet here,' Mark said as he looked around the car park.

'I'm on my way to you now with Eric. Don't go anywhere!' Joshua emphasised down the phone.

'Okay, but everyone has already'….*Beep Beep Beep*. A car alarm suddenly started up, and interrupted Mark mid-speech, 'They're here, I think they're going for Sally,' he yelled down the phone as he began to run.

Mark put his mobile in his pocket as he ran around the corner of the building. He was just in time to see Sally fighting with someone dressed in a black balaclava. He had just managed to get her into the car. The car door slammed shut just as he got to it.

As soon as Andrew was in the car with the Sally, Gary put his foot down. They had both seen Mark coming and they knew what he was by the speed that he was approaching. Fortunately he had just missed them.

Mark suddenly shot off overtaking the car, then jumped in front and onto the car bonnet. Gary put his foot to the accelerator and swerved sharply, sending Mark flying. He hit a tree backwards with some force and heard his neck crack on impact, and then everything went black.

The car was speeding out of the car park as Joshua and Eric arrived. Eric swerved to try and get in front of the kidnappers car, with Joshua clinging on to his seat for dear life. Gary managed to swerve around them, and shot off around the roundabout at the DIY store.

Eric did a handbrake turn and went off after them; this made Joshua slide around on the leather seat under his seatbelt. He threw Eric a sharp look while he was trying to reach Mark on his phone. He tried twice but couldn't get an answer. Joshua then rang the police. 'My name is Joshua Ellis; we are in pursuit of the kidnappers. They have just picked up another victim from the college car park. They're in a black Mercedes, heading towards Cowes, the registration number is covered over.'

Sally hadn't realised what was happening, until it was too late. She had just opened her car door, when she was jumped on from behind. 'Co-operate and we won't hurt you,' Andrew whispered into her ear as he put one hand over her mouth, the other held her arm behind her back.

Because she couldn't scream, Sally knew that the only way to get attention was to press the alarm on her key fob. The car's alarm began to sound.

Andrew began to pull Sally towards their car. She was desperately trying to bite him, but he had his little finger under her chin and her head partially pulled backwards onto his chest, making it impossible for her to open her mouth.

As Andrew pulled her into the car they both saw Mark running around the corner of the building. Andrew had to let go of her arm and slam the door closed. Before Sally could try and fight her way out, Gary had hit the accelerator, pinning both of them into the back seat with the force.

Andrew recovered fast and got hold of Sally by both wrists as she tried to scratch him. 'Calm down and I won't hurt you,' he said, as he was trying to put handcuffs on her.

They both heard the thud and looked round. Sally screamed for Mark as she saw him clinging onto the car bonnet. He had turned and his red eyes were staring in at them. Gary swerved sending them both sliding along the leather seating. This pinned Sally against the car door, giving Andrew a chance to handcuff one hand. At the same time she saw Mark disappear.

'Get off me!' she screamed, as she carried on fighting with Andrew.

Gary swerved again as a car tried to stop him just before the roundabout. This sent the fighting couple sliding once again across the seating. Andrew took advantage of this once more and forced Sally onto her back on the seat. Sitting on top of her, he managed to cuff the other wrist.

'That car is following us,' Gary shouted, over Sally's screams.

'Put your foot down and try and lose it,' Andrew shouted back, as he lifted himself from Sally's body to look out of the back window.

Gary headed away from Newport towards Cowes, speeding past the prisons and the hospital. He was slowly making the gap wider between them and the car following.

Andrew was trying to stifle Sally's screams with his hand but she was now trying to kick him furiously. He moved his hand to her throat and she stopped screaming. He was squeezing slightly, not enough to cut off her air supply but just enough to quieten her down. He leaned forward and looked her in the eyes through the gap in his balaclava. 'Stop struggling and calm down,' he said to her slowly and calmly. Andrew felt her beginning to relax. 'That's it calm down, I don't want to hurt you,' he said once again calmly and gently.

Sally didn't know what was happening, she couldn't take her eyes off his. Before she knew it she was relaxing, almost against her will and she could feel her eyes beginning to close. She shook herself the best she could and tried to stay awake. 'Stop fighting me and calm down,' Andrew said, once more, staring into her eyes. Sally heard sirens in the distance as her eyes closed.

Andrew climbed over into the front passenger seat. 'What have you done to her?' Gary yelled, as he tried to look back over his shoulder.

'Keep your eyes on the road, she's unconscious,' Andrew answered, sternly.

Gary looked at his partner. 'What did you do? Her blood has to be clean remember.'

'Just concentrate on the driving, will you? There are other ways of rendering a person unconscious, without using drugs. She's fine! Now drive.'

Gary approached the traffic lights at Northwood. There was a pub, on the left, and fields on the right. The road forked here, on either side of a garage. Right towards Cowes and left into Northwood. Northwood had a fairly new housing estate, off its main road.

They could now hear sirens coming at them from Cowes, beside the ones behind them. Andrew looked in the side mirror; he could see the other car coming up fast behind. 'I have an idea, go left, quick!' he shouted.

Gary swerved left into Northwood. 'Left again, here!' Andrew yelled. Gary swerved the car to the left, nearly missing the turn. 'Right!' Andrew yelled once more. The car tyres screeched as he made the right turn. 'Left again. And again,' Andrew kept yelling. He prayed that this would work, as he saw the cul-de-sac sign.

Both Andrew and Gary looked in their mirrors. They could see that they had temporarily lost the car behind and the police.

'Look for a driveway, and reverse up it,' Andrew ordered. Luckily there was a bungalow for sale with an empty drive. Gary quickly stopped and reversed up the drive. He turned his lights off and killed the engine.

Andrew jumped out of the car, 'Get down,' he said, to Gary as he left. Gary lay down across the front seats. He heard Andrew pull the cover off the front number plate, then silence.

Andrew had rolled behind a hedge in the garden. He saw a police car slowly creeping passed up the road. He then watched through the hedge as they turned around at the end of the street and came back again. Andrew breathed a sigh of relief as they carried on past and disappeared.

He sneaked back passed the car, around the back and looked in through a window. The bungalow was empty. Taking out his lock picks he opened the garage door.

Gary jumped as the passenger door opened. 'Jeez, you scared me,' he said.

'They've gone. Reverse into the garage,' Andrew said, as he closed the door again.

Gary reversed into the garage, as Andrew then pulled the garage door closed. He then watched as he unlocked the interior door into the bungalow. Then returned to carry Sally inside.

Luckily the previous owners had left curtains up. Gary drew them together, but they still didn't risk putting any lights on. They stayed in what looked like the dining room at the back of the house, just in case the police came back and looked into the front.

'It's freezing in here,' Gary said, wrapping his arms around himself and rubbing them with his hands. 'There's some blankets in the car, I'll go and get them.'

Andrew made sure that Sally was okay. She was sleeping soundly. When Gary returned they wrapped her up in a blanket. 'We had better gag her, she's going to scream the place down when she comes around,' Gary said.

'No need, she won't wake until I want her too,' Andrew answered.

'What!' Gary exclaimed. What have you done?'

'Stop panicking, and calm down. It's something I learned from the Master during my martial arts training,' Andrew said calmly.

'Well I've never come across it before,' Gary put in.

'I was trained in Tibet; it's something that they don't train over here, okay. Just trust me, she's fine.

'I wonder why the vampire was there?' Gary asked.

'He probably works there,' Andrew said thoughtfully. 'What I want to know is who was following us. Did that vampire manage to ring for help? If he did, how did they get there so fast? Unless they were close by.'

'Or did someone tip them off?' Gary said.

'I don't know, the only people that knew were us two and Edmond,' Andrew said, deep in thought. 'It's something that we'll have to watch.'

Eric hit the steering wheel with the palm of his hand. 'Damn it! We lost them.' He stopped the car; the police quickly surrounded them.

Tony Peters got out of one of the cars with two police officers. 'What happened?' the detective asked them.

'We lost them,' Joshua said, getting out of the car and throwing his arms up in the air.

'Don't worry about that, I have police cars all over this area,' the detective said. 'What were you two doing at the college?'

'We went to meet a friend of ours, when a car came speeding at us. We saw a struggle in the back seat and put two and two together, so we went after them,' Joshua quickly answered. Eric looked at him, knowing that this was a lie.

'Well it seems that this has just turned into a murder investigation. We have found a body in the college car park,' Peters announced.

Joshua looked at Eric baffled at first, then he realised. 'Who is it?' Joshua asked.

'You know that I can't tell you that, it's a murder investigation,' The detective answered, with a stern voice.

'The reason I'm asking is because we were supposed to be meeting someone there. He's a vampire and I can't get him on the phone. If it's him, your men are going to have a heart attack when he wakes up. Plus he's going to be very hungry as it takes a lot of our energy to heal,' Joshua said, in a panic.

'According to his I.D it's Mark Elliot, he has a broken neck,' Peters replied.

'He's going to wake up,' Eric said, relieved. 'We have blood in a fridge, in the car, we had better get back there.'

'You keep blood in the car?' the Detective said, in disbelief.

'Yes, I had a small fridge fitted. You never know when there may be an emergency. We always keep it stocked up with fresh,' Joshua answered.

They both got back into the car and drove off towards the college. 'You lied to him,' Eric said.

'I couldn't tell him about Stella. We now have her number on our phone records. She said she was in danger, if the police show up asking for her, she's in trouble. Besides it turns out that her information was correct, maybe she can alert us sooner next time. That is if they don't find them tonight,' Joshua explained.

'So what do we do now?' Gary asked.

'We wait a while, then we do exactly what we did before,' Andrew said, as he looked towards him.

'Are you insane?' Gary replied.

'Maybe. But the last place they will expect us to dump her is outside the Ellis place again,' Andrew said, with a smile.

'Really?' Gary said with sarcasm in his voice. 'How can you be so calm about all this?'

'I told you, martial arts. You should try meditating with nature sometime,' he replied with a grin on his face.

Eric and Joshua arrived just in time. Mark was just beginning to stir as they approached. '*Ow,*' he said, rubbing his neck. The police coroner was a visitor from the mainland and he nearly fainted when his dead guy suddenly woke up. The coroner looked at the detective with his mouth wide open in shock.

'Vampires.' Peters said, as if it was perfectly normal, opening his arms to take in the three of them, in front of him.

The coroner looked back down, as Joshua handed Mark a bottle of blood. He then looked back at the detective, his mouth still wide open and speechless. 'He needs it to fully heal,' Peters said, smiling at him

Tony Peters was beginning to enjoy this and Joshua could tell. He kept his face down along with Eric and Mark, laughing.

'*Ahhh!*' Mark said as he laughed, 'what the heck have you stabbed me with?' he said, looking up at the coroner.

The coroner glanced at him terrified. 'I had to check your liver temperature, to determine the time of death. It was the thermometer,' he said, backing away.

Eric burst into laughter even more. 'Thank your lucky stars that he didn't stick it somewhere else,' he said.

'So what happened, Mark?' Tony asked regaining his composure and watching the coroner walk away.

'Don't tell him about the tip off,' Joshua whispered in such a way that only they could hear.

'Where's Sally, have you found her?' Mark asked, to no one in particular.

'Is that the name of the woman who's been taken?' The detective asked.

'Yes, Sally Knox, she's on my computer study course.' Mark looked at them one by one, 'You haven't found her have you?' Mark said.

'Tell me what happened and what you saw, Mr Elliot,' The detective asked, once more.

'We were the last to leave the class. Sally had parked at the far side of the car park. I offered to walk her to her car, but she said that she would be okay. I heard a car alarm and went to investigate. I saw a man wearing a black balaclava forcing her into a black Mercedes. They drove off, I jumped onto the bonnet but they threw me off. I remember hitting the tree and hearing a crack. Shouldn't someone be getting in touch with her husband?' Mark said, in a panic. He felt guilty for not managing to rescue her and they knew it.

'It's alright Mark, calm down, I have a lot of police officers out there looking for her now,' Peters said. 'We got her address from her car registration number, there's an officer going to her home now to see her husband.'

'Sorry, we arrived just in time to see the car driving off, so we gave chase but we lost them,' Joshua added.

Joshua tried to ring Richard and Michael. But their phones were both switched off. Which usually meant one thing. They were working. So Joshua rang Michael's home phone and left a message.

Michael and Richard left the hospital later that night. It had proved to be a bad break in Cate's leg and had taken most of the night for Michael to patch her up. They both left the hospital exhausted.

'Do you mind if I crash out at you're place, as it's nearer?' Richard asked. 'I also don't want to disturb Sadie.'

'Yes, of course. Just follow me back,' Michael answered.

The first thing that Michael did when he returned home was switch off his phone. They were both so tired, they didn't want any interruptions. As he switched off his home phone, he didn't notice that his answer machine was flashing.

Michael poured them both a drink. They got halfway through them and fell asleep on the couch.

CHAPTER ELEVEN

'Okay, so how are we going to get to the Ellis residence, when this place is infested with police?' Gary asked.

'That's a good question,' Andrew replied. This wasn't the answer that Gary was looking for.

Andrew stood up and started walking slowly up and down the room. 'They're looking for a Black Mercedes with two men and one woman. We need to get my car from Firestone Copse. You stay here with her; I'll walk up the road and then call a taxi,' Andrew said, as a plan was coming together.

'What! I can't stay here with her. You know how you've knocked her out. You should watch her,' Gary said, in a panic.

'She won't wake up without me. She'll sleep soundly until then. I won't be long. Now stop panicking,' Andrew reassured him.

He sneaked out of the bungalow and up the road. Several police cars passed him as he made his way back through the side streets, towards the main road. When he thought that he was far enough away, he rang for a taxi. 'Hello, I would like a taxi please from Northwood to Wootton.'

Joshua and Eric had taken Mark home. He was living in a small two bedroomed terrace house, just a stone's throw out from the centre of Newport. He had a small comfortable lounge with a modern kitchen at one end. They were separate rooms when he moved in, but Mark had knocked the dividing wall out and fitted a new kitchen. This made the whole place look larger. They went into his fridge and got out some more of the red stuff and poured three drinks.

'What happened with you two then?' Mark asked.

Joshua sat on the couch next to him and pulled his knees up sideways, to make himself comfortable. 'When we arrived, a speeding car was heading straight for us. We knew straight away who they were. It's a wonder they got as far as they did. Their number plate was covered over. They could have been stopped at any time.' Joshua took a sip of his drink. 'Eric here took off after them like a bat out of hell – it was quite impressive.'

'I wish I'd been there to see it,' Mark said, smiling at Eric.

'It's what I was trained for. Unfortunately, this time they got away, despite having half of the Island's police force out as well. They seemed to just disappear,' Eric said, disappointed.

Andrew arrived at Wootton. He got out of the taxi at a pub by the creek. He thought that this would give him a cover if he needed it. He was just someone going out for a drink. It would have stood out if he had been dropped off at Firestone Copse.

When the taxi had disappeared, he walked over the bridge and headed up the hill at the other side.

Andrew's phone suddenly rang. It was Stella. 'Hi, are you okay?' he asked.

'Yes, but I don't think that I can carry on like this for much longer,' she said.

'Don't worry, I'm working on it,' he replied.

'Listen, I have discovered something that I think you should see. Edmond is away in London for the night with a client, Mr Weston. Can you sneak over,' she asked.

'I'll see what I can do,' he said thoughtfully. 'But I can't promise anything.'

'Okay, but it's really important,' she answered, as she hung up.

Andrew turned off onto a side street; the houses became more and more sparse as he walked along. Eventually the road was lined with trees. A little further on and he turned into a wooded area with a grass and gravel car park. Instead of going straight to his car, Andrew disappeared into the trees.

'How did you know that Sally was with them?' Mark asked.

Joshua took another drink. 'We didn't at first. We knew they were the kidnappers. So we figured that Sally was either safe with you. Or if she was in the car, we could either rescue her or at least capture the culprits. It wasn't until we had been chasing them for a short distance, when we heard her yelling. Eric put his foot down all the more, but we fell back on Horsebridge Hill.'

Mark put his head back and rubbed his neck. 'If I had insisted on seeing her to her car, this wouldn't have happened,' he said.

'You weren't to know; none of us would have thought that they would attack again so soon. And we did our best between us. If you had been human, you would be dead now,' Eric said.

'Eric, I am dead,' Mark answered.

'You know what I mean; we don't feel dead do we? I mean, we are still here,' Eric tried to defend himself.

'Where did you lose them?' Mark asked them.

'They took off into Northwood, when the police were coming towards them from Cowes. We saw them make a sharp left down there as we approached the traffic lights. By the time we got there, they had completely disappeared,' Eric informed him.

Andrew eventually made it back to the bungalow. 'At least they won't be looking for a silver BMW,' he said.

'This might look suspicious though,' Gary said, as he gave a nod towards Sally.

'She's going in the boot; we don't have far to go. We'll take the short cut on the floating bridge, instead of going through Newport – there could be more police that way,' Andrew said, whilst picking her up from the floor.

They laid Sally down in the boot and got into the car. Andrew drove out of the estate onto the main road. There were still a few police cars but they didn't give them a second glance.

'Well my idea seems to be working,' Andrew said, as he drove towards Cowes.

Gary was beginning to feel more thankful that Andrew was with him. His heart was in his mouth now, he would have been worse, if it weren't for the company.

The floating bridge was a small ferry that carried both cars and foot passengers over the river between Cowes and East Cowes. This avoided the need to go all the way around the River Medina, and through Newport, which was an eight-mile journey. They made it safely onto the floating bridge. 'You can pick your car back up again later, when everything has calmed down a bit,' Andrew informed Gary. 'Hopefully there will be no viewings. The last thing we need is an estate agent finding your car.'

Mark sat there thinking for a while, sipping his drink. His neck was feeling much better now, after drinking one and a half pints of blood. 'Maybe we should go and have a look around that estate,' he suggested.

'We were going to do that,' Eric answered, 'until we discovered that there was a body in the car park, with a broken neck. We had to get to you before you woke up.'

'Yes well, I must say that I liked the look on the coroner's face, when I woke up.'

'Do you feel well enough to go now,' Joshua asked.

'Yes, I'm fine, let's have a wander around.'

Before they set off, Joshua tried Michael's home number again and his mobile, but once again there was no answer.

Andrew and Gary made their way up the hill out of East Cowes towards Wootton and the Ellis residence. They had only seen one police car on this side and that was by the chain ferry.

When they had reached Wootton they turned down the unmade lane and carried on past the gates once more, then reversed into the field entrance.

Andrew lifted Sally out of the boot and laid her down on the grass. Gary handed him the fork. Andrew knew that he would have to miss the main blood vessels again and holding her head over to one side, he was about to pierce her neck when Gary interrupted him.

'Are you going to bring her around first,' he asked.

'No, it will be easier if I do this while she's still out, that way she doesn't move. This one is a real fighter compared to the other one,' he answered.

He also didn't want to hurt her, but he couldn't tell Gary that.

The three well-fed vampires had now arrived at the housing estate and were driving around slowly.

'What would we do?' Mark asked.

'We would want to blend in, that is presuming that they did get stuck on this estate. There is another way out at the bottom,' Eric said.

'Let's presume that they didn't know that. Or maybe knew that they would be spotted again on a long open road,' Joshua added.

'Well personally, I would find a drive to pull up. It would have to be where there was no one in, or an empty property,' Eric informed them.

They drove around and found two properties for sale. 'We'll start with these,' Joshua said.

They went to the first one and looked around, there was no sign of life. They listened at the doors and windows, but couldn't hear any heartbeats. Eric opened the garage - it was empty.

Andrew had pierced Sally's neck and they allowed her to bleed a little. After a while he picked her up.

'I'm coming with you this time,' Gary said.

'Why?' Andrew asked.

'Because I'm curious, as to how you are going to wake her up,' he replied.

'Now isn't the time for a demonstration, we need to get out of here. Drive my car back up the lane and wait for me,' Andrew ordered.

Gary reluctantly got into the car, while Andrew walked up the lane towards the gates. Gary then started the engine and drove passed him up the lane.

Andrew sat her up against the gatepost. He leaned in close and seemed to be whispering in her ear. Sally stirred and began to wake up. Andrew reached up and pressed the bell for the gates. He then walked away towards his car.

Lucy had just poured herself a drink. Mary was now hard and fast asleep. They had both been doing some more baking; she had cleaned up and was about to watch a film, when she heard the bell go for the gate.

She thought that it might be Joshua and Eric coming back at first. But they both had electronic keys, so she went to the office to have a look on the monitor. There was no one there, but she could see something on the floor by the gate. Lucy pressed a few buttons and zoomed the camera in. 'Oh no, not again!' she exclaimed.

Lucy grabbed her mobile phone, opened the front door and shot off down the drive. When she arrived Lucy pressed the button to open the gates, when they had opened a little way she squeezed through. Lucy then bent down to examine the wound just as Sally opened her eyes. 'Ahhhhh, get away from me!' Sally managed to scream. She raised her hand to her neck, and looked at the blood on her fingers.

Lucy suddenly realised that she was in vampire form. She was so used to it, she had forgotten. Realizing what this looked like she tried to calm her down.

'I know what this looks like, but I didn't do this to you, I swear. I'm not here to hurt you. Please let me help,' Lucy said, trying to calm her.

Joshua and the boys had made their way to the second bungalow. Again they had a good look round; there was no sign of life. Joshua was about to open the garage door when his mobile phone rang. It was Lucy.

'Lucy, hi,' Joshua said.

'Joshua, we have another victim at our gates,' Lucy said, in a panic.

'She's there!' Joshua exclaimed.

Eric and Mark heard him and returned to the front of the bungalow. 'Have they found Sally?' Mark asked.

Joshua nodded his head. 'How is she?' he asked Lucy.

'I think she's okay, but I can't get near her yet. She's in a bit of a panic. She woke up with me hanging over her, I'd forgotten about my form,' Lucy answered.

'Try and get her into the castle out of the cold and ring for an ambulance,' Joshua told her.

'Joshua, the wounds have missed the carotid artery again,' she informed him.

Joshua was stunned for a second. 'Okay get her indoors, we're on our way back to you,' he said, hanging up.

'She's turned up at the castle gates,' Joshua shouted as they ran back to the car.

'What? You're joking!' Mark exclaimed, as he ran after him.

All three of them got back into the car. As Eric drove off, Joshua rang Tony Peters to let him know.

Lucy rang for an ambulance, and then turned back to Sally having taken human form. 'Please let me help you, before you freeze to death. Let me get you inside. We need to put pressure on that wound as well. I'm Lucy,' she said. 'What's your name?'

'Sally.'

'Sally, please trust me, help is on its way.' Lucy knew that if she couldn't get Sally inside of her own free will, she would have to use her powers of suggestion.

'Where's Mark?' Sally suddenly asked, trying to remember what had happened.

This took Lucy by surprise. 'Excuse me, Mark who?' Lucy asked.

'Mark Elliot, I was with him at the college,' Sally said, confused. 'I'm in his class.'

'Come on let's get you inside,' Lucy repeated.

Sally allowed Lucy to help her to her feet. Lucy then picked her up, and ran at full speed back up the drive to the castle, leaving the gates open for the ambulance. This took Sally by surprise; she never thought that strength and speed also applied to the female vampires. It was something that she had never thought of before.

Lucy took Sally straight through to the kitchen conservatory and sat her down on one of the couches, putting a blanket around her shoulders. Sally then watched as Lucy took out a first aid kit and removed a large dressing. 'What are vampires doing with a first aid kit?' Sally asked.

'We have a lot of human friends visiting,' Lucy answered. 'Before I put this dressing on, I need to smell the wound. Please don't be alarmed, every vampire has its own smell and if it's one of us that has done this, we need to know who, okay?' Lucy continued.

Sally nodded. Lucy leant forward and smelt the wound. There wasn't any vampire saliva, just as she suspected.

'Well,' Sally asked, as Lucy applied the dressing.

'It wasn't a vampire that did this,' Lucy answered.

Sally remembered something, 'Wait a minute, this happened to someone else recently didn't it?'

'Yes, we're still looking for the culprit,' Lucy explained. 'How are you feeling?' she asked.

'Slightly light headed.'

'Here, put your feet up and sit back,' Lucy said. Sally looked at her unsure. 'It's okay, I've had my supper,' Lucy said, with a smile.

Sally did as she was told.

'Out there you mentioned Mark Elliot. What happened?' Lucy asked her.

'When I was dragged into the car, he jumped onto the bonnet and tried to stop them. I don't know what happened to him, one minute he was there, the next he was gone,' she said, worriedly.

Lucy picked up her mobile phone and rang Joshua. He answered on the second ring. 'Mark is in the college car park,' she said.

'No he isn't, he's with us, on our way back. We're nearly there.'

'Is he okay?' she asked. Mark could hear the conversation and smiled.

'Of course he is,' Joshua answered as he looked back at Mark.

'See you in a few minutes,' he said and hung up.

Lucy turned to Sally, 'Mark's fine,' she said. 'He's on his way here with Joshua and Eric.'

'Thank goodness for that,' Sally said.

They heard sirens as the ambulance turned up. 'That's not for me is it?' Sally asked.

'Yes, of course,' Lucy said baffled.

'But I'm fine, really. Just a little shaken, but there's no need for me to go to the hospital. Have I stopped bleeding?' She asked.

'Yes, you have, but the wound needs looking at. If it had been a vampire, you wouldn't need to go. We can't pass on any infections, because we don't carry any. But these kidnappers are using something to produce these wounds; goodness knows what's on it by now,' Lucy said.

'Hello!' Lucy heard the paramedic call out.

'Through here,' she shouted back.

It was the same paramedics as before. 'You seem to be making a habit of this, don't you?' he said to Lucy.

'Not us, honest,' she said.

Just then she heard Joshua, Eric and Mark return. Tony Peters arrived at the same time. She ran straight to Mark and threw her arms around him. 'Are you all right? Sally told me what you'd done.'

'I'm fine now, I got away with a broken neck,' he replied. The paramedics looked up dumbfounded. 'If you think the look on their faces is good,' he said indicating to the paramedics. 'You should have seen the look on the coroner's face when I woke up,' he laughed. This also cheered Sally up.

Mark went to Sally. 'Next time I offer to walk you to your car, you say yes, okay.'

Sally nodded.

'I'm detective Peters, 'Can you remember what happened?' he asked.

The paramedic interrupted him, 'I think the questioning will have to wait for later. We really should be getting her to the hospital.'

'Yes of course. Your husband has been informed; he's already waiting for you at the hospital. I'll see you there,' the detective said.

As the paramedics moved her into the waiting ambulance, she turned to Lucy. 'Thank you for looking after me,' she said.

'No problem,' Lucy replied.

The detective turned to Joshua. 'Have you any idea why someone may be targeting you?' he asked.

'No, not really. Obviously I took a few human lives in the beginning. But that was in the late 1880's. Unless it's a relative of one of them? But that's the only thing I can think of,' Joshua answered.

'Where did you come from?' The detective asked.

'A place called Newholm in North Yorkshire,' Joshua answered.

'And when were you turned?' the detective continued.

'1897,' Joshua answered slowly, wondering where all this was going. 'Do you think that this has got something to do with my past?'

'It's a possibility that I'm looking into,' he said, as he was getting into his car. 'In the meantime, try not to kill anyone.'

'I've been clean for over a hundred years!' Joshua exclaimed.

'I know that,' the detective shouted through his window as he drove off down the gravel drive towards the gates.

They all went back inside. Eric closed the gates after the ambulance and detective Peters had left.

'Tell me about her wound, Lucy,' Joshua asked.

'On the left but it had missed the main arteries again. It stopped bleeding when I put the dressing on and there wasn't any vampire saliva,' Lucy replied.

'Either someone doesn't know what they're doing or they're deliberately missing?' Mark said.

'Which doesn't sound good, if they strike again. If it is someone who doesn't know what they're doing, the chances are that they might catch the carotid artery next time.' Joshua answered.

Lucy walked over to Mark. 'You said that you had broken your neck. Is it all right now?' she asked him.

'Well it is a bit stiff,' he replied.

'Come over here,' she said, as she led him to a couch in the conservatory. She removed his shirt, whilst Joshua and Eric looked on smiling. She then moved behind him and started massaging his neck and shoulders.

'Oh, just there,' he said in ecstasy, whilst winking at Joshua and Eric. They both moved away with wide smiles on their faces.

119

Joshua turned to Eric, 'come on, we're going round to Michael's. Let's see if they are there.'

CHAPTER TWELVE

Andrew dropped Gary off at another guesthouse. 'Did you break into a caravan site, earlier on?' he asked.

'No, I found a suitable site and a caravan. But I thought we would break in if we needed to,' Gary replied.

'Good, so there is no evidence at a site then,' Andrew stated.

'No, there isn't. Where are you going now?' Gary asked, as he leaned through the window.

'I'm going to check into another guesthouse. I'll ring you tomorrow. We'll wait until dark to get your car back. Until then have a good night.'

Andrew drove off, but instead of finding a guesthouse, he drove into Cowes.

He left his car in a large car park at the side off Northwood Park. This was a large park, with playing fields and tennis courts, surrounded by trees. Its grounds sloped down to reveal a view of the sea and Southampton in the distance.

Andrew walked down the hill and eventually came into the town itself. He then turned right, under a small archway, which was built as part of a hotel. Then walked past the short row of shops to the passenger ferry.

He bought his tickets, and walked down the ramp to wait for the ferry coming in from Southampton. Then he took out his phone and rang Edmond.

'The second victim has been delivered,' he said.

'Good, I hope you made a better job of it this time,' Edmond replied.

'Yes, of course. Have you any other instructions for us?' he asked.

'Not at the moment. Just stay on the Island. I'll be in touch,' Edmond hung up.

Michael and Richard woke up to the sound of banging on the front door.

'Michael are you in? It's Joshua.'

Michael rolled off the couch, while Richard was stirring and trying to work out where he was.

He opened the front door and held onto the doorframe. 'What have you been up to?' Joshua asked, as he and Eric moved past him into the cottage.

They walked into the small front room, which was made even smaller by the large stone inglenook fireplace. Richard was sat on the couch rubbing his face with his hands. 'We both spent hours in theatre,' he answered.

'How come you're this tired? You're vampires, remember. You don't need that much sleep,' Joshua said.

'It takes a lot of concentration in theatre, and I'm 154 years old now,' Michael replied. 'Anyway what's wrong, it's not Mary is it?'

Joshua sat down. 'No, we've had quite an eventful evening though,' he answered. 'I've been ringing you and I left a message on your answer phone,' he said.

'We were so tired we didn't turn our phones back on, and I switched this one off,' Michael said, whilst indicating to the phone. 'Sorry, what is it?'

'I've had another delivery at my gates,' Joshua explained.

Michael and Richard suddenly woke up.

'Oh no,' Richard said.

Andrew got off the passenger ferry in Southampton and walked out of the terminal building. Once he was outside he rang for a taxi to the Parr estate.

Stella was in bed, but she couldn't sleep. Even after taking painkillers for all her bruises, they still hurt. She became aware of a tapping on the bedroom window. She opened the curtains slowly; Andrew was standing on the small balcony at the other side. 'I guess I should invite you in,' she said opening the window.

'It would help,' he replied. Andrew jumped in through the window. It was then that he noticed Stella's bruises. He took her hands in his. 'Did he do this to you,' he asked, whilst looking into her tear filled eyes.

'Yes,' she replied.

Andrew let go, and then placed one of his hands up the side of her face, under her hair, then around to the back of her head, slowly. He held her close to him with his other arm. Stella allowed him to bring her in close, and kiss her passionately. She felt herself melting into his arms.

Andrew then pulled away, 'I'm sorry that I'm asking you to put up with this a little longer,' he said. 'It's killing me to see you like this. But we must get enough evidence together to put him away for good. Otherwise, we'll never be free. I just hope that the Island vampires are as friendly as they're supposed to be.'

'I know, I hope that it won't be much longer,' she said looking into his eyes. 'Are the two girls okay?' she asked.

'Yes, but how did you know that there were two?' he asked, while holding her tighter.

'I heard Edmond talking to you about the second victim at the college,' she answered. 'I'm sorry but I panicked, I rang Mr Ellis and warned him.'

'It was you?' he said. 'It must have been him who turned up and chased us. Stella we nearly got caught,' he said, in disbelief.

'I'm sorry, but this isn't what we're supposed to be doing. We should be looking into those shipments, not kidnapping women,' she said, getting upset.

'I know that, he sent me off on this mission out of the blue. Those girls are not in any danger, trust me, I know what I'm doing. I keep botching it up so that they won't bleed to death. And using vampire hypnosis to keep them calm and avoid too much pain, but at least they're not dead. They would be, if Gary were doing the deed. Now I have two things to look into, the shipments and why he wants to destroy the vampires all of a sudden,' he said.

'That's why I've called you here,' Stella replied. 'I've found something in his office.'

Andrew followed Stella into Edmonds office. She opened the safe and took out the green folder that she'd found earlier. They turned the desk lamp on and took out its contents. Andrew found himself reading Edmonds Parr's family tree;

'Edmond Parr born 1955.

Father, Alfred Parr born 1930 died 1998 married;

Grace Hale born 1932 died 1990.

Grandfather, William Parr born 1908 died 1967 married;

Amelia Richards born 1909 died 1970.'

Andrew looked up from the pages. 'Carry on. Then I'll tell you what I've found.' Stella said.

Andrew looked down once more and carried on reading.

'Great Grandfather, Edmond Parr born 1884 died 1941 married; Charlotte Kenley born 1886 died 1946.

Great-great Grandfather, George Parr born 1864 died 1917 married;

Matilda Eliza Parks born 1865 died 1897.

Andrew studied the tree for a few minutes while Stella removed the remaining paperwork from the folder. 'I was going through the family's birth, marriage and death certificates, when I found this,' Stella said as she passed Andrew a marriage certificate. It was between Edmond's Great-great-grandfather George Parr and Matilda Eliza in 1883 at St Bartholomew's church in the village of Ruswarp.

'Where's Ruswarp?' Andrew asked, as he studied the certificate.

'It's in Yorkshire,' Stella answered.

'So where is this going?' he asked, baffled.

'Well maybe this will help,' she said, handing him a death certificate.

It was for Matilda Eliza Parr died in 1897 aged 32. From an animal attack.

'An animal attack,' Andrew said to himself, looking up.

'Yes, now look at the cause of death,' Stella said.

Andrew looked. *Complete loss of blood.*

He couldn't believe what he was seeing. 'It *might* have been an animal attack, that would have caused a great deal of blood loss,' he said to her.

'Yes I thought that, until I found a copy of an old newspaper clipping,' she said, handing him the copy. Stella waited while Andrew read through the clipping. When he came to the relevant bit, he read it out loud; 'No blood was found near the body.'

Andrew stood up from the desk. 'So now we know why,' he said.

'Yes, and why Edmond has developed a hatred for vampires so suddenly. It was after he discovered this in his family tree,' Stella said.

'I'm going to need a copy of all this,' he said picking up the papers and walking towards the photocopier.

'What are we going to do now?' Stella asked.

'Edmond needs to be caught in the act somehow. I don't know if our testimony will be enough to convict him sufficiently. I also need to know more about what he's importing,' he said whilst he busied himself making copies of the paperwork.

'Why don't you look now?' she said. 'His computers here, the records should be on there.'

Joshua and Eric filled Michael and Richard in on the evening's events.

'Sounds like we missed quite a party,' Richard said.

'How is she?' Michael asked.

'She seemed fine when she was taken away in the ambulance. In fact she didn't want to go,' Joshua said.

'In that case they might not keep her in for long. It looks like you and I are going back to the hospital,' Michael said, looking at Richard.

'Do you ever get the idea that we should take our sleeping bags with us,' Richard asked.

After several guesses, Stella finally came up with the correct password for Edmond's work files.

Andrew began to work his way through them until he found something that caught his eye.

'These are the imports that I'm interested in,' he said.

'The ones from Varna,' she said, looking over his shoulder.

'Yes. According to this, eleven crates of herbs and spices have just arrived in Southampton. I need to go further back through the details to find out, where the shipments are originating from before they reach Varna,' he said, partly to Stella, and partly to himself, as he worked through the file. After only about a minute he found the place of origin.

All Andrew could do was stare at the screen in horror. 'No, they can't be surely,' he said to himself.

'What is it?' Stella asked. 'Does that place mean something to you?'

'Yes, unfortunately it does. But first I need to know where these shipments are being stored over here? And where they are bound for?'

Andrew worked his way back through the files the other way. 'Here we are,' he said, as he found the address of a storage warehouse in Southampton. He jotted the address down on a piece of paper, then continued looking.

'He's sending them over to Cowes,' he said turning to Stella with a look of shock on his face.

'Have you heard Edmond mention Varna, at any time, to anyone?' he asked her.

'No, but I did hear his secretary mention that Mr Weston wanted to talk to him about Varna,' she replied.

'And Edmond is with him now?' he asked curiously.

'Yes. Andrew will you please tell me what's going on?' Stella said, getting irritated.

'I will, when I know for certain myself. First of all I must get a look at that shipment. According to this, Edmond is expecting another shipment, next week. Is your car in the garage?' He asked her, whilst shutting down the computer.

'Yes it is,' she replied.

'I will need to borrow it, to get to the storage warehouse.'

'I'm coming with you,' she said.

'I don't think so,' he said, forcefully.

'If you want my car I'm going with you. The staff will think that it's a little suspicious if my car were to drive off on its own, don't you think.

'Well okay then, but when we get there you stay in the car, understand?'

'Yes all right, she said reluctantly.

Michael and Richard soon arrived back at the hospital. They made their way through to the A&E department; looking on the computer they found that Sally had been treated, but was being kept in overnight to make sure that there wasn't any infection or delayed shock.

'We'll have to find out which room she's in,' Richard said. 'She's bound to be in a private side ward, probably under police guard as well.'

'Angela will know,' Michael said.

'Do you think that she'll still be here? Doesn't she ever go home?' Richard asked.

'No, you know how devoted she is to her work,' Michael said, as they made their way out of A&E.

'Are we sure that she's human?' Richard asked.

Michael just looked at him as they made their way down the corridor. As they got around the corner, they could see Angela at another reception desk filling in some paper work. The trouble was, the place was also full of police, including Tony Peters.

Michael pushed Richard very quickly towards a door. 'Oh no, not the bloody linen store again,' he said as he went crashing through the door. 'What are we doing in here again?' Richard asked.

'Shhhhh,' I'm thinking, Michael replied.

'The police know that we have nothing to do with this. So we don't have to hide,' Richard said.

'I know that, but I want us to talk to Sally on our own, without a police presence. You know I work better that way. Plus I want to know if Angela has found out anything from her,' Michael said, pacing up and down.

'Such as?' Richard asked, puzzled.

'I don't know, but you know as well as I do that some people will let something slip to the doctor that's treating them. Things that they never think about telling the police - it's the little details like that which I'm after.'

Michael looked out through the door, just in time to see Angela leave the desk and head their way. 'Angela's coming,' Michael said.

'Oh no, not again. Michael you're going to have this poor woman paranoid,' Richard said, as Michael dived out of the door.

When he shot back in, he had Angela wrapped in his arms once again. He let go and Angela turned around. She stood there glaring at him. Then she turned to look at Richard.

'Don't look at me, this wasn't my idea,' Richard said, putting his hands up.

'This had better be good,' Angela said, as she looked back to Michael.

'You have another bite victim, a Mrs Sally Knox,' Michael said.

'Yes I'm aware of that fact. But once again it wasn't a vampire bite and the police know that. So you don't need me to sneak you in again. You can just go and see her,' Angela said, trying to remain calm. She turned to walk back out through the door, but Michael stood in front of her.

'We know that. I want to know if she's told you anything about her ordeal that she may not have told the police'.

'I've dressed her wound, that's fine. I'm keeping her in for the rest of the night. She is so chirpy; I'm bothered about delayed shock. She can't tell the police much anyway, it seems that she passed out in the car and woke up at Joshua's gates. Now if you have quite finished, I have work to do.' Angela moved towards the door once more, but Michael caught her arm.

'What do you mean, she passed out in the car?' Michael asked.

'Did they drug her?' Richard added.

'I don't think so. I asked her that. In case I had to give her something. She doesn't remember any needles or anything. If there was she didn't feel it,' she said turning to Richard.

'Have you taken any blood samples?' Richard said, thoughtfully.

'Yes but I haven't got the results back from the lab yet,' Angela answered.

'In that case I'll taste it,' Michael said.

'What! You can't do that,' Angela cried. 'She's been through enough this evening.'

'I'll ask her first,' Michael said, trying to calm her down.

'Has she told you what she can remember up to her passing out?' Richard asked her curiously.

'What are you thinking?' Michael asked.

'Just a hunch,' he answered.

'When detective Peters was in there, I heard her say something about the man in the back seat with her was talking to her then the next thing she remembers is wakening up by the gates, bleeding,' she replied. 'Why?'

'Evie said that she thought that they had used some sort of sharp instrument to pierce her neck. That must have hurt. If they had used the same thing on Sally, and she had only passed out, she would have come around whilst he was using it. But if she was already bleeding when she came around, and she wasn't drugged.' Richard stopped and looked at Michael.

Angela saw the look on their faces, 'What is it?' she asked.

'Evie also said that one of them was kind to her and kept calming her down. He also whispered something to her, before he used the instrument. But she couldn't remember what it was,' Michael said, thinking out loud. 'He's one of us, He's using hypnosis and vampire sleep.'

'That would also explain the botched wounds. He's deliberately helping them, and saving them,' Richard said thoughtfully.

'You two are beginning to sound like Batman and Robin,' Angela said sarcastically.

Michael smiled at her, took out his mobile phone and rang Lucy.

She answered fairly quickly. 'Lucy what alerted you to the front gates, when Sally arrived? Were you watching the monitors?' he asked her.

'No, someone rang the bell, why?' she asked.

'We're just working on a theory,' he replied. 'Thank you,' then he hung up.

Richard had heard what Lucy had said, 'He's making sure that they're found quickly,' he said.

'If this guy is a vampire, and he's helping to save these women then why doesn't he get in touch with you or the police to say who is behind all this?' Angela asked.

'Maybe he has,' Richard said thoughtfully, looking at Michael. 'The whispers. He may have left us a message in each of the girls' subconscious.'

'We'll have to gain Sally and Evie's trust, see if we can find out anything,' Michael said.

'Let's start with Sally, we might as well while we're here,' Richard suggested.

They both made a move to leave, but this time Angela stood in the way. 'What's vampire sleep?' she asked.

Richard made a move towards her and smiled. 'Err, I know you're tempted, but now isn't the time.' Michael said, holding his arms up in front of his brother.

'But I want to know.'

Michael looked at her. 'It goes back to the days when we used to hunt. We used it to subdue our prey while we fed. It's a sort of instant hypnosis. We can either render someone completely unconscious or use it to control. But unlike normal hypnosis when a person will drift into normal sleep if left. Our victims stay under until we wake them up.'

'Oh,' she said' looking at Richard rather worried.

'Of course you have never seen me use it. I normally use it in theatre,' Richard added.

'One more question,' Angela said. 'Is there something in your offices that you don't want me to see?'

They both looked at each other baffled. 'No, why? Michael asked.

'Then can we stop meeting in the linen store?' she asked.

CHAPTER THIRTEEN

Andrew and Stella had managed to sneak out of the house unseen by any of the servants. Luckily they lived in quarters at the back and most of them would have been asleep anyway.

Managing to get the car out of the garage, they drove down the gravel drive and out through the gates, heading south for the A3024.

'Well that was easier than I expected,' Stella said.

Andrew was driving and Stella could feel the tension building in the car.

'Will they notice you missing?' Andrew asked.

'No, not until about eight in the morning, when Susan brings me my breakfast,' she answered.

'Well, hopefully, we'll be back by then,' he said.

'What are we looking for when we get there?' she asked.

Andrew glanced across, and looked at her, 'I'm not sure yet, until I get a look inside one of those crates,' he said, as he looked away to watch the road ahead.

'What if you're suspicions are correct? What do we do then?' she said, not looking at him.

'I'll have to destroy the entire shipment.'

'But won't we need it for evidence. I mean, if Edmond is smuggling something into this country illegally, we will need the evidence to put him away for longer. What with that and kidnapping, he'll never get out, surely?' she said.

'We can't, it will all have to be destroyed; besides I don't think that Edmond really knows what he's importing. That's if I'm right,' he replied.

'What makes you say that?' Stella asked puzzled.

'Because we know Edmond. Believe me, he would not be doing this,' he said seriously.

Andrew reached across and held her hand. 'It will be over soon. If necessary I'll get rid of this shipment and the other one next week. Then with our statements against Edmond for the kidnappings, we can get him put away,' he said, with a smile.

'What about you? You and Gary are the kidnappers, Edmond gave the orders, but you two carried it out,' Stella said. 'Won't you go down with them?

'No. The crime was carried out on the Island. As a vampire I'll be handed over to the Island vampires for judgment,' he answered.

'What are their punishments?' She asked.

Andrew didn't want to worry her. He knew that if he were found guilty, there would only be one outcome. He would be executed. Technically he was already dead, but he would be destroyed by fire. 'Everything will be fine. They will know that I'm on their side,' he said hopefully. If not he intended to ask them to look after Stella after his death.

'What about us two? Do you think that the nest on the Island will allow you to stay there,' she said, not daring to look at him as her eyes began to fill up with tears.

'Hopefully they will have realised by now that a vampire is involved. I deliberately messed up those wounds, to save those two women. They will know that a vampire would not make that mistake, unless it was for a reason,' he said, as he pulled onto the A35 and headed towards the A33.

'What makes you so sure that they'll suspect a vampire in the first place? The police didn't find vampire saliva on the wounds, so those puncture wounds could be made by anybody.'

'I have left clues with the two women that they will recognise and hopefully they will get my messages,' he answered.

'What? How?' Stella exclaimed.

'I guessed that their leader would want to question the two women. The police would allow them to, once they had ruled out a vampire. I deliberately used hypnosis on both of them, and vampire sleep on one, to calm her down. Hopefully the vampires will pick up on it,' he answered.

'What did you mean by messages?' Stella asked.

'Hopefully if they pick up on the clues I have left, they will hypnotise both women and find two messages from me. Then they will know that we are in fact on the same side,' Andrew said as he got closer to the warehouse address.

'That was crafty, wasn't it,' Stella said, impressed.

'I thought so,' he said to her, smiling.

'But wait a minute, you would have had to change. They would have seen your red eyes,' she said.

'I wore contact lenses the same colour as my own eyes. So they never saw them change,' he said, with a grin.

'What if they don't get those messages,' she asked.

'Then they can retrieve them later. They'll still be there, proving my intensions. I know that hypnosis can't be used as evidence in a human court, but a vampire court is different,' he said, pulling up to the warehouse gates.

When Michael, Richard and Angela walked out of the linen store together the coast was clear. Tony Peters had obviously got what he wanted from Sally as he had now left, leaving one police officer by the door.

'We had better go and collect our white coats,' Richard said to Michael as they walked down the corridor towards their offices.

'I will go in and see how she is,' Angela said.

Angela walked past the officer into the small private room. Sally was sat up in bed reading an old magazine. 'Hi Sally, how are you feeling?' Angela asked.

'A bit of a fraud really. I feel fine. Do I really have to stay here until morning?' she asked.

'Yes you do. You may not realise it now, but you went through a bit of an ordeal. The shock could hit you later.'

Just then there was a knock at the door. Michael put his head around the door. 'May we come in,' he asked.

'Yes,' Sally replied.

Both Michael and Richard entered the room. 'This is Mr Michael Moon our orthopaedic surgeon and this is Dr Richard Moon his brother, an anaesthetist,' Angela said, as she introduced them.

'Well you're looking chirpy,' Richard said. 'At least you can still smile.'

'I don't understand. I don't need you two do I?' Sally asked a little puzzled.

Before either of them could answer, Angela chipped in. 'They're both vampires and they're helping the police look into the recent kidnappings.'

'I hope that you don't mind, but Dr Carter here has told us that you passed out in the back of the car, when you were kidnapped,' Michael said, as he sat on the side of her bed.

'No I don't mind,' she said.

'Can you remember if your kidnapper said anything to you before you passed out?' he asked.

'No. All I can remember is that I was screaming at him to let me go. He had me held down on the back seat and had his hand at my throat,' she said, thinking back.

'Was he applying any pressure?' Richard asked her.

'No. Not enough for me to lose consciousness if that's what you mean,' she replied. 'He stared into my eyes and kept telling me to stop fighting him, and that he wasn't going to hurt me,' she said, as she sat there trying to recall everything. 'He kept telling me to calm down,' she said thoughtfully. 'His voice was calm and strangely relaxing, I felt myself drifting so I shook myself, but he told me to stop fighting him,' Sally continued. 'That's the last thing I remember until I woke up at the gates,' she said, as if coming out of a dream.

'What happened when you woke up at the gates,' Richard asked, as he moved closer to the bed.

'I woke up with him leaning over me as if he was talking to me. I presume he was trying to get me to wake up before he left me,' she answered.

Richard lifted his eyebrows up as he looked at Michael.

'The next thing I remember was Lucy standing over me. She scared me at first.'

'She scares the hell out of me at times,' Richard said, with a slight laugh.

'Sally, I need to ask you for a favour, but I need you to trust me,' Michael said.

'What is it?' she asked.

Michael knew that there was no easy way of asking her this. 'Will you allow me to taste your blood?'

Sally looked at him horrified and was about to say something when Michael held up his hand to stop her. 'I only want to prick your finger and have a taste. To see if he used any drugs, that's all,' he said to her reassuringly.

'Alright,' she answered, whilst nodding her head.

Michael cleaned her finger then removed a needle from his pocket. Sally watched him nervously as he pricked her finger then squeezed until a small red bead formed. 'You don't have to look so worried, I'm not going to take it all.'

He lifted her finger to his mouth and tasted the blood. 'Nothing,' he said turning to Richard and Angela.

'Sally,' Michael said, trying to think of a way to ask her. 'We now believe that the man who was in the back seat with you was, in fact, a vampire.'

'How do you come to that conclusion?' she asked.

'By the way you lost consciousness. It sounds like vampire hypnosis to us,' Richard said.

Sally sat there thinking for a few seconds. 'But they said that a vampire didn't make these wounds,' she said puzzled.

'Not with his own teeth anyway,' Richard added.

'We now think that he didn't want to harm you. He put you to sleep to avoid the pain and he deliberately missed your carotid artery,' Michael said.

'If that's the case, then why do it in the first place? And why didn't he use his own fangs?' Sally asked.

'We believe that he may be being forced into this, and if he bit you himself, he might have been tempted to feed.' Richard answered.

'The other kidnap victim mentioned that he kept whispering to her and calming her down. We now think that he may have left a message with both of you, for us,' Michael said. 'We will need to hypnotise you, to find out. The only problem is, that one of us will have to turn to do it.'

'You're joking aren't you?' she said, with a shocked look on her face.

Richard moved forward, 'I use it a lot in theatre, instead of using anaesthetic, but only on the Islanders because they know about us. If I tried it on a holidaymaker, they would have a heart attack,' he said with a smile, trying to reassure her. 'Would you allow me, please, it's safe.'

Sally looked at Angela, unsure.

'It's okay, you can trust him,' she said.

'Do you really think that he may have left this message?' Sally asked Michael.

'Yes, we think it's possible and it might help us to piece this thing together. You can trust my brother. Unless you would prefer me to do it?'

'No, it's okay, I'll let him do this,' she replied.

Richard removed the pillows from behind Sally's back. 'All you have to do is lay back,' he said gently.

The next thing that Sally knew she was looking into Richard's red eyes.

Andrew got out of the car, put his balaclava on and walked over to the gates. They were chained and padlocked. He took the chain in his gloved hands and pulled; it came apart easily. He then drove the car into the car park, keeping as far away as possible from the building to avoid any security cameras. Then he turned to Stella, 'Stay in the car. I mean it. You don't follow me in there, alright.'

'Alright,' she replied.

The storage warehouse was a large single story grey building, sitting in its own car park, just off the A33. Its location was ideally placed close to the river so that shipments could be moved straight in and out. What he couldn't understand was, why there didn't seem to be any guards.

Stella watched as Andrew ran towards one of the fire doors. He turned and used his vampire speed so the cameras wouldn't pick him up. He then used his strength to break the bar across the door and open it. If the place was alarmed, then it was a silent one. He could have heard a pin drop.

It was about the size of a football pitch inside and of course very dark. This didn't matter to him, as he could see in the dark, with his red vampire eyes. The place was empty apart from something at the far side under a tarpaulin. He quickly covered the distance and looked underneath the cover. There were eight wooden crates with paperwork stuck to the side of each one. He knew that he would have to work quickly. Pulling the tarpaulin off the crates he opened up the paperwork on one of them. Shipment from Varna to Cowes via Southampton. Herbs and spices. 'Yeah, right,' he said to himself sarcastically.

He moved to the side of one of the crates, put his fingers under the lid and lifted, pulling the nails out all at once. Looking inside, all he could see was, indeed, large bags of various herbs and spices. He had begun looking through them, when he noticed that the crate was deeper on the outside than it was on the inside.

He lifted the false bottom and found what he was looking for. 'Just as I thought,' he said to himself. 'Now I must destroy this lot before it gets to the Island.'

Stella saw Andrew come back out and dash back to the car. 'Do you have a spare petrol can in the car,' he asked.

'Yes in the boot,' she said as she leaned over and pulled the lever for him. 'Have you found what you were looking for,' she asked.

'Oh yes,' he said. Then he disappeared inside once more. He found the control box for the sprinkler system and ripped out all the wiring. He then poured the contents of the petrol can all over the crates and set them alight. Then watched as the flames took hold, just to make sure. He ran back to the car and threw the can back in the boot.

'Have you just set fire to it all?' Stella asked.

'Yes.' He replied, 'We have one problem though,' he said as he got back into the car.

'What's that?' Stella asked.

'There are three crates missing. I'm guessing they're already on the Island.' He removed his balaclava and drove out of the car park and back onto the A33.

'Did you take note of where they were going to be stored on the Island?' she said looking at him as he drove along.

'Yes I did. I will try and find an opportunity to take a look when I get back,' he said, glancing back at her.

'Are you going to finally tell me what it is, then?' Stella asked.

'No. I can't run the risk of you accidentally mentioning it to Edmond, during one of his rages,' he said.

'Do you think I would do that?' she exclaimed.

'Not intentionally, no. But it could easily happen. I'll choose my moment don't worry.'

Stella went quiet.

'What's wrong,' he asked.

'I hope that this will all end soon. I fear that he's going to kill me. When he finds out that someone has just torched his shipment he's going to fly into a rage,'

Andrew reached across and squeezed her hand. 'I know, I'm really sorry, but we have to hang on in there for a little longer. Do you still have Mr Ellis's phone number?' he asked.

'Yes, I've programmed it into my phone, why?

'Here take my phone and programme it into mine as well, just in case,' he said, as he passed his phone over. 'If anything happens to me, I want you to call him for help, okay.'

'What do you mean if anything happens to you? What are you planning?' she said, in a panic.

'It's just a backup plan that's all, I want you safe.'

Stella gave him his phone back once she had programmed the

number in. 'He offered to help me when I tipped him off about the last pickup,' she said.

'Good, I think you can trust them. I did a lot of research on them before Edmond got me into all this. I was planning on approaching them for sanctuary anyway. For the both of us.'

Sally was soon relaxed and asleep. 'Can you hear me Sally,' Richard asked.

'Yes I can hear you.'

'I want you to go back to your kidnapping, to just before you fully woke, outside Joshua's gates. You heard someone whisper something to you. What was it?' He asked.

'I have to keep up this pretence, while I find out what is going on besides the kidnappings. Meanwhile I will endeavor to keep any future kidnap victims safe. Then I will contact you.'

Angela had been writing this down. 'What does that mean? What else is going on?' she asked.

'We don't know,' Michael answered as he looked at Richard.

Richard shook his head and shrugged his shoulders. Then he turned back to Sally.

'Sally can you hear me?' he asked once more.

'Yes.'

'I'm going to wake you now. On the count of three you will wake.'

'One, Two, Three, Wake,' he said.

Sally opened her eyes and looked up at Richard. 'Are you okay?' he asked.

'Yes, fine. Did you get what you wanted?' she asked.

'Yes, thank you, we did. Even though it has now thrown another mystery at us,' Richard said.

'What's that?' she asked.

'We don't even know ourselves,' Michael replied.

'This could be because this is the second message. It could all make more sense when we have heard the first one,' Richard added.

'We'll see if Evie will see us tomorrow. Meanwhile you had better get back to Sadie. If she has woken up, she will be wondering where you are?' Michael said, as he re-read what Angela had written down.

Stella and Andrew eventually made it back to the manor. They hadn't spoken much on the way back. Each of them was in their own world. Stella was dreading Edmond coming back home and finding out that someone had torched his shipment. She knew that he would fly into a rage and that she would be on the receiving end. Andrew wanted to get back to the Island as soon as possible. He knew that he wouldn't make it back now before dawn and he couldn't run the risk of breaking into the warehouse in daylight. He would have to wait until dark.

'Andrew I'm scared. He's going to be in a terrible mood tomorrow,' she said, as they put the car back into the garage.

'I know, and I wish I could get you out of here. But if you leave now he will be suspicious of you. Not to mention the fact that he won't let you go. He will hunt you down, you know that. We have to see this to the end and get him locked up for good.'

Andrew took out his mobile phone and rang for a taxi, arranging to be picked up further along the road. He then turned to Stella. 'Try and get some sleep before he comes back. Believe me I don't like leaving you like this,' he said, pulling her close to kiss her. He then turned around and walked across the lawn and disappeared into the bushes.

CHAPTER FOURTEEN

Ann woke up the following morning feeling a lot better. She had been taking the antibiotics now for a few days and was beginning to feel like her old self again. Her mother had returned home the previous evening after much persuasion. Ann had to convince her that she wasn't going to do a lot, and would rest. After taking a shower, she went downstairs and poured herself a coffee and a bowl of cereal.

Sitting down in the lounge, she switched on the local radio, just as the news was coming on.

'Another woman with a fake vampire bite, was found last night outside the home of Mr Joshua Ellis. The woman in question, was kidnapped from the college car park earlier that evening. Mr Ellis and his driver happened to be at the college meeting a friend, at the time when the incident took place. They gave chase along with the police, but the kidnappers managed to get away. The police are now looking into why both women were left on Mr Ellis's doorstep. The woman is said to be fine and is recovering in hospital.'

Ann sat there stunned, 'What's going on,' she said to herself, as she switched the radio back off again. Ann had only met one vampire on the Island, Michael. She couldn't vouch for the rest of them, but if they were all as friendly as him. Why would anyone want to victimise them like this? Unless it was some sort of vendetta against Mr Ellis - did he kill someone before he settled here on the Island? She soon found herself feeling sorry for Michael, and felt guilty for the way that she had treated him. Maybe she did owe him that drink after all. It might take his mind of his troubles for a while. After all when, one vampire's reputation is in question, surely it would affect them all.

Evie had spent the night in her own apartment. She thought that she had better do it now; otherwise she would never go back there again. She had kept herself busy the night before, clearing the mess up in the hall. As she did, flashes of memory kept flooding back. The struggle in the hall. The other kidnapper coming in. Evie had tried to stop thinking about it, but she knew it would take some time before she settled back down again. Moving out of the hallway, Evie had got her duster out and had cleaned up all the finger print dust that the police had left behind. She had worked hard trying to scrub the place clean as if trying to scrub away the memories as well. Having worked herself deliberately to the point of exhaustion, she had gone to bed.

As Evie sat there the following morning, having breakfast, she was stunned by the news. Another woman had been found. Her memory of Joshua's visit to the hospital came flooding back. Evie picked up the mobile phone he had sent to her and rang his number.

'Hello, Mr Ellis?' she asked tentatively.

'Yes,' came an unsure voice on the other end.

'It's Evie,' she said, a little shyly. 'How are you?'

'Hi Evie, I'm fine, how are you?' he asked, cheerfully.

'Probably a lot better than you at the moment. I've just heard the news, about another victim,' she said. 'Have the police worked anything out yet?'

'If they have, they're not telling me,' he replied. 'Have you managed to return home yet?' he asked her.

'Yes, last night. I cleaned the apartment to within an inch of its life. I didn't go to bed until I was absolutely exhausted, to make sure that I could sleep,'

'You can't do that every night; you'll drive yourself insane. Try not to let it rule your life. I know that it's easy for me to say. Maybe you have gone home too early?' he suggested.

'No, I had to do it, otherwise I never would have,' she answered. 'I would like to get back to work tomorrow. Something normal and it would tire me out.'

'You can if you're sure. Do me a favour though; keep your mobile under your pillow at night. If you feel that you need someone, even if it's just for someone to talk to, ring me. We vampires don't sleep that much, maybe we could keep each other sane,' he said.

'Thank you,' she said.

'No, thank you, you're one of only a few that has asked me how I am,' he answered. 'Now take care and remember what I've said, I mean it.'

'Thanks, bye,' she said as she put the phone down.

Evie decided that she needed some fresh air and peace. Whenever she felt low, she sat on the promenade opposite her apartment taking in the sea view. It was like a tonic, and right now she needed it. Putting on her coat she left the apartment building and crossed the car park. She then sat on one of the benches and turned her mobile phone off; she needed to clear her head.

Edmond had risen early that morning to catch his coach back to Southampton. After breakfast he was packing whilst listening to the Island radio station on his lap top, when the news came on. He was seething. He couldn't let his anger out because he was in a hotel. 'Those idiots have done it again and nearly got caught,' he said, under his breath. 'Well next time I'll do it, and do the job properly,' he cursed.

After breakfast Michael had first rung the castle to ask Mary if she was all right staying with Lucy. He felt guilty leaving her there but with everything that was going on at the moment, he was here, there and everywhere, and at least he knew that she would be safe at the castle. Sadie could watch her during the day of course, but not at night, that would be too dangerous for her. He wasn't about to add his sister in law to the casualty list; it was getting bad enough as it was.

Once he had made sure that Mary was all right, he then tried to ring Evie but he couldn't get through. He wanted to make arrangements for Richard and himself to go and see her. Then they could hopefully get the other half of the message. Michael was about to jump into the shower when his phone rang.

'Hello Michael, it's me, Ann,' she said, cheerfully.

'Hello, you're sounding better,' he said.

'I am thank you, I've always been a quick healer, I'm not coughing as much now' she replied. 'I wondered if you were available to go for that drink? Of coffee, I mean. Well what I mean is, it's a bit early to go for a glass of wine somewhere. Do you drink wine?' she asked, fumbling over her words.

'Red,' he replied, laughing.

This also made Ann laugh, followed by some coughing. 'I'm sorry, I'm not doing very well at this am I,' she said, a little embarrassed.

'You're doing fine. Your place or mine. Or would you rather go out somewhere?' he asked.

Ann wanted to ask him so much, so she knew that they would need privacy. But on the other hand, was she beginning to trust him? This was stupid. 'You can come here if you like, I'm more likely to have coffee,' she answered.

'You would be surprised, he said.

141

'Right,' Ann said, laughing. 'I will see you soon then.'

'Yes I'll just have a quick shower. Then I'll be right with you,' he said, then hung up. He jumped into the shower, with a smile all over his face. He needed this tonic to help break up the frustration he was feeling over everything else. He was wondering if Joshua *was* keeping something from him. He left the cottage and got into his car. Although Ann only lived further down the hill, he wanted his car with him, just in case something else cropped up. That was happening a little too often recently.

He didn't notice the car following along behind him, which had set off at the same time. He pulled up outside Ann's and got out of the car. The other car pulled in a little further on. As Ann answered the door, they couldn't see that they were being photographed through the car's tinted windows.

'Hi, come in,' she said, a little nervously.

This made him smile; he could hear her heartbeat. The only problem was, he didn't know if this was nerves or excitement. He only knew that if his were beating, it too would be beating rather fast right now.

She led him through to the kitchen and put the kettle on. 'Sorry, I don't seem to have anything as posh as a percolator,' she said apologizing.

'That's no problem,' he answered. 'It's good to see you up and about again.'

'Yes, I feel a lot better now,' she said, removing two cups from the cupboard. 'Do you take milk and sugar?'

'Black, with no sugar thank you,' he answered. 'So what's your story then?'

Ann looked at him. 'Sorry.'

'Well this is rather a large house,' he said.

'Divorce settlement, wealthy but nasty ex-husband,' she replied, whilst pouring out the hot water.

'Oh, I see. I'm sorry I shouldn't be so nosey,' he said, feeling a little embarrassed.

Ann handed him his coffee and led the way to the lounge. She allowed him to sit down first and then proceeded to sit on the other couch. Michael put his head down slightly as he placed his cup on the coffee table in front of him, smiling to himself. It was obvious that she didn't fully trust him yet.

'That's okay, I'm a little curious about you,' she said, putting her cup down. 'You must have a long story to tell. Not that it's any of my business of course.'

'That's okay, I'll tell you mine if you'll tell me yours,' he said, smiling.

'That sounds fair,' she answered. Ann studied for a little while, trying to decide where to start. 'I got married to a guy called Carl Bray seventeen years ago. Everything was all right at first. But when the honeymoon period was over, he began to change. Carl was one of those people where only his opinion mattered. He ruled over not only me but his friends as well,' she said thoughtfully, as if in a trance, reliving everything. 'He owned a small transport business, which was quite successful so we never really wanted for anything. I did work, at a local bakery, but Carl didn't like it. He didn't like the fact that I had my own friends and a bit of independence. He just wanted me to do as he ordered all the time, especially if his friends were around.'

'Did he ever hurt you?' Michael asked.

'He didn't hit me if that's what you mean,' she answered. 'It was all mental abuse. But I did worry that one day he might turn on me, she said then started to cough a little.

'Did his friends ever say anything to you? Michael asked, curiously. 'I know that I couldn't have stood by and kept quiet.'

'No. They did notice of course, but most of them were as bad as him and the others seemed to be too scared of him themselves. Things gradually got worse and I became ill because of the stress and eventually I found myself a room to rent and walked out.' She took a drink of her coffee before continuing. 'I had also put some money into that house but he made me fight through the courts to get it back. After a further year of arguing, I eventually received some money and I was able to move away and start a new life for myself down here. That was a year ago now.'

'Do you think that he would ever come after you? I mean, he must know that your parents are living on the Island?' Michael asked.

'I think that he would have come for me by now if he wanted too. He's probably found someone else to bully by now anyway. So what's your story then?' she said, with a smile, changing the subject.

Michael could tell that Ann didn't want to discuss Carl any further and he didn't want to push her if this was the case. 'My story is a bit longer. Over a hundred years in fact,' he said, smiling.

'That's all right. I can drink my coffee slowly,' she said with a laugh.

'Okay, but remember, you asked for this,' he answered. Michael sat back with his cup in his hand and began his story. 'I was born in 1856, my brother Richard was born the year after, in a little village in North Yorkshire, called Ruswarp.

Ann looked at him open mouthed, 'Wow I didn't realise that you were that old,' she said.

'Thanks, I think. I don't look bad for a 154 year old do I,' he said laughing.

'No you don't,' she said. 'Sorry, please go on.'

'Our sister Alice, was born in 1862. We all grew up on a farm. It was mostly a vegetable farm, but we did have a little livestock. Such as a few cows and chickens, mainly to keep us fed really. Our livelihood came from the vegetables.

'I must say, I can't imagine you as a farmer,' Ann said.

Michael smiled back at her. 'Some of our money came from our mother. She used to treat the locals with a little herbal medicine.'

'So that's where your interest in medicine has come from,' she said.

'Yes, there was a nasty accident on the farm, which involved a farm hand and a hayfork. He got it stuck in his foot somehow, but not too deep. Richard and I came to the rescue. Of course we didn't know then about tetanus, like we do now. But using what knowledge we had learnt from our mother about herbs, we stopped the bleeding and treated the wound using a herbal poultice. Our mother supervised but didn't interfere. She could see that our interest in medicine had been fueled. In the end we stopped any infection and saved his foot.'

'How old were you?' Ann asked.

'I was eleven, Richard ten,' he answered. 'It was strange really; the accident provoked an interest that neither of us realised was there. It became a sort of challenge to both of us, getting this man's foot to heal. I became fascinated by the body and disease. Richard, seeing how much pain this man was in became interested in anaesthesia. As we grew up, the people in our village used to come to us. We gradually learned all sorts of things, mostly about the use of herbs at first. When I was sixteen I left the farm, much to the disgust of our father, who wanted us both to take up the family tradition. But I did get a lot of support from our mother. I managed to get into medical school. Over the years I learnt new techniques as medicine advanced. Some of it not very glamorous as a lot of medical research involved dissecting corpses. My brother Richard followed suit not long afterwards, learning about the merits of chloroform. Did you know that chloroform was used on Queen Victoria herself, when she gave birth to Prince Leopold in 1853?' he asked.

'No I didn't. I thought that women in those days had to suffer childbirth. It's something that we take for granted these days I suppose,' Ann answered.

'Well it was because of the queen that other women started to follow suit, those who could afford it that is. The poor still had to grit their teeth, as it were. But they soon discovered that in some cases it could stop the heart, so they had to find an alternative.'

Ann was totally engrossed with Michael's story and sat there listening intently.

'Gradually we both learned about the human body, disease and infections. We studied and worked together, sharing what we had both learned. After fourteen years we decided to move back home to our village. Only to discover that they had a barber-surgeon operating there.'

'What! Do you mean a barber, as in haircut and shave?' she asked, shocked.

'Yes, It used to be quite a common practice at one time,' he answered.

'That's horrendous! It's like something from a horror movie!' Ann exclaimed.

'And I'm not?' Michael said, raising his eyebrows and smiling at her. 'Well by then the practice had long been dissolved, but we found our village a little behind times. He wasn't performing surgery but was still practicing bloodletting. Have you ever heard of bloodletting?' Michael asked.

'No,' she answered, a little embarrassed.

'It was commonly believed that all diseases and illnesses were caused by a buildup of blood in the body. This was even blamed for headaches at the time. A physician would recommend bloodletting, but the barber would carry it out. They used different veins and arteries, to cure different problems.

Ann couldn't believe that she was having a conversation about bloodletting with a vampire, and was beginning to feel a little uncomfortable. She picked up her cup and had a good drink of coffee.

Michael could see that she was looking a bit anxious. 'Are you all right, I can stop if you are feeling a little uncomfortable,' He said.

'No I'm fine. It just seems a strange conversation to be having with you,' she answered then began to cough once more.

'Don't worry, it's not making me hungry, if that is what's worrying you,' he said, with a laugh.

Ann smiled, but couldn't look him in the eyes.

'Have you ever noticed the red and white signs outside barbers' shops?' he asked.

'Yes I have, but I've never given them much thought,' she answered.

'Not a lot of people have. Well the red strips represent the blood. The white strips, the tourniquet or bandages. The pole itself represents the stick a patient squeezed in their hand to dilate the veins and increase the blood flow. This is also why I am a Mr and not a Dr, because in the UK, this is still used to describe a consultant or registrar in surgery.'

'Well I never knew that. That's fascinating. So the reason why you are a Mr is because barbers used to perform the surgery,' she said, now totally engrossed again and forgetting about her nerves once more.

'Yes, I'm glad I have your interest. The last thing I want to do is bore you with my story. Anyway we both settled down in the village. Getting rid of the barber surgeon and giving the villagers the best possible care we could. Eventually our sister Alice was married to David in 1889 at our local church, St Bartholomew's. Then two years later Mary was born. In fact we both helped with the birth. It was frowned upon by the local gossiping women,' he said laughing. 'But Alice would only have David and ourselves in attendance. Of course Richard was able to help with the pain. Then everything changed in the summer of 1897. After a great storm, a plague spread through the neighbouring town. It arrived here after a ship was wrecked on the coast. We went to help and our sister was there visiting a friend at the time. Luckily our mother was looking after Mary. What we found there was what you now know as vampirism. We learned a lot about the disease from a foreign gentlemen who was staying in the town. He had witnessed this problem in his own country. Our sister soon became a victim she then turned David and Mary. Richard and I knew what they had become but we couldn't bring ourselves to do anything about it. So we began to cover for them instead, by bringing them fresh animal kill. Because we were feeding them, they managed to survive by only taking a small amount of blood from humans, without the humans remembering. Not long afterwards Richard and I were called to a neighbouring village to help a man with a fever. When we returned home, we found their cottage on fire. The locals had discovered our secret. I managed to save Mary whilst Richard went for Alice and David but he couldn't get to them. We took Mary and fled the village.'

Ann was listening to all this as if caught in a spell. She just couldn't believe what they must have gone through. When she looked at him, she could see the sadness in his eyes. He had lost his sister all those years ago, and it was still raw.

'We gradually made our way slowly down the country. Using our combined skills as doctors we earned money and managed to keep Mary well fed. After a few months I began to realise that we couldn't go on like that forever. We both knew that Mary would always be six years old and that we would age. Eventually she would be left to fend for herself. We couldn't let that happen. So I made the decision and asked Mary to turn me.'

'Mary turned you!' Ann exclaimed.

'Yes, because I asked her to.'

Michael took another drink of his coffee, and then looked up at Ann. She had tears in her eyes, and she looked miles away. There was a box of tissues on the table. He reached forward and handed her the box. 'Are you okay, I didn't mean to upset you,' he said.

'Sorry,' she said, feeling a little embarrassed. 'You gave your life for Mary?' Ann said, sadly.

'Yes we both did in the end. After a few weeks Richard decided that it would be best if he were a vampire too, in case anything happened to me. So I turned Richard.'

'Before Richard was turned, weren't you and Mary tempted to feed from him?' she asked.

'No, we were both well fed. After being turned myself, I soon discovered the instinct that allows us to use, what we call, vampire sleep. We could feed from our patients without them ever knowing what we were. Don't believe what you see in the horror films. We do know what we're doing. We can control our hunger with willpower. We simply took a little from each patient. We didn't have to kill.

'So you can feed from someone, without them remembering any of it,' she asked in disbelief.

'Yes.'

'But that's like rape,'

'Please remember, this was a long time ago. We had to do it to survive. This way we could feed without killing. We took a vow, to preserve life, not take it. It wasn't easy all the time, but we managed.'

He was watching her as she reached up and touched her neck. 'We haven't done it for a long time. We don't need to on the Island.' He leaned forward on the couch. 'Ann, look at me,' he said in a soft voice.

She slowly lifted her head and looked into his eyes. 'I would *never* do that to you, you *can* trust me.'

Ann somehow knew that he was telling her the truth. She *could* trust him. Something connected between them. She couldn't put her finger on it. It was as if she fully understood his condition, but she didn't know how. She relaxed and they smiled at each other.

'Have you and Richard never taken a human life, then?' Ann asked.

'I can honestly and proudly say, no.'

'There can't be many of you that can claim that. What about other things, like garlic and crucifixes?' she asked, through another cough, breaking the spell.

Michael smiled. 'Made up by Hollywood, along with holy water and sunlight. But I must say that a stake thought the heart would tend to ruin anyone's day, including a vampire's,' he said laughing, trying to cheer her up. 'We eventually ended up in Southampton,' he said, deep in thought. 'All this time we had kept up with medical advances. We knew that we couldn't continue feeding the way we were, it wasn't right. We had to find another source. Somewhere, where we could keep it reasonably quiet and under control. I had an idea, but it would take some time to put into practice. I saw an opportunity after seeing the Isle of Wight. We stayed in Southampton, but took it in turns to visit the Island and offer our medical expertise. It wasn't long before our reputation grew and we were well respected and trusted on the Island. When the time was right. I organised a meeting with the Island's officials. It was during this meeting that I made them an offer. I revealed the fact that we had skills that would help the Islanders, health wise. I also told them what we were. I expected complete panic and braced myself for it. But it never came; probably because they trusted us, plus I don't think that they believed me at first. There were some people who didn't like the idea of course. All I asked was that the Islanders embalm some of their dead. This drains out the blood, which we use to feed. In return we would use our combined medical skills.'

'They accepted, just like that?' Ann asked.

'Of course not, it took a little while longer. But eventually they began to trust us, even as vampires. The more lives we saved, the more we were accepted. Eventually we moved to the Island permanently. We eventually earned our freedom and Mary got her security.

'But what made you both so popular with the Islanders as doctors? Surely there were other doctors on the Island?' Ann asked.

'Yes, there were. Don't get me wrong, we didn't stand on their toes, we worked together. After all they had got to know us over a number of years. Ironically our popularity grew because we were vampires. Not because they were fascinated with us, but because of our extra skills,' he answered.

'You mean the blood tasting bit?' Ann asked.

'Oh, so you remember some of what I said that night, do you?'

Ann didn't answer him. She looked at him and went slightly red as her thoughts went back to that night.

Michael continued. 'Besides the blood tasting, and using it to diagnose, we also have good hearing, eyesight and sense of smell. Body odours can also tell us things. In surgery we can hear the patient's heartbeat and breathing. Also Richard uses vampire sleep to anaesthetise *some* patients, which is a form of instant hypnosis which used to be used to subdue our prey.'

'What do you mean, *some* patients?' she asked.

'We have to be in vampire form to do it. So we can only use it on people who know about us. If we tried it with a tourist, they would panic. Although it would only be for a split second.'

'But why would you use it in the first place? When there are plenty of drugs available.'

'Okay, I'll explain it to you. If no drugs are used to anaesthetise, then the liver can go to work on the healing process straight away. The result is, the patient heals quicker, and therefore recovers faster. There also tends to be less bleeding so the surgeon has a better view of what he or she is doing. This makes the operation a little faster as well. The use of hypnosis in surgery is slowly becoming more popular, especially in Belgium.'

Ann had sat there listening to every word. 'Don't they feel the pain and wake up?' she asked.

'No, when a human performs hypnosis, they use deep relaxation techniques, and teach the patient to block the pain. When Richard does it he knocks the patient out as completely as if they had had an anaesthetic.'

'I think I prefer Richard's way,' she said, thoughtfully.

This took Michael completely by surprise. 'You mean to say that you would trust us in a crisis? You haven't even met my brother yet.'

'I know. It's just that the more I get to know about your past, the more I understand you,' she said.

'Well the good thing, or bad depending on which way you look at it, is that with vampire sleep you wouldn't wake up until he woke you. Although, we can put a patient to sleep for a certain amount of time. This allows them to wake by themselves.

Ann sat there thoughtfully for a little while. 'Michael, where is our friendship going?' she asked, looking down at her now empty cup.

Michael placed his cup back on the table. Then he stood up and walked towards her. Sitting down beside her, he sat sideways with one knee up on the couch so that he could watch her. 'Where do you want it to go?' he asked her softly.

'I don't know?' she answered, still looking down at her cup.

Michael reached across and removed the cup from her hand placing it back on the table. He could hear her heartbeat and breathing getting faster. 'I'm not going to deny that I have strong feelings for you,' he said, as he reached up and turned Ann's face to look at him. 'I think that you are beginning to have similar feelings for me?' Ann opened her mouth to say something but he put his finger to her lips to stop her, and then removed it again. 'Please let me finish. I know exactly what's going through your mind. The future. You are going to get old and I'm not, which means that you would have a decision to make. I know that this isn't easy for you, and I fully understand. But I would still like us to at least remain friends. If you feel it might help, I can arrange for you talk to someone?'

'Who?' Ann asked.

'My sister in law, Sadie, she's human,' he said, still looking into her eyes.

'What,' she said, baffled. 'You mean that this sort of thing is common.'

'Yes, we have a lot of successful vampire-human relationships going on, on the Island. Richard and Sadie have been together for 18 years.'

'You're joking!' she exclaimed.

'No,' he said, and then laughed.

'How many are there of you on the Island?' She asked, her voice having now gone up a pitch as she tried to stifle another cough.

Michael moved his hand away from her face and sat back. 'There are a few of us, but not too many' he said looking at her. 'We gradually made friends as we moved down the country. Such as Joshua Ellis and his housekeeper Lucy. I keep a strict control of things. All vampires are vetted and they have to prove that they are in a correct form of mind to live here. I wouldn't allow a serial killer onto the Island, or someone like that. In fact, we don't accept vampires from the mainland now, unless there are special circumstances. Our new vampires come from loved ones. But even then they have to ask my permission, then it goes through to the vampire council.'

'Why you? And who is the vampire council?' Ann asked.

'I was appointed vampire leader a long time ago. We set up a council to make sure that we could keep everything under control, to protect the humans. Any vampire turning a human without permission is punishable by death. It also applies if they take a human life.'

'That's a bit strong isn't it? I can understand the killing bit, but not the turning of a loved one,' she said.

'I have to have such severe punishments to make sure that the killing doesn't happen. We haven't had a vampire death all the time that we've been here. As for turning a loved one, we have strict measures in place to make sure that the human isn't being forced into it. They must turn of their own free will, so we have both human and vampire councillors in place. It's a big step to take. Plus I have to make sure that our numbers never exceed our food demand. For example, I know that we would all be in trouble if I turned you,' he said, with a serious face.

'What do you mean?' Ann said, looking at him horrified.

'Well after that big breakfast you ordered the other morning, we'd starve,' he said laughing.

'You cheeky rat!' Ann yelled, and started to hit him about the head with a cushion, and laughing.

'What is it with you and cushions?' Michael yelled, as he made a dive for her. Ann screamed as he managed to get hold of both her wrists and hold her down on the couch. They both stopped and looked into each other's eyes. Michael saw Ann briefly look down at his lips and her breathing increased. He leaned in close slowly; it was then that his phone rang.

Michael bowed his head forward and gave a sigh. It couldn't have come at more inappropriate moment. Letting go of Ann's wrists he sat up and looked at the caller's name. It was Sadie.

'Hi Sadie, what can I do for you?' he asked.

'Is Richard with you?' she asked.

'No, why?'

'He got up early this morning to try and get hold of Evie. He couldn't get through to her and got a bit frustrated. Not being able to stay still for five minutes, he's gone off on his pushbike,' she said, rather quickly.

'I've tried to get hold of Evie this morning myself, and got no reply. I was thinking about turning up at her apartment this afternoon. But what's the panic all about?' he asked.

'He went out for a ride to clear his head, and to try and calm down. That was three hours ago; he would normally be back by now and I can't get a connection to his phone. Michael I'm worried,' Sadie said, now becoming a little upset.

'Sadie try to calm down, I'm sure that there is a rational explanation for this,' he said trying to calm her down.

'I would normally think that, but with everything that has been going on…. I'm sorry you're probably right,' she said.

Michael looked at Ann and had a thought. 'Hold on a minute Sadie,' he said, as he put his hand over the phone. 'Would you like to meet Sadie?' he asked Ann.

'Yes I would,' she said.

Taking his hand away from his phone, he said, 'Sadie I'm on my way to you, all right.'

'Yes, okay, I'm sorry.'

Michael thought that there may be an opportunity to kill two birds with one stone here. It would give both Ann and Sadie someone to talk to; at the same time it would take Sadie's mind off things. He was convinced that she was panicking over nothing, although he knew that Richard wasn't normally this long whilst out cycling.

CHAPTER FIFTEEN

Tony Peters arrived to work that morning with a lot on his mind. Was Joshua telling him the truth? He would like to believe that he was. The Island vampires had proved themselves trustworthy now for over a hundred years. It certainly looked like someone was setting them up. What he couldn't work out was, who and why?

He had managed to get some colleagues on the mainland in Southampton to look into the tattoos, but they had come up with nothing. They had come across a few tattooists who had seen the tattoo on a few of their clients and thought that it was a new gang. But they didn't know much about it, and no one on the mainland had ever heard of the *Action Against Vampires* group.

Sally hadn't been able to tell him much except that the two men were wearing black balaclavas. She had also informed him about the man in the back seat who was trying to calm her down and the mysterious way that she had passed out. One thing seemed to stand out though. Was this the same kidnapper who showed Evie so much compassion? It was obvious to him that this guy didn't want to be doing this. So why was he continuing?

Tony stared at the file for some time, but he just wasn't getting anywhere. He thought that it was time to look into Joshua Ellis's past.

Ann was very quiet during the journey into Shalfleet. 'Are you alright?' Michael asked, 'you haven't said much.'

'Yes, I was just thinking about how much you and Richard gave up for Mary,' she said, watching the country road in front of her.

'She means a lot to us, she's all we have left of our sister. We didn't spend much adult time together but we got to see our niece being born. We also felt guilty for not being able to save them,' he said sadly.

'You've both made up for it since. She's a lovely child, a credit to you both. And look at what you've achieved for her. Mary's a lot more secure now,' she said smiling at him.

'Thank you,' he said.

'You're not as frightening as the horror films are you?' she said.

'We would be if we didn't have enough to drink. I also try my best to make sure that we all behave ourselves. That's why this latest incident shook us so much. It will only take one vampire to upset the order of things and it would cause a bloody war,' he said.

'If there's anything I can do to help? Just ask me, she said.

Michael changed down a gear as he approached a tight bend in the road. He then reached out and squeezed her hand.

It wasn't long before they pulled up outside Richard and Sadie's cottage.

'Wow, it's gorgeous,' Ann said, with a smile.

Michael allowed Ann to go in front of him, through the gate. They walked up to the little front door. Michael knocked but didn't wait for it to be answered, he opened the door and they both walked in.

They walked down the narrow passage into the small kitchen at the back, with a conservatory beyond it. As soon as Sadie saw him, she had her arms around him. 'Thank you for coming, I'm pacing the floor here,' she said.

'I'm sure that there's a logical explanation for all this. It's the humans that have been targeted, not the vampires. And what if it is an accident? He can't die,' he said, holding her close.

'I know, I'm sorry,' she replied.

'This is Ann, by the way,' Michael said, gesturing with his hand for her to come closer.

Sadie let go of Michael and put her hand out to shake Ann's, 'Hello, it's nice to meet you. Are you feeling better?' Sadie asked.

'Yes, I'm still feeling a little rough, but I'm on the mend thank you. I think that having your own personal doctor helps,' Ann answered.

'Yes, I find that too,' Sadie said, with a slight laugh.

'I'll put the kettle on shall I?' Sadie said as she began to fill it under the tap.

'Have you any blood?' Michael asked.

'Yes there's plenty in the other fridge, help yourself.' Michael went to the small fridge, which was only used for Richard's blood supply. It was unhygienic for it to be stored along with Sadie's food.

'What route does Richard normally take when he goes on one of his cycle runs?' he asked, as he opened a fresh bottle.

'Normally just as far as Yarmouth and back,' she answered.

'I'll just drink this, then I'll go and see if I can see him,' he said. Sadie nodded.

Ann watched as Michael drank. Sadie noticed and thought that it would be best to distract her. 'I hear that you saved Mary the other night,' she said.

'Yes, but I didn't do much really,' Ann answered.

'Oh, you would be surprised. With these guys such an act towards a vampire earns a great deal of respect,' Sadie answered.

Ann couldn't take her eyes off Michael as he was drinking. 'Don't worry about that,' Sadie said, indicating with her head. 'You soon get used to it.'

Michael was about to say something when the conservatory door slid open and Richard walked in, pushing his pushbike. He was dripping wet from head to toe. The front wheel of his bike was all buckled and had seaweed stuck in the spokes.

'Don't say a word!' Richard exclaimed. 'Just don't say a word!' he repeated, as they stood there staring at him. Michael nearly choked on his blood as he began to laugh hysterically. This also set the other two off. 'Oh, I'm so glad that you find this so funny,' Richard said, sarcastically.

'What happened to you,' Sadie managed to say.

'I was cycling along the footpath at the back of Fort Victoria, when I saw a rather nice yacht sailing passed. Before I knew it I was in the sea,' he answered.

'Was she worth the cold dip?' Michael asked, still laughing.

'Who?' He asked.

'The blond at the wheel,' Michael answered.

Richard looked at his brother disgusted. 'I'm going in the shower,' he said, ignoring him, as he squelched his way along the kitchen floor towards Ann. 'You must be Ann,' he enquired as he approached her and held out his hand. 'I'm the nice looking one of the two.'

'Yes, I'm pleased to meet you,' she answered, trying her best to keep her face straight.

'I tried to ring you, but I couldn't get through,' Sadie said.

'That's because my phone is at the bottom of the sea,' he answered, whilst still looking at Ann.

Ann could no longer hold it in and almost collapsed in a heap in front of him, laughing and coughing. 'The shower is calling me,' he said, as he walked away from Ann squelching once more.

Once Richard had disappeared upstairs, the three of them had a good laugh and Ann soon forgot what Michael was drinking. 'I see you're feeling better now,' Michael said to Sadie.

'Yes except the stomach ache,' she replied.

'I think he'll have to buy a new bike now, don't you?' Michael said, trying to calm down and wipe the tears from his eyes.

'I've been trying to get him to buy a new car,' Sadie answered.

'Well maybe he will meet you halfway and buy a three-wheeler,' Michael answered, and burst once again into hysterics.

'If he does that, I'll stake him myself,' she said.

Michael's phone rang as he finished drinking his blood. It was Joshua. 'Hi, I wondered how you got on last night at the hospital,' Joshua asked.

'Oh, sorry Joshua, I got a little waylaid,' he answered. Michael went on to tell Joshua about their hypnotic message theory and how they had managed to get the second half of a message from Sally.

'We're going to see if Evie will allow us to hypnotise her and find the first half. Maybe that will throw more light on the matter. We have both tried to ring her this morning, but we couldn't get through.'

'She rang me this morning. She's moved back into her flat but is having trouble sleeping,' Joshua said.

'Well as soon as Richard has warmed up in the shower we will go over there,' he said.

'Why, what's Richard done?' Joshua asked.

'He took an unexpected dip in the sea,' Michael said, with a laugh, just as Richard came back down stairs.

'Oh, I'm so glad that you find this all so amusing. I could have got hypothermia out there,' he said, sulking and getting himself a drink from his fridge.

'I will speak to you in a bit Joshua,' Michael said, and hung up. 'Hypothermia is what humans get, so stop playing for sympathy,' he said to his brother.

Michael walked across the kitchen to Ann, who had been listening to Michael's conversation. 'Will you be alright staying here with Sadie, it will give you a chance to talk things through,' he said.

'Yes, I'll be fine. But who's Evie?' She asked.

'The second kidnap victim.'

'Will she let you do this?'

'Well, we'll soon find out,' he answered.

'Of course she will, I'm used to talking patients round,' Richard said, trying to sound convincing, whilst giving Ann a wink.

They both left the cottage. 'Nice girl,' Richard said, as they walked down the path. 'I take it that she's more comfortable with you now.'

'I think so. I've told her the family history,' Michael said, as they got into his car.

'So you brought her to see Sadie for a chat, I guess?' Richard said.

'That's the idea,' he answered.

As they drove away they didn't see the car parked up the lane with a single occupant inside, on the phone.

Edmond hadn't been home long when he had a visit from two customs officers. There had been a fire in a warehouse during the night. The only person using the warehouse in question at the time was himself.

For a second or two he was totally shocked by the news. 'Are you telling me that the shipment I had in that warehouse has been destroyed?' he asked.

'Yes I'm afraid it has,' one of them said. 'We need to know if the records are correct. So I need to ask you what you were storing in there.'

'Herbs and spices,' he said.

'Thank you.' The officer made a note in a small book. 'That's what the fire brigade have confirmed.'

'So, why are customs involved?' Edmond asked, a little baffled.

'Well, we would like to know why someone would disconnect the sprinkler system and deliberately set fire to eight crates of herbs and spices.' the officer said, whilst watching Edmond's reaction.

'So would I,' he answered.

'Have you made any enemies recently?' The officer asked him.

'No, not that I know of,' he replied. Of course he knew that this may be a lie. But there was no way that the vampires would know that it was him behind the recent kidnappings. Unless he had a leak?

'Well, if you remember anything get back to us. The forensics team are looking into it, of course, just in case there are drugs involved. In the meantime, we suggest that you get in touch with your insurance company.'

Edmond saw the two officers to the door. He knew that they

weren't satisfied and were still suspicious. But so was he. Who would destroy crates of herbs and spices and why? Was Patrick Weston using him to smuggle drugs? If he was, who knew about it? He would have to wait for Patrick to contact him again, then confront him.

Stella had been listening from the top of the staircase. She thought that she had better keep out of his way for a while, so she went for a walk in the grounds to give him time to cool off.

Edmond was walking up and down his office cursing and trying to decide how he was going to tell Mr Weston about his lost shipment and confront him with his suspicions when his phone rang. 'I think we've just dropped lucky,' the voice on the other end said. 'The two women, Ann Grayson and Sadie Moon, have just been left alone together. If you like, your plan could come forward a little. They could be taken together now.'

'What an excellent idea,' Edmond answered. 'Where are they?' he asked.

The person on the other end gave Edmond Richard's address.

'I'll ring the boys and let them know,' he answered.

'Do you want me to help them?' the voice asked.

'No, I want you to get the boat ready. Gary and Andrew will handle the pick up. It's the fake bite that they're not too good at. This time I'll do it over here. That way I can make sure that the job is done properly.'

'Very well,' the voice said, and hung up.

This cheered Edmond up. Once the Islanders thought that the Island vampires had turned against their own human close family, his project would be complete. Then he could sit back and watch the fireworks. It wouldn't matter that the police knew that the bites were fake; the seed of doubt would have been planted.

CHAPTER SIXTEEN

Tony Peters sat in his office looking through a file that had just been handed to him. It was about Joshua Ellis.

Joshua Ellis was born in Newholm, North Yorkshire in 1869 and worked in his father's tailoring shop from a very early age. *Well that would account for the interest in the fashion business,* Tony thought, as he read further. There didn't seem much at all, not even a record of him ever being married.

He found a copy of a newspaper cutting, the year was 1897. It mentioned an illness that killed several people in the village. It was thought to be a form of anaemia. The son of the local tailor also caught the illness – however, he disappeared whilst he was still ill and was missing. It was a local mystery. How could someone so ill suddenly disappear? He didn't show up again on any paperwork until 1901 when he moved to the Island along with Michael and Richard Moon. But was Joshua responsible for those deaths? He doubted it. From the sound of things he was ill at the same time.

Delving further into the file, the Detective found another paper cutting from 1898. It mentioned the deaths of some local vagrants in various villages a little further down the country, due to animal attacks, but because they were vagrants, there were no names. He was going to have to find out more from Joshua himself.

Andrew had managed to return to the Island without raising any suspicion. He hadn't had much sleep and although he didn't need a lot, he thought that he would get his head down for maybe an hour or two before checking up on Gary.

He walked back up the hill out of Cowes town centre towards the car park. As he made his way along, he thought about Stella's safety and hoped that all this would be over soon for her sake. All they wanted was the freedom to live together. Andrew left the car park and headed for what had become his favourite place on the Island, Firestone Copse. Having a large gravel car park, surrounded by trees with various nature trails out into the woods, it had given him sanctuary for just over a week. There, he had been able to clear his mind and feed on the wildlife. It was a popular area for dog walkers, and dogs may be man's best friend but not vampires. So he had had to be careful, but in winter with the night's drawing in so soon he had found his freedom. It was here that Andrew decided to put his head down for a few hours.

Michael and Richard were on their way into Cowes, hopefully to retrieve the first message from there unknown vampire.

'I hope that Evie will allow us to do this,' Richard said, thoughtfully.

Michael glanced across at his brother. 'I'm sure she will; after all we did help her in the hospital. That should account for something,' he answered. 'We'll see how she is when we get there.'

'What if she won't do this?' Richard asked.

'She has to. There's too much at stake here. I wouldn't like to force her into this, but if we have to, we will,' Michael said, regretfully.

They eventually arrived at the promenade car park in front of Evie's apartment block. 'That's Joshua's car over there!' Richard exclaimed, a little puzzled.

'Well he did visit her, and from the sound of it she got on well with him. Maybe he's come here to give her some support. He might be able to help, actually,' Michael said, as he parked his car next to Joshua's.

They made their way to the front entrance and rang Evie's intercom. It wasn't long before she answered. 'Hello.'

'Hello Evie. It's Michael and Richard Moon. May we come in?'

'Of course you can,' she said cheerfully.

They both looked at each other and raised their eyebrows as the buzzer sounded.

'She sounds a bit cheerful,' Richard said, as they entered the lift. 'I wonder what Joshua has been up to?'

'I dread to think,' Michael answered.

Evie opened the door to her apartment and invited them in. 'Can I get you two a coffee at all,' she asked, as she led them through to the lounge.

'Thank you, that would be nice, both black' Michael said.

Joshua was sat there on the couch with a drink already in his hand. 'What are you doing here?' Richard asked.

'Well when I visited Evie in hospital, she warmed to me. I think she trusts me, so I came to give you guys some support. I know how important this message might be, that's if he left one with her,' he explained.

'Have you mentioned anything to her at all?' Michael asked.

'No I just said that I'd come in response to her phone call, and that I was worried about her,' Joshua said, as he drank some of his coffee.

'And are you?' Richard asked, lifting his eyebrows.

'As a matter of fact I am. She's very jumpy at the moment, so go easy on her, okay,'

'She can't be that jumpy, she's just knowingly invited three vampires into her apartment,' Richard answered. 'We know that she can trust us,' indicating to Michael and himself. 'But we also know what you're like.'

'What do you mean?' Joshua exclaimed, a bit loudly. 'What do you mean?' he whispered.

'What Richard is trying to say is, you like to womanise,' Michael explained.

'What! Me! Never!' Joshua exclaimed.

'Yes' they both said in unison.

Evie returned with the coffee and looked at their faces. 'Did I miss something?' she asked.

'We have something to discuss with you,' Michael said.

Andrew had managed to get about an hour and a half sleep when his phone rang. He struggled to sit up on the back seat of his car and remove his phone from his back pocket. Looking at the display he saw that it was Edmond.

'Hello?' he said, a little groggy.

'I have another job for you both. Do you have pen and paper?' Edmond asked.

'Just a minute,' Andrew said as he climbed into the front seat and found paper in his glove compartment. 'Right, fire away.'

'I want you both to go to this address in Shalfleet,' Edmond said, smiling to himself. He read out the address to Andrew. He couldn't believe his luck. The two women that he was after had been left alone together.

'You'll find two women there, left alone. I want you to pick both of them up. You can use drugs this time if you wish. Then I want you to bring them back over here,' he explained.

'To your place?' Andrew inquired.

161

'Yes. My informant will meet you in East Cowes on the far side of the car ferry terminal. He will moor the boat up at the slipway by the toilets. I want you and Gary to come back here with them,' he said.

'What about our cars?' Andrew asked.

'Okay, get Gary and one of my men at the harbour to bring them both back over here. But I want you back here.'

'Okay, who are these two women?' Andrew asked.

'You don't need to know that, just get them here!' Edmond shouted down the phone and then hung up.

Andrew thought for a minute or two. This was the first time that Edmond had chosen a target. Who were these two women? And why did he want them off the Island?

He dialled Gary's number. 'Where have you been all morning, out with nature again?' Gary asked.

'Yes, I have, actually. Edmond just rang, he has another job for us,' Andrew said. He then went on to explain everything.

'He's risking it, isn't he. So soon after the last one, and two together as well,' Gary said.

'Yes I know. But we have to act now while they're alone,' he said. 'I'm on my way to pick you up.'

Andrew was getting hungry, but there wasn't time for him to disappear into the woods again.

Sadie sat Ann down with a drink and a sandwich at the kitchen table, and explained how she and Richard had met.

'Wow, they both like to play the hero don't they,' Ann said.

'Yes, totally different to what you would imagine,' Sadie replied.

'So during the last eighteen years, they've never given you cause for concern?' Ann asked.

'No, they haven't. The only thing that you have watch is Mary. She can turn in her sleep if she is having one of her nightmares. Apart from that, I've never witnessed anything gruesome. The nearest I come to that, is pouring Richards meals out,' Sadie said, with a laugh.

'I guess I'll have a lot to learn, if I decide to take Michael, on that is,' Ann said, thoughtfully.

'I happen to know that he's extremely fond of you,' Sadie informed her.

'What's he like, Sadie? Can I really trust him?' Ann asked, with a concerned voice.

'He's a really thoughtful, caring person. I think that it comes from both their medical backgrounds. They must have been like that before, to go into such a profession. When they became vampires it didn't change them. Probably because they never had to kill to survive, like a lot of them had to. Has he told you about how they survived in the early days?' Sadie asked.

'Yes, he did. I've had that lesson. Not literally of course, thank goodness,' Ann replied.

Joshua moved across to where Evie was standing. 'Please come and sit down,' Joshua said, as he guided her to the couch and sat down beside her.

'Now you're getting me worried,' she said.

'I can assure you that there's nothing for you to worry about. And you can trust us. We're not here to hurt you, okay.'

Evie looked at all three of them and nodded her head.

'You know that there has been a second kidnapping,' Joshua began.

'Yes,' she replied.

'Well Michael and Richard have discovered something. One of the kidnappers is a vampire, and we believe that he may be the one who was being kind to you.'

Evie shook her head. 'No, It was definitely an instrument of some sort that he used, not his fangs,' she said, with certainty in her voice. 'It must have been the other one.'

'You said that one of them was making you feel comfortable all the time,' Michael asked.

'Yes he had a strange calming voice. He was never nasty towards me. Even when they first picked me up. He spoke gently and calmly to me all the time. It was as if the panic I felt temporarily disappeared each time. I didn't mind him being near me. Not like the other one, he didn't seem to be bothered as much about my welfare. Before they took me out to the car, it was the kind one who went off to find a blanket to wrap me up in. I think he could see that I was in shock,' she said, staring at her coffee, recalling that night.

'It's definitely him that we're interested in. We believe that he was calming you with vampire hypnosis,' Michael said. 'Did you notice anything strange about his eyes?'

'Such as?' she asked.

'Were they the same as Lucy's; red,' Michael asked.

'I know that he was wearing a balaclava, but I could see his eyes. They looked normal to me,' she answered.

'That's what Sally said,' Richard added. 'He must have definitely been wearing contact lenses to cover them up,' he said looking at Michael and Joshua.

'Do you have to change to do that, then?' she asked.

'Yes we do,' Joshua answered.

Andrew had picked Gary up from his hotel and explained where they were going.

'So who are these women?' Gary asked.

'I don't know, he wouldn't tell me. We're just following orders as usual,' Andrew replied.

'So do we have a plan then?' Gary asked.

'Not yet, I want to see the house first, see what we're dealing with,' Andrew replied, as he drove towards Shalfleet as fast as he could. 'We don't know how long we've got.'

Sadie had a drink of fresh orange then looked at Ann. 'You can trust Michael with your life. I mean that. He would never hurt you. None of them would,' she said.

'It's the future that worries me,' Ann said.

'Yes, I know what you mean; I'll have to make that choice very soon,' she said thoughtfully. 'Don't get me wrong, I fully trust Richard, he'll be the one who would do it. First I have to ask Michael's permission to join the nest. Then it would go through to the vampire council.'

'Surely Michael wouldn't refuse you?' Ann said.

'No, I don't think he would. That is if he were certain that I was sure.'

Michael sat there thoughtfully, and then he glanced across at Evie. 'We need to ask you a favour,' he said.

'What's that?' she asked, a little worried. Joshua took hold of her hand reassuringly.

'He left a message for us with Sally, the other girl,' Joshua said.

'What do you mean? He didn't leave a message with me,' she said, looking at Joshua.

'You wouldn't remember,' Richard added.

Evie turned round to Richard.

Michael leaned towards her a little. 'It was deliberately hidden for us. If the message were for the police, Sally would have remembered it and would have told them. As it was, he hypnotised her and left signs that only we would recognise, so that we could retrieve it. We very nearly missed it though. It wasn't until we saw Sally and retrieved her message, that we realised that you may have one as well,' Michael said.

Evie pulled her hand away from Joshua, then stood up and walked towards the window and watched the ferry sail passed. 'I don't like where this is going,' she said.

'All we're asking is that you allow us to use hypnosis to retrieve the message. It may be something extremely important,' Richard said. 'I do this every day at the hospital, you'll be fine, I promise you.'

Joshua moved towards her and put his hands on her arms. 'Turn around Evie,' he said. But she didn't move.

'Evie, please turn around and look at me, I'm not going to do anything, I promise.'

Evie slowly turned around and looked at him. 'Would you feel easier if I did this?' he asked her.

'Are you sure that he has left a message with me?' she asked.

'We're almost certain that he has,' Michael said.

'Do you mind if Joshua does this?' she asked Richard.

'Of course not. Whoever you feel happier with,' he answered.

'All right then I'll do it. What do you want me to do?' she asked.

Sadie was putting the plates in the dishwasher.

'Do I have a lot to learn about vampire etiquette?' Ann asked.

'No, not really. You just have to try and remember that they don't follow our rules and regulations. They may live in our world, but when we are taken into their nest as a friend or even a wife, we are the guests in their world and we must respect that. A vampire doing wrong will be tried by and punished by them. We may not like it, but it's their rules, and they are strict. Likewise a human in their midst would be handed over to the police,' Sadie explained.

'Yes Michael explained all this to me this morning,' Ann said. What bothers me is that he's their leader. How do I treat him? I don't want to upset any of them,' she added.

'Just be respectful and don't interfere with any of his judgments, at least not in front of the others,' Sadie said, as she came to sit down beside her. 'Sometimes you'll see something that you don't like. But above all you must trust him. Don't always believe what you see with your own eyes, especially if it's something that looks bad. Michael and Richard are masters at deception, mainly when it comes to interrogation techniques.'

'Interrogation techniques?' Ann exclaimed.

'Because they have their own rules and regulations, they do their own inquiries and interrogations. They have to, to protect humans and their own kind,' Sadie answered.

'Why do they have to use interrogation techniques, when they can use vampire hypnosis?' Ann asked.

'I'll let you in on a little secret that I discovered when Richard and I were messing about one day. He tried to put me under because he wanted to watch the football. I wanted him to fix the toilet cistern that had been playing up for weeks. So I kept my eyes closed,' she said, laughing. 'They can't do it providing you don't look into their eyes. Once they have held your gaze you can't look away.'

'You're kidding me,' Ann said.

'No, that's why sometimes they use other techniques. Either the person has realised this weakness, or they want their victim to sweat a bit.'

'So what happened over the football,' Ann asked.

'I got my toilet fixed, rather fast,' Sadie answered. They both started laughing. 'Would you like another coffee?'

Andrew turned down a narrow lane just before he drove into Shalfleet itself. He soon found the little cottage and parked up just a little further on.

'One of us should go in through the front while the other goes in through the back, just in case they make a run for it,' Andrew said, as they got out of the car. 'We'll grab one each. When I've rendered mine unconscious, I'll then help you with yours.'

'I won't need you to help me, I can cope on my own with one woman,' Gary said, as he put on his balaclava.

'You weren't doing too well with the first one when I turned up, were you?' Andrew remarked.

'That's because we weren't allowed to put her to sleep. These two we can,' he said, as he removed a cloth and a bottle from his pocket.

'What are you doing?' Andrew asked, as they sneaked in through the front gate.

'Chloroform,' Gary answered. 'What do you think I'm doing?'

'We're not using any of that,' Andrew said. 'It's dangerous stuff, we do it my way.'

'Who put you in charge anyway? I'm getting rather fed up with this. This was supposed to....' Gary was cut short by Andrew, as he pinned him up against the sidewall of the cottage.

'Do you want to be put on a murder charge?' Andrew asked him quietly.

'No, what are you on about?' he answered.

'Chloroform can stop the heart. Let me do it my way, it's harmless,' Andrew said, staring at him.

'How come you're such an expert?' Gary asked.

'I know all sorts about a lot of drugs,' Andrew said. 'Now can we get on with this? Go around to the back and see if the back door is unlocked. If it is, ring me; my phone will be on silent. I'll check the front, if they're both unlocked we go in at the same time, all right,' Andrew asked.

Gary nodded, and Andrew let go of him. 'What if one of the doors is locked?' he asked.

'Then we improvise somehow. Just ring me and let me know how things are around the back,' Andrew said, getting a little annoyed.

They both parted company. Andrew went back along to the front of the cottage and listened at the door. He could hear both women chatting away. From this he could tell that they were a little way off, probably in the back half of the cottage. *I hope that Gary doesn't mess it up back there*, he thought to himself.

Gary sneaked around to the back of the cottage. It had a small garden, which looked out onto a wooded area, so he wasn't overlooked. There was a small conservatory, but its lower half was brick. This gave him some cover as he crawled along underneath the window towards the back door. He slowly raised his hand and very gently tried the handle. The door was unlocked. Gary closed it gently again, and then sat down on the path, to ring Andrew.

Andrew had made his way back around to the front. Then he

first made sure that there was no one about before he tried the door. It too was unlocked; just then his phone vibrated. 'It's open at this side,' Gary said.

'Open here too,' replied Andrew. 'Remember, no chloroform.'

'Yes, I know!' Gary exclaimed.

'Right let's do this, now!' Andrew shouted down the phone.

CHAPTER SEVENTEEN

Joshua got Evie settled on the couch, and sat on edge at the side of her. 'Now I'm going to turn, there's no need for you to worry, I'm in full control, okay?'

Evie nodded.

Joshua turned away from her for just a second then turned back. Evie found herself looking into two red eyes – she found it frightening and began to panic, trying to sit up. Joshua took hold of her hands and held them gently against her stomach. 'It's all right, lay back, I'm not going to attack you. It's still me behind all this,' he said smiling. But this made her panic all the more as she caught sight of his fangs.

'I've changed my mind,' she said, in a panic, trying to get up again.

Richard moved forward and knelt down at the side of the couch. Taking hold of her shoulders he gently laid her back down again. 'It's okay Evie; I know that you're not used to seeing us like this, but we wish you no harm. Please trust us. We really do need to get this message if he has left one with you. Another female's life could be at stake as we speak,' Richard pleaded.

Evie looked from Richard to Joshua and nodded, 'I'm sorry,' she said.

Joshua let go with one hand and placed it at the side of her face. 'That's okay, I know I look ugly like this,' he said, smiling again.

This time it didn't bother her. Richard let go of her shoulders.

'All you have to do is look into my eyes and relax,' Joshua said to her. 'Just keep looking into my eyes and allow your eyelids to get heavier.'

Evie could feel herself getting more and more tired. In a matter of moments she had allowed her eyelids to close and she had drifted off into a trance. Joshua changed back to human form as he had now got her into the trance he wanted. 'That's it you're doing well just relax. I want you to go back a few days, to the night that you were abducted. This time there is nothing to fear, you are merely recalling a memory so you're not in any danger,' he said gently.

Sadie and Ann were enjoying their cup of coffee when they heard the front door burst open.

Sadie looked down the hall straight away. She saw a man making his way quickly down the hallway towards them, wearing a black balaclava.

'Ann, get out of the back door, quick!' she yelled.

But before Ann could make a move, the conservatory door slide open and there was another man standing there, blocking their way.

'What do you want?' Sadie yelled.

Andrew came towards her down the hall. 'We want you two to come with us. We won't hurt you. Now, we can do this the easy way or the hard way. Which is it going to be?' Andrew asked.

Sadie looked round for a weapon and spotted a large pan. She picked it up and threw it at him. Andrew brought his arm up and knocked it away with side of his fist.

'Now that wasn't very nice was it? I said that we won't hurt you,' Andrew said, as he moved closer.

Gary made a move towards Ann. She picked up the frying pan and hit him with it across the face. His ears began to ring.

'Ooooh, I felt that. You're not having much luck are you, first a baseball bat now a frying pan,' Andrew said.

'Next time I'm wearing a helmet!' Gary exclaimed.

They both made their move together towards the two girls. Sadie brought her knee up between Andrew's legs, but she wasn't quick enough. He twisted his body to one side and caught her leg.

Meanwhile Ann picked up her coffee and threw it into Gary's face. It soaked through his balaclava. While he was wiping his eyes she took off down the hall towards the front door.

Andrew now had Sadie by the throat and was pinning her up against the cupboards. Meanwhile Gary took off after Ann.

Andrew stared into Sadie's eyes. But somehow she sensed what was coming so she closed them. She knew he was a vampire. The one that Michael and Richard were after. She hadn't seen his red eyes but she knew. He was too quick to be human.

'You'll regret this,' she said through clenched teeth.

'Open your eyes,' he asked, calmly. Andrew started to get a bit suspicious, did she know what he was and what he was trying to do? Or was she keeping her eyes closed through fear?

Gary had managed to get to Ann before she reached the door. He had grabbed her from behind. She kicked back with her heels and caught him on the shin just as he was dragging her into the lounge.

'Ow, you little bitch!' He yelled. As he turned around and threw her onto the couch he hit his head on one of the low beams. 'Shit,' he yelled, seeing stars once more and letting go of her.

Andrew could hear what was going on in the lounge. 'It sounds as though my partner is going to get very angry soon. I need you to co-operate with me so that I can help her. I don't want either of you hurt, but I'm having trouble controlling him. So please open your eyes.'

Gary made a dive for Ann as she tried to get up of the couch. He managed to get hold of one of her wrists. Ann was trying to push him off her with her other hand whilst he was trying to get the handcuffs out. 'I'm now beginning to get a headache,' he said, under his breath to Ann. 'I have chloroform in my pocket. If you don't calm down, I'll use it. Do you understand?' he asked her.

Andrew heard what Gary had said. He let go of Sadie's throat. Before she knew it, he had got hold of her wrist and had pulled her over his shoulder.

'Put me down!' she yelled, as he carried her down the hall and into the lounge.

Andrew got there just as Gary was fishing in his pocket. 'The handcuffs, nothing else, I mean it! Andrew yelled at him, as he put Sadie down on the other couch and held her down by her wrists. 'I won't hurt you, but I need to get your friend here away from my partner before he does something stupid.'

Sadie realised that he was telling the truth. There was something about the tone of his voice. The other girls had been right, it sounded as if he didn't really want to be doing this. So why was he? The only way that she could help Ann was to give into him. She opened her eyes and looked into his.

'It's all right,' he said, 'calm down and sleep.'

Sadie felt herself relax, and everything went black.

Andrew let go of Sadie and moved towards Gary who by now had managed to get one handcuff onto Ann's wrist. Leaning over, Andrew managed to hold Ann down while Gary moved out of the way.

'It's okay, calm down, we're not here to hurt you. Ann moved her head so that she could see Sadie. 'What have you done to her,' she screamed.

'She's okay, she's sleeping,'

'How?' she yelled, still struggling against his grip.

171

'Ssssh, calm down and look at me,' Andrew said.

Andrew realised that Gary was watching over his shoulder, 'Go and bring the car closer to the front door. Then come back in.'

'You're really going to have to show me this trick of yours sometime you know,' Gary said, as he opened the front door and made sure that the coast was clear before he went out.

'Relax,' he said gently. 'Come on, stop struggling, you're not getting anywhere, look at me.'

Ann started to get suspicious and remembered what Sadie had told her, but she found that she just couldn't close her eyes. She looked into his and lay still.

'I know that you don't believe me, but you're going to be all right,' he said calmly. 'Now sleep.'

Ann fell unconscious. He then removed the handcuff that was dangling from one wrist.

Gary came back in and between them they carried both the girls out to the car. Luckily for them it was a very quiet lane. The car was parked under a large overhanging tree, which gave them some shelter from any nosey neighbours. They gently placed the girls in the back seat of the car. Whilst Gary got in, Andrew had a quick scan round to make sure that there weren't any witnesses.

CHAPTER EIGHTEEN

Evie had been under hypnosis now for about fifteen minutes. Joshua was gradually taking her back through her abduction. 'The kind one came back into the bedroom of the caravan,' Evie recalled.

'Did he say anything to you?' Joshua asked.

'He said that they had their instructions, and that soon it would be all over,' she answered.

'What happened next,' Joshua asked, as Michael and Richard watched and listened.

'He made me look into his eyes. He told me that he had a message that I must remember,' she answered.

Michael and Richard sat forward on the couch. Joshua looked up at them. Richard quickly, took a pen and paper out of his pocket and nodded to him to say that he was ready. Joshua then went back to Evie.

'What was the message?' Joshua asked.

'My name is Andrew; I'm a fellow vampire who won't take human life. But I have to cover myself. There's a human working with me, her name is Stella. If anything should happen to me please make sure that she is safe. My boss is human; he's trying to discredit you with the humans on the Island, but I don't know why. I have a feeling that something else is going on, something larger.'

Joshua looked up at Michael. 'That's the woman who rang and warned me about the second kidnapping.'

'Well, now we know that they're working together. It also sounds as though he's willing to trust us with her if anything should happen to him,' Michael said. 'Bring her back round.'

'Evie, can you still hear me?' he said.

'Yes,' she replied.

'I'm going to wake you now. I'm going to count to three, after three you will be fully awake,' he said. 'One, two, three wake.'

Evie opened her eyes and looked up at Joshua who was smiling at her. 'Did you get it?' she asked.

'Yes we did. You did well, thank you for trusting us.' Joshua said moving to one side to give Evie room to sit up.

'What was it?' she asked curiously.

'Well let's find out shall we,' Michael said. 'Put both messages together,' he said looking at Richard.

Richard pulled the other piece of paper out of his pocket and began to read.

'My name is Andrew; I'm a fellow vampire who won't take human life. But I have to cover myself. There's a human working with me her name is Stella. If anything should happen to me please make sure that she is safe. My boss is human; He's trying to discredit you with the humans on the Island, but I don't know why. I have a feeling that something else is going on, something larger. I have to keep up this pretence, while I find out what is going on besides the kidnappings. Meanwhile I will endeavour to keep any future kidnap victims safe. Then I will contact you.'

'I can't believe that I was carrying that message around in my head,' Evie said to Michael in disbelief.

'Well you were, the first part anyway,' he answered.

'But I can't remember any of it,' she said.

'You weren't meant to. It was so you wouldn't tell the police; the message was meant for us,' Richard answered.

'But why won't he reveal who his boss is, and what he is up to?' she asked.

Michael looked at her. 'He's probably still collecting all the evidence together,' he said.

'But the mystery is, what is it?' Richard added.

Michael stood up, 'Thank you for what you've done Evie, it means a lot,' he said to her. 'We had better get back to the girls,' he said turning to Richard.

'The girls?' Joshua asked, knowing that Mary was with Lucy at the castle.

'Yes, Ann is with Sadie,' Michael said.

'Oh, getting to know the family is she?' he said smiling.

'Sort of,' Michael said. 'I take it that you're staying here a bit longer?' he asked Joshua, with raised eyebrows.

'Yes I am if Evie doesn't mind,' he answered, glancing towards her.

'No not at all, as long as all you want to drink is a coffee,' she said.

Michael and Richard made a move to leave, but Joshua stopped them. 'What are we going to do next?' he asked.

'We'll have to wait for Andrew's next move; it sounds as though we can trust him. I just hope that I'm right,' Michael said thoughtfully. 'There's a lot at stake here.'

'I could ring Stella of course and ask her to get a message to him. I'm sure that we would like a word with him,' Joshua said.

'I don't want to risk blowing her cover unless it's absolutely necessary,' Michael said. 'But give me her number, just in case.'

Joshua gave Michael Stella's number. He programmed it into his phone and then they left.

'Joshua is getting a bit friendly with her isn't he,' Richard remarked, with a smile.

'He seems to be, maybe love is in the air at the moment,' Michael answered.

'What's that supposed to mean,' Richard asked his brother with a grin.

'Nothing,' Michael answered, with a wink as they both got back into the car.

After ringing Edmond to let him know that the job was done, Andrew headed out towards East Cowes via the main town of Newport. Gary looked towards him curiously, 'What is it?' Andrew asked.

'This,' Gary indicated with his head towards the two sleeping passengers.

'I told you, Edmond didn't tell me who they are,' he answered.

'Not that,' Gary replied a little impatient. 'This trick of yours.'

'What about it? I've already told you how and where I learned it,' he answered.

'I don't believe you,' Gary snapped. 'If I didn't know you better, I would say that you were a vampire.'

Andrew laughed. 'You're kidding. Look I studied for several years in Tibet with the monks there. Besides learning Tai Chi and various martial arts, they also taught a form of meditation and hypnosis. I can't teach you how to do it, it takes several years to master, all right,' he said, glancing across at Gary, hoping that he had convinced him. The last thing he needed now was for Gary to realise what he was. If he did of course he would have to do something about it now. He couldn't risk being exposed now when he still had another shipment to sort out. Not to mention trying to find out who Mr Weston was?

'How come you know so much about drugs?' Gary asked, a little curious.

'I trained as a dentist some years ago,' Andrew replied.

'Why did you give it up?' Gary pressed.

175

'I never really got around to starting my own practice after my training,' Andrew explained.

Gary was looking once more at the road ahead, deep in thought, 'I wish I had known about those monks, I might have been able to avoid that frying pan across the face,' he said, in a dreary tone of voice.

This made Andrew laugh once more. 'How is your face?' he asked. 'I can't see any bruising yet. Would you like me to have a look at your teeth? You do seem to have all the bad luck.'

'It stings a bit, and no thank you,' Gary answered.

'What's wrong now, don't you trust me?' Andrew asked.

'No. I still think that there's something that you're not telling me,' he replied.

Once they were in East Cowes, Andrew headed for the car ferry. When he approached the small roundabout just before the ferry he turned right and headed down the road behind some industrial buildings and passed the new supermarket. He then turned left into a dead end and parked the car. 'If I were a vampire, I would have had you for lunch by now,' Andrew joked, as he got out.

'Yes, I suppose you would,' Gary replied, as he also got out of the car.

They both walked the short distance around the corner to a jetty. This was a small jetty hidden from the Ferry by a high pile of rocks used as breakers on one side and hidden partially from the road by the toilet block on the other. Other boat users didn't normally use it, so their boat was the only one there. Theirs was a small cabin cruiser, with a small galley and seating area and one cabin in the bow with a small shower cubical and toilet.

A medium built male with fair hair was sitting on the deck. He was dressed warmly in dark clothing and it looked as though he hadn't shaved for a few days. 'Hi Martin, long time no see,' Andrew said, as he approached and shook his hand.

'Hello, Andrew, Gary, still having fun on the island?' Martin asked.

'Yes, something like that,' Andrew answered.

'Speak for yourself,' Gary said under his breath.

'What's up with you,' Martin asked.

Before Gary could answer, Andrew did for him. 'He's had a close encounter with a baseball bat and a frying pan so far.'

'Oooops, that sounds like fun,' Martin replied. 'Have you got the girls then?'

'Yes, in the back of the car, sleeping soundly,' Andrew said.

'How long for?' Martin asked.

'Long enough,' Andrew replied.

'Good I wouldn't like to think that you couldn't cope if they woke up halfway across the Solent,' he remarked. 'I understand that I am to bring one of the cars back to Southampton.'

'Yes, but we can't get mine back until nightfall,' Gary explained.

'Right, I guess that we are stuck with each other until then. It's a good job that it's only about an hour and a half away,' Martin said.

Gary hated working with Martin, he was a real know it all, pretending to be an expert at everything, whilst actually knowing nothing. At times he found Andrew annoying the way he took over things but at least he knew what he was doing. They made sure that the coast was clear while they carried Sadie and Ann across to the boat and down into the cabin.

'We're using the usual marina at the other side. My car's waiting for you. I've left the keys under the wheel arch,' Martin said.

'Thanks, I'll see you two in a few hours,' Andrew said, as he fired up the boats engine.

Gary and Martin watched as Andrew set off towards the exit buoys of the harbour.

'So who are these two women?' Gary asked.

'You mean you don't know?' Martin said.

'I wouldn't be asking if I did, now, would I,' Gary said sarcastically.

'One of them is the new girlfriend of the Island's vampire leader, the other is his brother's wife,' Martin informed him.

'You're joking,' Gary said, in disbelief.

'No. Edmond has had me following the wife for a few weeks. We were only going to take her. But then the other one came on the scene. Edmond thought that this was even better. Then when they were left together on their own, well, Edmond thought that he'd won the lottery,' Martin explained.

'What does he have planned for them?' Gary asked.

'Oh something gruesome no doubt,' he replied. 'Well let's go somewhere while we wait for nightfall shall we?' Martin said.

Joshua was enjoying a drink and a chat with Evie, getting to know her better when his phone rang. Looking at the caller display, he saw that it was Eric. He looked at Evie, 'I'm sorry, you'll have to excuse me a moment,' he said. 'Yes Eric, what is it?' Joshua asked.

'Peters has been asking questions about you,' he said.

Joshua moved out into Evie's hallway. 'What kind of questions?' Joshua asked.

'He wanted to know about your past,' he answered. 'I told him that he would have to speak to you about that, and I didn't know where you were,' Eric said.

'That's okay; I get the impression that he thinks that all this is linked to my past,' Joshua said. 'I'll have a word with him later.

'Are you still at Evie's?' Eric asked.

'Yes, Why?' Joshua asked.

'Oh I just thought that you may want to join me,' Eric replied.

'Now why would I want to join you?' he asked, 'when I'm working on a very nice young lady.'

'Oh, I just thought that you might want to see what I can see?' Eric said in a smug voice.

'What's that?'

'The kidnappers' car,' Eric said, in a calm voice.

'What! Where?' Joshua exclaimed.

'We never did finish checking out those bungalows, did we. We got interrupted. So I thought that if I were them and I had had to abandon the car temporarily, then I would wait until nightfall. So I came to have a look, and guess what?' he asked.

'It's still there,' Joshua answered.

'Yep, got it in one. It's at that last bungalow we were at, in the garage.'

'I'll be right there. Ring Michael,' Joshua said, and then hung up.

Michael and Richard pulled up outside the cottage. 'I wonder what the girls have been up to while we've been out?' Richard asked.

'Hopefully having a good chat,' Michael answered. 'I do hope that Sadie hasn't put her off me,' he said as he got out of the car.

'I doubt that, Sadie loves you to bits,' Richard said, as he moved to his brother's side of the car.

'She does?' Michael asked, as they set off down the garden path.

'Yeah, every time I misbehave, she tells me that she married the wrong brother,' he replied, as he stopped dead in front of the door. Michael nearly walked straight into the back of him. They had been so busy talking, they hadn't noticed that the front door was wide open. They both stood there and looked at each other.

Richard moved forward slowly, 'I'll go around the back,' Michael whispered to him.

Richard listened but he couldn't hear any heartbeats. He glanced into the front room first of all. The cushions on both couches were all over the floor as if there had been a struggle. He suddenly panicked and dashed down the hall into the kitchen. Not really noticing the smell in the lounge. He got there just as Michael came in through the conservatory.

They began to take in the scene before them. A pan and the frying pan were on the floor. The floor was wet with coffee. Despite that they both could smell the same two men that they had smelt on Evie and Sally.

Richard flew into a rage, 'shit!' He yelled. 'We shouldn't have left them alone.'

Michael was still in shock.

'If they hurt just one hair on their heads I'll kill them!' Richard continued to yell.

'Wait, Richard, calm down a minute. We have to think this through. This must have been planned. They must have been watching our every move,' he said.

'So what are you getting at? When I get my hands on Andrew, I'm going to rip his head off,' Richard went on.

'Richard sit down!' Michael yelled at the top of his voice. Richard did as he was told.

'We know that they were taken by Andrew and the guy he is working with. We can still smell them both. If we can trust Andrew; then we know that they're safe for now. But what I don't understand is, why he didn't warn us?' Michael said.

'What if he doesn't know who they are?' Richard suggested.

'What do you mean?'

'Well someone has been watching us, if it wasn't Andrew then who was it?' Richard asked.

'You mean that Andrew may have simply been given the order,' Michael asked.

'Yes.'

Michael got his phone out of his pocket and dialed Stella's number. It rang several times but he got no answer.

'We have to get hold of Stella and try to get a message to Andrew or even try to talk to him ourselves,' he said.

'What about Tony Peters,' Richard asked. 'We must ring him.' But before Michael could answer, Richard began to sniff the air again.

'What's wrong?'

'Can you smell that?' Richard asked as he dashed back down the hall. 'I would recognise that smell anywhere. I used to use it,' he yelled.

'What?' Michael said, as he went after him, trying to sniff the air as well. As Michael got halfway down the hall he also picked up the scent. He got into the lounge just as Richard threw a cloth in his direction, his eyes were blazing. 'Why would a vampire need to use chloroform?' Michael asked.

'Because at least one of his victims knows that if she closes her eyes he can't use vampire sleep,' Richard answered. 'But we also know that one of these guys is a human - it could be his.'

Michael's phone rang; he answered it quickly. It was Eric. 'Michael, I've found the kidnappers car,' he said.

'Where?' Michael asked.

Eric gave Michael the address. 'We're on our way,' he said.

Richard didn't have to ask – he had heard the conversation. He locked up the cottage and went out after Michael.

Andrew had made it to the other side of the Solent and into the harbour. He moored the cruiser up in a quiet area, and then went looking for Martin's car. He eventually found it parked up alongside a large boat on its trailer. He knew that he had to move the car nearer to cruiser, so that he wouldn't be noticed carrying two unconscious women. Then, after successfully transferring Sadie and Ann to the car, he began the final leg of his journey.

Michael and Richard had joined Eric and Joshua at the bungalow.

'You two look a little flustered, what's wrong? Eric asked.

'They took Sadie and Ann while we were at Evie's,' Richard answered.

Eric and Joshua glanced at each other, then back at the two

brothers. 'How long have they been following you and planning this?' Joshua asked.

'No idea,' Michael replied.

'If this was planned though, why didn't Andrew or Stella warn us?' Eric asked.

'Maybe they didn't know until the last minute. And it could be possible that Andrew doesn't know who he has,' Michael said. 'After all when you're running an operation like this, the less your people know the better. You can cover things up.'

'Where's the car?' Michael asked.

'In the garage of that bungalow over the road,' Joshua answered.

'We should ring the police and let Peters know,' Joshua said.

'No, we do this our way,' Michael said.

'What!' Richard put in.

'The police will do what we are about to do and wait for them to come back. They will end up at the police station being questioned. It will take a lot longer for them to question them than us. In the meantime Sadie and Ann are in danger,' he answered.

'They had better not be long,' Richard said, impatiently.

Michael turned to face Richard and took hold of his shoulders. 'We have to be calm about this Richard, if we lose our temper, we won't get anywhere and we lose our girls, okay,'

'Right,' he answered, taking a deep breath.

'Talking of which,' Joshua said. 'I'm going to pick Evie up. I'm not risking it, just in case. I'll take her to the castle then I'll come back and join you.'

'I've never seen the boss that smitten with a human, apart from Sadie,' Eric commented.

'Yes, we did notice,' Richard said.

'Okay, you two park the cars at the bottom of the cul-de-sac, where you can see them coming. I'll hide in the garage. Let me know when they arrive,' Michael said.

They took up their positions and waited for the sun to go down.

181

CHAPTER NINETEEN

It wasn't long before Joshua returned. He parked up at the entrance to the estate. 'Can you hear me? I'm back,' he said, without using his phone.

'Yes,' they all said in unison.

'I've parked at the entrance, where are you?' he asked.

They explained where everyone was. 'Is Evie alright?' Richard asked.

'Yes, she's at the castle with Lucy and Mary,' Joshua answered. 'She's a bit nervous of Lucy. They've only met briefly in the shop, but hopefully she should be all right.'

'I hope that it isn't Andrew that comes back for this car,' Michael said. 'Because he's going to hear us warning each other and it will also mean that he isn't with the girls.'

They didn't have to wait long. Just as the sun was going down, Joshua spotted someone being dropped off on the main road at the entrance to the estate. 'Someone's here, he's on his own. Tall, medium build, dark brown hair and a moustache, wearing a long dark coat.'

'It's a good job that he's tall, then,' Richard said.

'Why?' Joshua asked.

'Well you wouldn't have been able to see him out of your windscreen otherwise,' he answered.

Michael smiled at this. At least Richard was becoming his normal self again.

'I'm sat on a cushion, if you must know,' Joshua answered then quickly moved on. 'According to the reflections in the bungalow windows, this guy is human, and he's heading in your direction.'

'Yes, we have him in sight,' Eric answered.

Eric and Richard watched as he walked towards the bungalow that was for sale, looking around as he did so. He then stopped and had a good look around once again before walking down the drive towards the garage.

'This is him,' Richard said. 'He's about to open up the garage.'

Michael heard the garage door open. Glancing underneath the car he saw his two feet approach the driver's door. Before Gary could open it, Michael had shot around the other side and came up behind him.

'Hello, we meet at last,' Michael said.

Gary jumped and spun around, dropping his keys on the floor as he did. Michael was stood there staring at him. He was about to make a run for it. When he saw a slab of a man blocking his way at the door – it was Eric. 'Don't even think about it,' he said.

'What's your name?' Michael asked.

'Gary,' he replied.

Richard approached from the other side.

'Who are you?' Gary asked.

'I think you know that,' Richard said. 'Now, where are they?'

'Who? I don't know what you're talking about,' Gary exclaimed, looking round just in time to see Joshua appear at Eric's side.

'Yes you do,' Michael said. 'Tell us now and we'll hand you over to the police. If you don't we'll question you further and believe me that's the last thing that you want.'

'You can't do that, I haven't done anything,' he replied.

'We got your scent off the other two victims, so it's no use lying to us,' Richard said. 'And my patience is wearing thin.'

Michael knew that Richard was now putting on a show to try and frighten Gary into a confession.

'I have had enough of this,' Richard said, as he moved forward and put his vampire face on.

Gary knew that Edmond would have him killed if he said anything. But how long could he hold out against the vampires? 'I really don't know what you're talking about,' Gary said turning his head away from Richard and closing his eyes.

'If you are really telling the truth, then you have nothing to fear,' Michael said.

'Open your eyes,' Richard ordered.

'No,' Gary said trembling.

'I'm asking you nicely, where is my wife and my brothers girlfriend?' Richard asked through his fangs.

Gary just stood there with his eyes closed, not saying a word.

Michael and Richard looked at each other and raised their eyebrows. 'Plan B?' Michael asked.

'Plan B,' Richard answered, nodding his head.

Joshua looked up at Eric, 'Plan B?' he whispered, a little baffled.

Eric shrugged his shoulders, 'Plan B?' he whispered back. 'I didn't even know that there was a Plan A.'

'Keep him here, Richard, while I go and bring the car closer,' Michael said, as he walked out of the garage.

Joshua stopped him 'Plan B?' Joshua asked.

'Yes, we'll have to take him somewhere private. He's keeping his eyes closed here, so we can't use our usual talents. We need somewhere to question him further,' Michael answered.

'Where?' Joshua asked.

'My place.'

'You will need somewhere more secure than the cottage, you have neighbours. Someone will hear him scream,' Joshua said.

'Oh, he won't be doing any screaming and I don't want you involved. This is kidnapping.' Michael answered.

'What are you two going to do?' Joshua asked.

'Use his own imagination against him,' Michael said, as he walked away to the car.

Joshua followed him. 'Michael use the castle, it's secure. We're talking about Sadie and Ann here; they are part of our family. We're behind you both. I know that we haven't got time to go through the normal channels. After you have questioned him, if we are fast we should be able to catch him out and use vampire hypnosis. He won't be expecting it. We can make him forget all this, bring him back here. Then leave a message for the police to pick him up,' Joshua suggested.

'Are you sure about this?' Michael asked.

'Yes, come on, time might be running out,' Joshua emphasised.

Richard and Eric had been listening into the conversation. They never said a word. This told both Michael and Joshua that they were in agreement. Michael reversed the car up to the bungalow's garage. Richard had returned to human form.

'Come on Gary,' Richard said, taking hold of his arm.

'Where are we going,' he asked, opening his eyes at the same time.

'Somewhere private, where we can have a little chat,' Richard answered.

Michael got out of the car with a pair of handcuffs and put them on Gary. 'Does Ann know that you keep a pair in the car?' Richard asked him, with a mischievous smile on his face.

'No,' Michael said smiling back, whilst opening the car door for them both. 'I like to be prepared for every emergency.'

Stella had returned from her walk and had fallen asleep on the bed after a shower. She was woken up by Edmond.

'Had a nice walk?' he asked.

'Yes,' she replied. 'All that fresh air made me fall asleep.'

'Good, I want you nice and refreshed for later. I'll want to celebrate,' Edmond said with a big smile across his face.

'What will you be celebrating?' Stella asked.

'My final victory,' he answered.

'Your final victory?' Stella asked puzzled.

'Yes, Andrew is on his way back from the Island as we speak with two new victims. Ann Grayson the new girlfriend of the vampire leader and his brother's wife Sadie Moon,' he boasted.

Stella's mouth dropped open, stunned for a second. 'What do you plan to do with them?' she finally asked.

'Kill them of course,' he replied, happily.

'What!' Stella exclaimed.

'Oh come on, I can't leave this one to botch it and bugger it,' he said, referring to Gary and Andrew. 'They've already botched up two jobs. I have to make sure that this one is done properly. This time I intend to have the pleasure of bleeding them myself. Then I'll take my pleasure out on you,' he said with a grin.

'What are you going to do with them after you've killed them?' she asked.

'Dump them back on their own Island somewhere,' he answered. 'When they are found, it will cause uproar amongst the Islanders. I mean if they are willing to attack their nearest and dearest, what hope do they have?' He said.

'But won't they be able to prove that it wasn't a vampire bite?' she asked.

'That won't matter. The people will believe what they want to believe,' he said, getting hold of her by the hair. 'I'll be ready for you then,' he said through his teeth.

Stella knew that she couldn't let him get away with this. She had to warn Andrew.

It wasn't long before Andrew arrived and Edmond went out to meet him. 'Where are they?' he asked.

Andrew opened the back door of the car. Sadie and Ann were still unconscious. 'When will they come around?' Edmond asked.

Andrew wanted to keep the girls unconscious until he found out what Edmond wanted them for. Not to mention who they were - he didn't want them awake and panicking. He had a feeling that whatever Edmond had planned for them, he would want them awake. So the longer he could stall the better. 'A little while yet - why?' Andrew asked.

Edmond just looked at him. 'Take them inside to the guest room and don't ask questions,' he said.

Andrew walked in carrying Ann. Taking her into the guest room he laid her down on the four-poster bed.

Stella had opened her bedroom door just a crack and had seen him walk passed. 'Andrew, I hope that you can hear me,' she whispered. 'I need to talk to you urgently.'

On his way back from the guest room, he slowed down and looked around. There was no one else on the landing. He quickly opened Stella's door a little further. 'Keep talking to me; I can hear you, even outside,' he said.

Stella proceeded to tell Andrew everything that she knew; who the two women were and what Edmond had planned for them.

When Andrew had brought Sadie upstairs he sneaked in to see Stella. 'I can't stay in here for too long, Edmond will wonder where I am,' he said. 'Are you sure about all this?' he asked.

'Yes, he bragged about it to me himself,' she replied.

'I need time to think,' he said. 'We may have to end all this now and get Edmond arrested. Hopefully, there will be enough evidence on his computer to convict him of illegal imports, besides the kidnappings,' he said thoughtfully.

'The police will surely look at his next shipment,' Stella said.

'I'll have to go back downstairs. We can't be found together. Keep your phone handy and stay within sight of me if you can. You might have a better chance at raising the alarm than me. If I give you the nod, sneak away and ring Joshua Ellis. Tell him where we are and put your phone on vibrate in case he needs to get hold of you,' he said, giving her a quick kiss.

Gary had a horrified look on his face as Michael drove through the gates of the castle. One look at the high wall surrounding this place told him that there would be no escape. He knew that one way or another he would end up telling the vampires what they needed to know.

Edmond had done his homework when he looked into the Island vampires. He had found a weakness in their ability of mind control. They had to turn to be able to do it. This enabled you to see it coming. 'If you keep your eyes closed they can't hold you with their gaze,' Edmond had told his men early on. Of course this is what Gary had done in that garage. But where had it got him? He now wondered what they would do to him now - what form of torture awaited him?

Michael and Richard smiled at each other as they escorted him from the car into Joshua's office. They both knew that their form of interrogation had already begun. They knew that his mind was now racing, as they could both hear his heartbeat and breathing. They could also smell his fear. His own body was already working against him, before they had even started.

Richard disappeared out of the room while Michael removed Gary's handcuffs and coat. 'Sit down, make yourself at home' Michael said, as he threw Gary's coat over a chair.

Gary did as he was told; he sat down on the couch and tried to focus past Michael to the view out in front of him, but all he could see was his own reflection. It was now too dark to see out of the window. He could see that Eric was guarding the office door out of his eye corner. They had removed his handcuffs, but why? Probably because he didn't need them on - they were stronger than him and he couldn't out run them.

After what seemed an eternity, Richard returned followed by Joshua.

Michael pulled up a chair in front of Gary and sat down. 'Where are they?' He asked. Gary stayed, silent, his throat was beginning to go dry.

'I'm sure that you don't want to suffer over this. Is your boss really worth it?' Michael asked.

Gary looked at him; he was still in human form. 'I don't know who you're referring to,' Gary answered, and then swallowed, trying to ease the dryness.

'I'm not going to waste my time turning and trying to hypnotise you. You've already shown your knowledge over that one. Let's see how long you last with something else shall we?' Michael said, as he stood up and moved the chair.

Andrew returned downstairs and went into Edmond's office. 'Did everything go according to plan?' Edmond asked.

'Yes, we didn't have too much trouble,' Andrew answered.

Stella walked in, sat herself down on a couch and picked up her book. Edmond looked at her. 'What are you still doing up?' he asked.

'I won't be able to sleep, so I've come down to read my book,' she said, glancing at Andrew.

'Why don't you read in bed?' he asked.

'Because it makes my neck ache, and it isn't as if I don't know what's going on, is it?' she replied.

Edmond looked back towards Andrew. 'How long will the girls be unconscious?' Edmond asked.

'A while yet. I gave them a second dose on the way here they were coming around. I didn't want any trouble in the car, I was on my own,' he lied.

'Good idea,' Edmond said. 'What did you give them?'

Stella sneakily glanced over the top of her book at him. Andrew could see her out of the corner of his eye.

'Does it matter? I have quite an extensive knowledge of drugs. I wouldn't want to bore you. What matters is that what I have used is effective, safe and has no side effects,' he answered.

Stella smiled, behind her book.

'Very well,' Edmond answered, as he began to tidy his desk.

Andrew smiled back at Stella. Maybe that was convincing because it wasn't a lie. It was just that Edmond thought he was talking about something else.

'Maybe I should let you loose on this one, then?' Edmond said, indicating with a nod towards Stella. 'She says that she can't sleep, although I think that she's just being nosey.'

Stella looked at Edmond and then to Andrew, with a worried look on her face.

'But I'll need her conscious for later,' he said, as he sat down by her side and sneered at her.

Andrew wanted to rip his throat out, but he held his ground. He promised himself that Edmond would pay before the night was out. He wanted to see him squirm.

'And where's Gary?' Edmond asked.

'He had to wait until nightfall before he could recover his car. He should be following Martin back. He's probably on the next ferry,'

Andrew answered.

'You must be hungry; you will want something to eat. The cook will have gone to bed, but I don't think that Stella here will mind supplying you with something,' Edmond said. 'I'm going to bed to get a little sleep, but I want waking up as soon as those girls have come round.'

'Thanks, I am a little peckish,' Andrew replied.

Andrew and Stella left the office and headed for the kitchen. Stella looked round at him, he had turned and was smiling at her, flashing his fangs. 'Don't even think about it,' she said.

'Well, he did say that you wouldn't mind,' he replied.

Andrew sneaked outside to his car and retrieved his own emergency supply from the boot. Stella made a ham sandwich to cover for him just in case Edmond came back downstairs.

Gary saw Richard hand something over to Michael. When he turned round he had a syringe in his hand. Before Gary could make a move, Eric had hold of his shoulders from behind. 'Hold out your arm,' Richard said, holding a tourniquet in his hand.

Gary smiled, 'Do you think that this will work? I've already told you, I don't know who you're talking about,' he said, trying to sound convincing.

Eric squeezed his fingers into a pressure point on his neck. 'Arrrrgh,' the pain shot through his shoulder and down his arm.

'Put your arm out,' Richard repeated.

Gary did as he was told. Richard put the tourniquet around his arm and forced his hand into a fist using his own hand, until he saw a vein stand up.

Michael moved forward with the syringe. Gary kicked out but Eric applied pressure to his neck once more.

'I suggest you relax – once I've given you this, Eric will let go,' Michael said, as he moved forward once more. This time Michael managed to administer the injection. Richard removed the tourniquet and Eric let go.

'You see, that was no problem, was it?' Michael said, smiling. 'I know that you're lying about the girls, because I can smell them on you. But for some reason I can still smell Evie on you, and it's very strong.'

'Who the hell's Evie?' Gary asked.

'Your first victim,' Michael answered. 'You mean that you didn't even bother to find out her name?'

'What have you given me?' Gary asked.

'Oh you will find out soon enough,' Michael said with a smile. 'She's here you know, Evie. I have a good mind to let her in here so she can tear you limb from limb. Now let's find out why you smell so strongly of her shall we?' he said nodding to Eric, who put on a pair of gloves then picked Gary's coat up. It wasn't long before he found Evie's mobile phone. He held it up for Michael to see. 'You had better put that in a plastic bag,' Michael said. 'Preserve the evidence.'

Gary couldn't believe that he still had Evie's phone in his pocket; he had forgotten all about it. He started sweating and both Michael and Richard noticed.

'Feeling hot are we?' Richard asked. 'It's started working already,' he said, looking at his brother.

'What has?' Gary asked.

'The poison I've given you,' Michael answered.

Michael reached back with his hand and brought out another syringe. 'This one is the antidote, if you want this, you will tell us where the girls are,' he said.

'You're lying to me, you're a doctor, you wouldn't take human life,' Gary said.

'But I'm also a vampire.' Michael said glaring at Gary. 'That reminds me, I'm getting hungry are you?' Michael said turning to his colleagues.

'Yes I am a bit,' Richard replied. 'Eric would you mind, and in glasses please.'

Eric left the room. Joshua was still puzzled about what the two brothers were up to. He knew that they liked to use deception in their interrogations, but this one was new to him. He was fascinated.

Gary now found himself short of breath. 'Stage two,' Richard said, looking at Michael.

'Yes, it looks like it,' he answered.

Andrew returned from the car with a bottle of blood. 'What do you want to do?' Stella asked.

'We go into his office and see if we can find out where those other three crates have disappeared to,' he said.

They returned to the office. Stella brought the ham sandwich with her and started tucking into it. 'What if he comes back down and catches us?' she said.

'I'll hear him coming,' he replied. 'Now get me back into his business files.'

Stella eventually got through to his business files. She then moved over to allow Andrew access.

'Open his safe, see if there are any clues in there,' he said. 'I took the shipping details from one of the crates. It gives the address of a warehouse in Newport, but just in case I want to see if there are any further addresses.'

Andrew was working once more through the files when Stella interrupted him. 'I have something here,' Stella said, moving over to him. 'It's for an address in Shorwell. It looks as though it's being rented by Mr Weston,' she said, smiling at him.

'Well done, are there any more?' he asked.

'Yes, Thorley and Nettlestone,' she said.

'That's three, good. Let's get those photocopied,' he said as he shut down Edmonds computer.

'What next?' she said, as she photocopied the three rental agreements.

'We make a phone call,' he said, smiling.

Eric returned with a tray of glasses full of blood and handed them out, taking one for himself. This made Gary feel queasy even more, and he started to retch.

'Stage three already, that was quick,' Michael said.

Michael's idea was working; soon Gary would tell them what they needed to know.

Joshua's office phone began to ring. He looked at the others and then to his watch. *Who's ringing at this time?* He thought.

'Hello,' Joshua asked.

'Is that Joshua Ellis?' a male voice asked.

'It is, who is this?' he replied.

'It's Andrew. Hopefully by now, you will know who I am?'

Joshua clicked his fingers at Michael and Richard and pointed to the other phone. They both picked it up quickly.

'Yes we know who you are, we found your messages,' Joshua answered. 'Are the girls all right?'

'They're fine. I'm having to keep them both in vampire sleep, to stall for time. Edmond thinks that I've drugged them. I believe that he wants to kill them when they wake,' Andrew said.

'What? If he touches one hair on their heads I'll rip him apart,' Richard shouted down the phone.

'Who's that?' Andrew asked.

'Richard Moon, Sadie's husband,' Richard said, in a threatening voice.

'Edmond Parr won't be coming anywhere near them; I can assure you of that. If you don't get here in time, I'll get them out of here myself. Do you have a pen?'

Joshua picked up a pen. 'Go on, I'm ready,' he said.

'We're at the Parr manor in Bitterne, Southampton. It's just south of the airport.' Andrew then went on to give them directions.

'You mentioned that something else was going on?' Joshua asked.

'Yes I have that information now, I'll fill you in on that when you get here,' he answered. 'I can assure you that you'll understand why I couldn't pull out until now. I had no choice, I had to carry on until I gathered all the evidence together,' he explained.

'Why Sadie and Ann?' Joshua asked.

'I didn't know who they were until I got back here and Stella told me. Edmond just gave us the order. We didn't hurt them, but you must get over here soon. Use Stella's number to get in touch when you arrive, it will be on silent. She'll have a better chance than me to sneak away, so she'll let you in through the gate. But please, do me a favour?' he asked.

'What's that?' Joshua asked.

'Don't let her come back in. Edmond will kill her, if he finds out that she's been helping me,' he said.

'Okay, you've got it,' Joshua answered.

Then Andrew hung up.

Michael put the phone down. 'Joshua, can we use your jet?' Michael asked.

'Of course you can,' he answered.

'I'll get George, David and Mark out of bed,' Richard said.

'Tell them to meet us at Bembridge Airport,' Michael said to him.

'How many cars will you need me to hire from Southampton airport?' Joshua asked.

Michael did some quick calculations in his head. 'Three.'

'Right, I'll get on with that,' Joshua answered.

'Will they be open at this time of night?' Richard asked.

'The hire company that I use is always open,' Joshua said. 'They will be waiting for us at the terminal.'

'What about me?' You can't leave me?' Gary said, in a panic.

'You're right,' Michael said. 'We will drop you off where we found you and call the police to pick you up.'

'But the antidote, I need it,' he said.

Michael broke the needle off the end of the syringe and squirted the liquid into the plant pot. 'You won't need this,' he said. 'All you were injected with, was water. Your own imagination did the rest. When you started sweating we convinced you that it was the poison. Same with the shortness of breath, as you began to panic even more. Then when we brought the blood into the room, we knew that it would make you feel ill if you were squeamish. We merely used your own imagination and body against you,' he explained.

Gary sat there open mouthed; he couldn't believe that he had fallen for it.

Richard had alerted the rest of the team. 'They're all on their way to Bembridge airport,' he informed his brother.

Michael then phoned Tony and informed him about Ann and Sadie's kidnapping and asked him to meet them at the airport.

'Well done, I'm impressed,' Joshua said after Michael had rung Tony.

'With what?' Michael asked.

'With that technique!' he exclaimed. 'Do you two sit together each night and dream all this stuff up?' he asked.

'No, we just work well together that's all. Plus, you know as well as us how imagination can run away with you. All you have to do is plant a little seed. The mind will do the rest,' Michael said with a grin.

'Right, Richard and I will take Gary back to his car. Joshua, Eric, you go straight to the airport, we will meet you there,' Michael said. 'There is just one thing that we need to do before we go, though. Eric, watch Gary for a couple of minutes before you go will you. Richard come with me.'

'What are we doing now?' Richard asked, as they began to climb the stairs.

'Giving Mary a kiss,' he replied.

'You don't expect to come back from this, do you?' Richard asked.

'I'm hoping that this isn't a trap, and we do come back. But just in case...' Michael didn't finish his sentence. He didn't have to, Richard understood.

They both walked into Mary's room. Joshua had had it painted up as a forest with fairies hidden in the trees. He had also had a special coffin made for her, made to look like a tree trunk so that she could hide inside. Michael gently lifted the top half. Mary was sound asleep inside; he leaned over and gently kissed her on the cheek and whispered something in her ear. Then Richard did the same. They both quietly left the room and returned back downstairs.

Eric then left with Joshua, they both knew where they had been and smiled.

Michael took hold off Gary and stood him up. 'Now let's get you back to your car,' he said, as he replaced the handcuffs.

Gary couldn't speak; his mind was racing once more as he was pushed into the back seat of Michael's car.

CHAPTER TWENTY

Michael and Richard arrived back in Northwood at the bungalow. They removed Gary from the car and took him into the garage, placing him into his own car.

While Richard removed his handcuffs, Michael changed. As soon as Richard moved, Michael moved around in front of him, he held Gary's gaze before he realised what was happening; this time he hadn't been expecting it. 'We found you here, and questioned you here. Do you understand?' He asked.

'Yes,' Gary answered.

'You will remember nothing about the injection. You will sit here and wait for the police to pick you up. Do you understand?'

'Yes I will wait here.'

Michael picked Gary's car keys up off the floor from where he had dropped them earlier on and threw them onto the passenger seat along with Evie's mobile phone. He then closed the car and garage door, changing back into human form as he did.

Michael then rang the police and told them where to find him. 'Let's get to the airport, and sort this Edmond Parr out,' Michael said.

By the time they arrived at the airport everyone was waiting for them.

'Are we ready to go?' Michael asked.

'It will be about five more minutes,' Joshua answered. 'George is just doing his pre-flight checks on the jet.'

'Good,' Michael answered, as he moved over towards Tony Peters.

'Why didn't you tell me sooner about this latest kidnapping?' Tony asked.

'Because we didn't know that they had gone straight away – we were busy doing something else at the time. We had left Sadie and Ann together at Richard's cottage in Shalfleet, that's where they were taken from,' he answered.

'So how do you know where they are now?' Peters asked.

'Because we received a tip off,' Michael answered.

'So what were you doing at the time?' Peters asked.

'Well that's another story,' Michael said. 'We discovered that one of the kidnappers is a vampire.'

'How did you find that out?' he exclaimed.

'When we realised that he had left a message with both Evie and Sally for us,' Michael replied.

'What do you mean, they never said anything to me about a message?' he said baffled.

'That's because it was meant for us. He placed a message with both of them, using hypnosis,' Michael answered. 'When we realised, we were able to retrieve it.'

'So what's the message?' Peters asked.

Michael walked across to Richard and retrieved the two pieces of paper. Then he handed them to the detective.

'We're all ready to go,' George said, as he approached the group.

'Shall we?' Michael said to the detective, indicating to the door of the jet.

Tony looked up, 'Oh, yes,' he said, engrossed with the message and followed Michael on board.

The jet was white and large, with twin engines. It was the largest that Joshua could buy that Bembridge airport could accommodate on its runway. The airport was only small situated between Brading and Bembridge; it was close to the coast, surrounded by fields. The airport was largely used for pleasure flights and also had its own inn.

The jet inside was very spacious. It had large cream leather seating, which could swivel around. Further down the aisle there was three-seater leather couch near to the cockpit, where there was a wide screen TV mounted onto the wall. Looking around Tony could see that there was several security cameras mounted in various places along its length.

'I'm in the wrong job,' Tony said, as he boarded the jet and looked around.

'I'm glad you like it,' Joshua said. 'Please take a seat.'

The detective took a seat, buckled up and read the message through. 'So do we know what this other thing is that's going on?' he asked.

'No, we don't yet,' Michael replied.

Eric closed the door, everyone was on board. 'Okay George,' he said, into the intercom.

They began to taxi to the runway. 'May I ask where we're going?' Tony said.

'Southampton airport, then onto the Parr manor in Bitterne,'

Michael said.

'What!' Peters exclaimed.

All the vampires looked round and the detective started to feel a little uneasy. How had he landed himself in this position? He put his head in his hands and took a deep breath, as the jet took off.

'I take it that you know him?' Michael asked.

Tony looked up, 'Oh I know him all right, he's a nasty piece of work. He loves to play the bully and I'll love to take him down. He particularly likes to treat women as his slaves, turning them into robots if you like. Let's just say that I owe that guy a lot of pain.'

'So what's your history with this man,' Michael asked.

'He's my father in law,' Peters answered.

Michael and the others were stunned. 'He's what?' Michael said.

'My father in law,' he repeated. 'Let's just say that I rescued Clair from him. She was an absolute nervous wreck. I still believe that there's a lot that she won't tell me,' he said.

'Right, so I gather that you're on our side then?' Michael asked.

'Put it this way, if you end up killing him, I didn't see anything,' he said, with venom in his voice. 'I would love to see him squirm in pain after what he's done to so many others in the past. Let him know what it feels like for a change.'

'Then I think that you'll have to leave this to us, stay here on the jet. Let us bring him to you. Then you can surprise him,' Michael said.

'Why?' he asked.

'I don't want you forgetting yourself and killing him. You have a wife and children. He isn't worth it. Let us go in, we can make him squirm,' Michael said.

'But why has he suddenly started picking on you? He normally only picks on his employees – and women of course,' Peters said.

'That we don't know yet,' Michael answered.

'It's the vampire who has tipped you off, isn't it? Let me guess, he doesn't know that he has a vampire working for him does he?' Peters said, with a laugh. 'Oh I would love to see his face when he finds out.'

Michael looked around the jet; they all had amused looks on their faces. None of them expected this reaction from the detective. They all knew that they would have to keep an eye on him. It was supposed to be them who were the bad guys. Tony obviously had a lot of bitterness for Edmond Parr.

'I take it that you've been to the Parr manor?' Michael asked.

'Yes of course, many times,' Tony answered.

'Can you give us a rough layout,' Michael asked.

'It would be my pleasure.'

'Joshua, I take it that this jet has pen and paper?' Michael asked.

'Yes, it's in the overhead locker above Mark's head. But don't ask me to get it down for you,' Joshua said.

They all laughed, including Tony. 'How do you normally cope on board?' Michael asked.

'Eric,' Joshua answered, indicating to his driver and bodyguard with a movement of his head.

Mark got up and retrieved a pen and paper. He handed it over to Peters, who immediately got to work on the drawings.

'There's a high wall around the grounds with an electric gate. I guess that this won't be a problem to you,' he said.

'No, our contact will be there to let us in,' Michael answered.

'I meant, climbing wise,' Tony added, glancing at Michael, who was smiling at him.

Martin had returned to the Parr manor and disappeared upstairs to his room, they heard the shower running.

Andrew put the kettle on. 'How does Jack in the gate house take his coffee?' he asked Stella.

'One sugar and milk, why?' she asked, as she watched him make a drink.

'I want you to take this to him and make sure that he starts to drink it,' he said, as he put a few drops of something into the cup. 'We don't want him stopping you from opening the gate do we?'

'No, we don't, do we?' she said with a smile.

Stella disappeared out of the front door with a hot cup of coffee in her hand.

George interrupted them on the speakers, 'Approaching Southampton Airport,' he announced.

Tony continued to draw plans of the Manor and its grounds.

'Do you know how many guards he has?' Eric asked.

'I only know of six,' he said. 'Gary, Martin and Andrew, are normally in the house. Jack in the gatehouse and two others in the grounds,' Tony said.

They all looked at each other. 'Well this just gets better,' Eric said.

'What does?' Tony asked, as they approached for landing.

'The fact that we have now narrowed that down to four,' Michael answered.

'How have you done that?' he asked.

'Gary will be in custody by now and Andrew is on our side, he's the vampire.'

Peters looked at him in shock, 'I've known Andrew for years, I never knew that he was a vampire,' he said, as he felt the tyres hit the tarmac. 'Oh it's a shame that I won't see Edmond's face,' he said, with a laugh once more. Then he suddenly came out of his dream. 'What do you mean Gary is in custody?' he asked.

'We found his car, in that estate. But he came back before we could contact you. We questioned him a bit then made sure that he stayed there for the police to pick him up,' Michael explained. 'This was just before we rang you. We thought that you would rather be with us to bring Edmond in.'

'That's true,' he answered. Then he seemed to remember something, 'There's a woman at the manor,' he said, 'her name's Stella. I'm guessing that she's one of his victims too, by now?'

'It's alright, we know about Stella, we'll look after her,' Michael answered, as the jet came to a stop.

They all prepared to leave the jet. 'You stay here and sit in the cockpit with George. Wait for us to return, and stay in there out of sight,' Michael said, to Peters.

'Why?' he asked.

'You want to surprise him don't you, after you've seen him suffer a bit,' Michael said, pointing to the cameras

'You mean you have something in mind?' Peters asked.

'I'm working on an idea,' Michael said, as he went to the jet's first aid box and removed a syringe. Peters watched him with a worried look on his face. Michael noticed. 'Don't worry, this isn't for you,' he said.

Richard watched his brother, wondering what he was up to.

'Joshua do you have any clean blood on board?' Michael asked.

'Yes on the top shelf of the fridge,' he answered.

Joshua quite often kept a supply of clean blood. This was blood that had been tested after harvesting from a body, to make sure that there were no impurities in it including embalming fluid. It cost a lot more, but they regarded it as being claret of high value. It was drunk on special occasions. The only thing that was higher than that was human champagne, fresh blood, straight from the artery. Only Joshua did this from time to time. He had special ladies, all volunteers who got paid a lot of money for half a pint. They not only got paid, they also found it erotic. He never forced anyone into it and he only fed from the same woman once a month. This allowed their bodies to recover.

Michael took out a bottle and filled the syringe with blood, then he filled a small phial with it, and then placed it down the side of one of the chairs. Richard smiled; he knew exactly what he was up to.

'What do you need that for?' Tony asked.

'You'll see when I get back. That is of course if get permission to pull it off,' he answered. 'But I must ask you to trust me, no matter what you see. Now sit tight and don't move that phial, we'll be back shortly.'

CHAPTER TWENTY-ONE

The three hire cars were waiting for them as they exited the terminal building. The private jet had taxied to a private part of the airport.

All three cars were BMW's 'Why does this not surprise me?' Richard said.

'Our girls will return home in nothing but the best,' Joshua said, smiling.

Stella was pacing up and down the kitchen, 'Sit down they'll be here soon,' Andrew said.

'I can't, I'm nervous, I've never met them, only read about them,' she said.

Andrew stood up and stopped her from pacing. 'Look at me, you'll be fine, they know about you, they won't hurt you,' he said.

Just then Martin came into the kitchen. He had returned about a half hour earlier. 'How come you two are still up? He asked.

'I'm waiting for Gary to get back and Stella is having sleeping problems. So we thought that we would keep each other company,' Andrew answered.

'Shouldn't those two girls be coming around by now?' he asked curiously.

Andrew looked at his watch. 'Yes, you're right, they should be, I'll go up and check', he said, as he left the kitchen.

'Do you need a hand, just in case they have?' Martin shouted after him.

'No I'll be fine,' Andrew replied.

'We wouldn't want them hiding behind the door with a vase in hand, now would be?' Martin shouted, and then laughed.

Stella just looked at him, 'What?' he asked. 'How come you can't sleep anyway?'

'I don't know, I'm wide awake,' Stella replied.

'How come you're dressed?' he asked looking at her curiously.

'I gave up in the end, so I thought that I might as well,' Stella answered, wondering if Martin was beginning to get suspicious.

Andrew went into the bedroom where the two girls were still sleeping. He took his phone out and rang Joshua. 'Where are you?' he asked.

'We're on the A3024, we'll be with you shortly, about five, ten minutes,' Joshua replied. 'How many guards are there?'

'There's only Martin and myself in the house, but there are two patrolling the perimeter. We have dealt with Jack at the gate house, he's sleeping soundly.' He replied.

'Where's Edmond?' Joshua asked.

'He went to bed, he wants me to wake him when the girls come around,' he replied. 'I'll have to wake Sadie and Ann up shortly, Martin is getting suspicious.'

'Okay, I'll let Michael know,' Joshua said, as he hung up.

Michael was driving one of the other cars, so when his phone rang he handed it over to Richard, who put in on speaker. Joshua explained what Andrew had just said. 'Okay, when we get there I want you to stop outside the gate a little further up the road. You, David and Eric go over the wall and take out the two perimeter guards. No killing, use vampire sleep, time them for two hours, we'll leave them for the police to pick up. Then join us in the house. But I want you to sneak in through the back, just in case this is a trap. That way we can cover ourselves. Andrew doesn't know how many of us are coming,' Michael explained.

'But he's trusting us with Stella when she lets you in through the gate. If it was a trap, they wouldn't hand Stella over as a hostage surely,' Joshua said.

'Not unless she's being used as a pawn and they don't care about her,' Richard answered.

'Right,' Joshua said.

'I would rather be safe than sorry,' Michael added.

Andrew walked around the bed and noticed that one of them was wearing a wedding ring. He knew then that this was Sadie and handcuffed her to the front. Holding onto the cuffs he leaned over her. 'Can you hear me, Sadie?' he asked.

'Yes,' she replied.

'I'm going to count to three. On three you will wake. You're safe with me, I'm on your side. Do you understand?' he said.

'Yes I understand,' Sadie answered.

Andrew put his other hand over her mouth just in case. He didn't want her to wake Edmond up or alert Martin downstairs. 'One, two, three wake, he said.

Sadie opened her eyes and focused onto Andrews face. He let go of the handcuffs and put his finger to his lips. 'Shhhh,' he said, 'I'm Andrew. Rescue is on its way trust me. But you must be quiet.'

Sadie nodded her head and Andrew moved his hand away from her mouth, slowly.

'What's going on?' Sadie asked.

'I'll explain in a minute, right now I need to wake Ann up. Then I'll tell you both together.' Andrew then moved to the other side of the bed. 'Ann, can you hear me?' he asked.

Sadie lay there watching him as he went through the same process as he did for her. 'You must be very quiet,' he said, to Ann as he removed his hand.

'Are you all right?' Sadie asked her.

'Yes, Where are we?' she asked Sadie.

'You're both in Southampton,' Andrew replied. 'This is the Parr manor.'

'The what?' Ann asked.

'I'm Andrew; I'm the one who kidnapped you. You've probably realised by now what I am. I was under orders from my boss, Edmond Parr. I had no idea who you were,' he said.

'Oh, so that makes it okay, does it?' Sadie said angrily.

'No, please, listen to me, we don't have much time. I had to go along with these kidnappings while I did some digging of my own. I now have the evidence. Michael knows where you are, he's almost here, and I'm helping him now. I'm the one who rang him,' he explained.

'And how do we know that this isn't a trap? Your boss hates vampires,' Sadie said.

'I'm sure that Michael will have thought about that. He'll put measures in place just in case. I know that you don't trust me right now and I don't blame you. But I'll not betray my own kind. Especially not a nest that shows so much compassion towards humans. You see, I'm also in love with a human.'

Just then he heard footsteps outside on the landing. 'Shhhh,' Andrew said, as he moved over to the door. Just before he got there it opened, it was Martin.

'Ah, they're finally awake, I see. Whatever you gave them must have been strong to last this long. Does Edmond know that they're awake yet?' he asked.

'No, he doesn't, I was just about to let him know,' Andrew said.

'I'll go and give him the good news. Why don't you take them down to his office?' Martin said. 'I know that the boss is really looking forward to meeting them.'

'What does he plan to do with us?' Ann asked, as Andrew moved them both out onto the landing.

'You don't need to know, because it's not going to happen,' he answered.

When they got to the bottom of the stairs Stella appeared, 'My phone's vibrating,' she said.

'That means that they're at the gates, Go and unlock the back door and then go out to the gates and let them in. Jack should still be asleep but watch out for the other two. Quickly before Martin and Edmond see you,' he said.

Stella disappeared towards the back of the house. Andrew took Sadie and Ann into Edmond's office.

David pulled up about a hundred yards back from the gates, while the other two cars continued. He got out of the car, along with Eric and Joshua. David and Eric jumped and landed on top of the high stone wall. Joshua stood there and looked up. 'Come on what are you waiting for? You're a vampire, you can make this easily,' Eric said.

'You're not this short, looking up at that monstrosity,' Joshua complained.

'Come on, just jump,' David said.

Joshua leapt and landed on top of the wall easily. 'You see,' Eric said, slapping him on the back.

'I can't believe I made it,' Joshua said, in disbelief.

They all sat quietly on top of the wall and turned into vampire form. With their eyes they could now see in the dark. They could see the two guards patrolling the perimeter and a female heading for the gates who they guessed   must be Stella. 'One of them is going to see her,' David said.

'Okay, David you go for that guard. Joshua you go and help Stella then get her safely into one of the cars and I'll get the other guard,' Eric said.

Stella was moving as fast as she could towards the gates. She didn't see the guard until it was too late. 'Stella what are you doing out here?' he asked.

'Hi, I was just coming to see if Jack needed another drink,' she said.

The guard looked over her shoulder to the gatehouse. 'Well it looks as if he's fallen asleep on the job,' he said.

As he moved forward, David came up behind him. Stella gasped as she saw him. She had seen Andrew change but not very often. David hit him in the face but he didn't go down. He staggered backwards and was stunned at first at what he was looking at, adrenaline coursed through him. He spun around with one leg in the air to try and knock David off his feet. But he was too fast for him and moved out of the way. This made the guard fall to the floor. David dived for him but the guard rolled to one side quickly and David missed him. Looking around quickly the guard found a tree branch, he grabbed it and jumped to his feet. David rushed towards him, putting one hand around his throat and grabbing the arm holding the tree branch at the same time with the other. He kept going until the guard found himself pinned up against a tree.

'I do hope that you were not planning to stake me with that,' he said, with his face only inches away from the guard's. The guard couldn't speak. He then began beating the guard's hand against the tree trunk until he dropped his weapon. David then held his gaze and said a few words. The guard suddenly went limp and David allowed him to fall to the grass.

Joshua grabbed Stella by the hand. 'Come on,' he said, as he dragged her towards the gates. 'Is there an entry code for these gates?' he asked, as he turned round.

Stella was looking down into the red eyes of the smallest vampire she had ever seen. 'What?' she asked.

'Hello,' he said, waving at her. 'What's the code for the gates?' he asked, once again.

Stella came to her senses and punched in the code and the gates began to open. She couldn't take her eyes off Joshua, until she heard another voice. Looking up she saw two cars enter the grounds, one of the cars stopped and someone had got out. It was Richard. 'Stella?' he asked.

'Yes,'

'Get into the car,' Richard ordered. Joshua opened the door for her and indicated with his head for her to get in. She got into the car and was now shaking.

Michael opened his window, 'Joshua, go into the guardhouse and see if you can find something to tie that guard up. Then go around the back and meet up with David and Eric,' he said.

Michael then turned around to face Stella 'Where are Andrew and the girls?' he asked her.

'They're in the office, second door on the right,' she said.

'Where's Edmond?' he asked.

'He was in his room asleep, but Martin went to wake him to let him know that the girls were awake. I think that everyone will be in the office by now,' she said, so fast and in a panic that they could barely understand what she was saying.

Richard turned round to her, 'It's okay Stella, calm down, you have no reason to fear us, but we want you to stay in the car. We promised Andrew that we would keep you safe, all right.'

'Yes,' she said, taking a deep breath.

Eric had gone after the other guard. He began stalking him from behind but the guard sensed that he was there and turned around. He lifted his arm up to throw a punch but Eric suddenly disappeared. The guard felt someone tap him on the shoulder, he turned around and found Eric stood there waving at him. 'Hi,' he said. The next thing the guard found himself on his back. Eric had spun around low to the ground with one leg out, taking out the guard's legs. Before he could close his eyes, Eric had his gaze. 'Sleep, two hours,' was all he had to say, and the guard was unconscious.

Eric then headed for the back door.

Andrew sat the girls down in two chairs. 'The cavalry is here by the way, I can hear them,' he whispered.

Martin walked into the office. 'Hello girls, had a good nap have we? I don't know what he uses but it's good stuff.'

'Martin, back off,' Andrew said.

'Only paying you a compliment,' he answered. 'Edmond won't be long, he's just putting some clothes on. He's really looking forward to meeting you two.'

'You're going to regret this,' Sadie said to him.

Martin just laughed it off. 'Where's Stella gone?' he asked, looking around the room.

'She went out to see if the boys would like a hot drink,' Andrew answered.

Just then Edmond entered the office. 'Well, we meet at last,' he said. 'Is Gary back yet?' he asked, looking around then turning to Andrew.

'No, I haven't heard him?' Andrew replied.

'That's strange. I just thought that I saw the gates open a few minutes ago, through the bedroom window,' he said thoughtfully. 'Martin, go and have a look will you,' he ordered.

Martin wasn't pleased with the order, why him, he was about to have some fun with the girls. Andrew noticed and threw him a sarcastic smile.

Edmond looked at Andrew 'Do you have our little toy?' he asked.

'No,' Andrew lied, 'Gary has it.'

'And where is he?' Edmond yelled, then stared Andrew in the eyes.

The girls jumped, but Andrew never flinched. 'I don't know? He should have been right behind Martin,' Andrew said, calmly.

'I guess we can have a little chat while we wait. Maybe even have a little fun,' Edmond said, moving towards Ann. She went to kick him but missed. 'Oh, you're going to regret that,' he said, to her.

'I don't think so,' a voice behind him said. It was Michael; he was holding Martin by the throat with one hand.

Ann breathed a sigh of relief, even though she was seeing Michael for the first time as a vampire.

Richard and Mark soon appeared behind him, also in vampire form.

'Andrew don't just stand there, do what I employ you to do!' Edmond yelled.

'No, I just quit,' he answered, whilst putting on his vampire face at the same time.

Edmonds jaw dropped, he couldn't believe what he was looking at. 'How long have you been…?' but he couldn't finish his sentence.

'All the time,' he replied, whilst taking the handcuff keys out of his pocket and walking towards Sadie and Ann.

'Where's Stella?' Edmond yelled.

'Our hostage,' Richard said, smugly

Andrew looked worriedly at Michael, who managed to give him

a slight nod without Edmond seeing him. Andrew got the message. He was up to something, so he said nothing. He bent over and unlocked Sadie and Ann's handcuffs. Then he threw a pair to Richard who put them on Martin.

Michael let go of him and he fell to his knees coughing. 'Are you both alright?' Michael asked, looking at the girls.

'Yes,' they both replied.

Richard and Michael headed straight for them and held them tight. Ann didn't know how to respond, it was the first time that he had held her in this form. She started to shake and couldn't look him in the eyes. 'It's okay, we're going to take you home,' he said gently. He hadn't realised that she was shaking because of him and not because of her ordeal.

While Edmond thought that the girls were distracting them, he made a run for it. Michael, Richard and Mark let him go. Andrew made a move to go after him but Michael put his hand up to stop him and shook his head. 'So you're Andrew,' Michael asked.

'Yes,' he replied.

'I'm Michael,' he said, 'I believe that we have a lot to discuss.'

'What about Edmond?' Andrew asked.

'Oh don't worry about him, he won't get very far, I have it covered.'

'Is Stella all right?' Andrew asked.

'Of course she is, I've kept my promise and I can see that you have kept yours,' Michael said looking down at Ann in his arms.

'Get off me you sodding hobgoblin!' Edmond was yelling as Joshua was dragging him back into the office along the floor in handcuffs. Eric and David appeared in the doorway, laughing.

'What did you just call me?' Joshua asked, bending down over him and grabbing him by the throat.

Sadie hid her face in Richard's chest and was trying not to laugh.

'I'm sorry,' Edmond squeaked.

'Yes, you definitely did have it covered,' Andrew said.

'Okay, have all the guards been sorted out?' Michael asked Eric.

'Yes they're all bundled up and are waiting for the police to pick them up,' he answered.

'Right then, let's get everyone home shall we,' Michael said, changing back into human form.

He looked down at Ann in his arms. 'I need you to travel with

208

Mark and Sadie. Richard and I need to question Andrew and Stella on the way in another car. I'm putting Edmond in the car with Eric, David and the hobgoblin,' he said. This made Ann smile. 'Will you be okay?'

'Yes, I'll just be glad to get back to the Island,' she replied.

David brought their car into the grounds. Edmond got in, handcuffed to Eric. 'Where are you taking me?' he asked.

'To where your crimes were committed,' Eric said.

Andrew joined Stella in the back seat of one of the other cars. Michael got into the passenger seat so that he could turn around and question Andrew. While Richard drove.

'Okay, what's your story?' Michael asked Andrew.

'I've worked for Edmond for a few years as one of his bodyguards. He never knew what I was. It wasn't long before I befriended Stella. I didn't like how he was treating her. After a while our relationship became strong. Being a vampire was something I had to tell her, It wouldn't have been fair on her if I had allowed our relationship to continue without her knowing,' he said.

'So you trusted her?' Michael said.

'Of course. I knew that she would either stay by my side or tell me to get lost. But what I did know was that she wouldn't tell Edmond or the others,' he replied.

Michael looked at Stella; and smiled. She was holding onto him in the back seat.

'What are you going to do to Andrew?' she asked.

'He's a vampire and he committed a crime in my territory. He will have to stand trial by our council,' Michael answered.

'But he was forced into it and he saved the lives of those girls,' Stella pleaded.

'I know that. It will all be taken into account, I can assure you,' he answered.

'We only wanted the opportunity to live together and be left alone. We both knew that Edmond would hunt us down and I feared for Stella's life, knowing that I couldn't be with her twenty-four hours a day. After doing some digging I found out about you. I was going to get in touch with you for help. Then the next thing I knew Edmond was ordering all these kidnappings. He was trying to set you up and destroy your reputation. We thought at first that he had found out about us and was doing it on purpose. But then Stella found something in his family tree,' Andrew said.

'What did you find?' Michael asked, looking at Stella.

'It will be easier if I show you,' Andrew said, going into his pocket and taking out the photocopies of Edmonds family tree and the newspaper cuttings. He then handed them over to Michael.

Michael read through the family tree and the paper cuttings. The look on Michael's face worried Richard. 'What is it?' he asked.

'Do you remember Matilda Parr?' Michael asked.

'Yes. And I remember what happened. Is she one of Edmond's ancestors?' Richard asked.

'Great, great, Grandmother,' Michael replied.

'You two knew her?' Stella asked, in shock.

'Yes, but we can assure you that it wasn't us that killed her. We were turned after we had left Ruswarp.'

'Do you know who did?' Andrew asked.

'There was only one family of vampires living in Ruswarp at the time. And I can assure you that none of them took human life,' Michael said.

'How do you know that for sure?' Andrew asked.

'Because we were supplying them. They had no reason to kill,' Richard answered.

'So Edmond must have found out that you two were from Ruswarp and thought that you were responsible,' Stella said.

'But why was he picking on Joshua?' Michael asked Richard.

'It's something that we'll have to ask him. Maybe he thinks that it was Joshua who was responsible,' he replied.

'Edmond only asked us to drop the first one at Joshua's gates. I made the decision to leave the second one there, knowing that she would be found quickly,' Andrew said.

'So Edmond was only looking for initial media impact, to test the Islanders' reaction,' Richard asked.

'Yes,' Andrew replied.

'Are you sure that he doesn't know about you two?' Michael asked.

'Yes, if he did I wouldn't be alive,' Stella said.

'Does he love you?' Michael asked.

'Yes he does. But he has a strange way of showing it. I hate him – he makes me sick. I'm black and blue,' she said clinging onto Andrew.

'What are you thinking?' Andrew asked.

'We have a private jet waiting for us at the airport. There's a police detective on board; he's hiding in the cockpit. I believe that he would like to hear a full confession from Edmond. I do know that he would also like to see him suffer for personal reasons,' Michael said.

'Why, what's Edmond done to him?' Andrew asked, puzzled.

'I can't tell you that, it's something personal,' Michael replied.

'I wouldn't mind seeing him suffer either after what he's put me through,' Stella said.

'But if you torture him into a confession, the detective won't be able to use it in court,' Andrew said.

'We all know that. But it's about time someone gave him a taste of his own medicine, Michael said.

'Oh, I would pay to see that,' Stella said.

'Unfortunately, you won't see it,' Michael said.

'What do you mean?' Andrew asked, now on guard.

'Let me tell you what I have in mind,' Michael said, with a smile.

CHAPTER TWENTY TWO

They arrived at the airport. Joshua had phoned ahead to George, to let him know. He had also asked for Tony Peters to clear it with airport security, as they would be coming through with someone in handcuffs.

They all walked out onto the tarmac towards the jet. Michael took Sadie and Ann over to one side. 'Something is going to happen on board. I will need both of you to trust me. I know that you know me, Sadie, and you know how Richard and I work together. It's you that I'm worried about, Ann, Please trust me,' he said, taking hold of her hand and leading her on board.

When she was on board, she looked around, 'Does this belong to Joshua?' she asked open mouthed.

'Yes,' Michael answered.

Edmond was led on board by Eric. 'Whose wallet did all this come from?' he asked, looking around.

'The smallest!' Joshua shouted at him, still annoyed at what he had called him.

When they were all settled, Michael went through to the cockpit to let George know that they were ready. Before he started up the engines George pressed a few buttons and Tony found himself looking at a TV monitor on which he could see the jet's cabin.

The detective smiled at Michael. 'I take it that you didn't have any problems,' he asked.

'No, none at all,' Michael answered. 'Enjoy the show and remember you can trust us.' He returned to his seat as the aircraft taxied to the runway, they joined a queue and waited. He leaned forward and glared at Edmond. 'So what's all this about?' he asked.

'What are you talking about?' Edmond asked.

'Oh come on, you were caught red handed. You kidnapped our girls,' Michael said, as the jet moved forward in the queue.

'I didn't know that I had a vampire working for me. I got up this evening and he had brought his dinner home,' he said' sarcastically

'Ha Ha,' Michael laughed. 'Nice try, now try again - and this time tell me the truth,' Michael said, with force.

The jet began to move once more, this time onto the runway.

'I'm not responsible for kidnapping those two,' he continued to lie.

'We know what this is about Mr Parr,' Michael said, taking out the pieces of paper that Andrew had given him.

'What's that?' Edmond asked.

'Your family tree!' Michael exclaimed.

'Where did you get that from?' he asked.

'I found it,' Andrew said.

Stella stayed quiet, but began to get a little nervous.

'What have you been doing snooping in my office!' Edmond yelled.

'Gathering information,' Andrew answered.

'So what does that prove?' he asked.

The jet set off down the runway picking up speed as it went, then took off.

'It tells us that you're great, great, grandmother Matilda Eliza Parr was supposedly killed by a vampire,' Michael stated, mainly for the cameras.

'So what? That was a long time ago. I have a business to run. I haven't got time to be running backwards and forwards taking revenge on every vampire,' Edmond said, getting anxious.

'No you didn't, you got someone else to do that for you, didn't you?' Michael said.

'This is stupid, it's him you should be questioning, not me,' he said, indicating towards Andrew.

'I've already done that,' Michael replied. 'Now tell me why you did it.'

Edmond now chose to be silent.

'Richard,' Michael said, indicating to Stella with his head.

Richard moved around to the back of Stella's seat. He looked over her shoulder at Edmond and turned into vampire form.

Ann looked across at Sadie, who very slightly shook her head at her to tell her not to interfere.

'I know what you do for a living, you wouldn't hurt her,' Edmond said, in a smug voice.

'Oh, so now you admit to doing some research on us do you. Now why would you do that I wonder?' Michael said, as he turned towards Richard and nodded.

Richard put his hand under Stella's chin and turned her head to one side, then leaned over her neck moving her hair out of the way as he did so.

'Are you sure, we won't?' Michael asked.

Edmond looked towards Andrew. 'Don't look at me, you just accused me of kidnapping without orders,' Andrew said.

'Okay!' Edmond yelled.

Michael put his hand up to stop Richard.

'I found out that Matilda lived in Ruswarp when she was killed. Then I discovered that you had also come from Ruswarp,' Edmond said nervously.

'Go on,' Michael said.

'You are living on that Island freely; as if you've done nothing in your past to be ashamed off. You've killed innocent human beings,' Edmond shouted.

Michael remained calm. He could see Ann out of the corner of his eye; she had tears in her eyes. 'If you had done your homework properly, you would have discovered that both Richard and myself were turned after we had left Ruswarp behind,' Michael said. 'We are not responsible for the death of Matilda. In fact, because we're doctors we were able to feed ourselves through bloodletting, so we didn't have to kill.'

'Okay I did the research, but I don't know anything about the kidnappings,' Edmond said.

'You know what; I'm beginning to get a little tired of this. All I want you to do is admit to the kidnappings. Because we all know that you gave the orders. Then I want you to tell us what your objective was.' Michael said, as he stood up and walked towards Richard and Stella at the front of the jet.

Richard stood Stella up in front of Michael. He held her with one arm around her neck. Ann began to panic and was about to stand up but Sadie put her hand on hers and stopped her. Ann looked round at her. Sadie was shaking her head, 'trust them,' she mouthed.

When Michael turned round he was a vampire once more. 'Last chance Edmond, what's it going to be? I thought that you loved her,' he said.

'You're bluffing. You're a doctor first, even I know that,' Edmond said.

'So why accuse us of taking human life then?' Michael asked. 'Which is it Edmond, are you going to take the risk? Did you order the kidnapping of Evie Martin?'

Edmond just looked around the jet, as if asking for help. Then he saw Michael turn back towards Stella.

Stella looked into Michael's eyes, and tears began to stream down her face. He gently wiped them away with his fingers and whispered something to her. Edmond couldn't see what he was doing as Michael was blocking his view. Richard let go and gave Stella over to Michael. 'Okay,' he whispered to Richard, 'I've got her.'

Edmond looked on in horror, as Michael was about to bite down on Stella's neck.

'No!' he cried, as he watched Michael. 'I did give the order, to kidnap Evie Martin. But Gary had chosen her, he'd been following several girls around to find the ideal victim.'

Michael lifted his head, but didn't turn around. He could feel Stella shaking and her knees were beginning to buckle. Michael was gently massaging the back of Stella's neck to try and get her to relax a little. 'Who did you have kidnapped next?' he asked.

'I didn't know her name, Gary and Andrew went out scouting and told me when they had found someone,' Edmond said.

'Is this true?' Michael asked, turning his head slightly to look at Andrew.

'Yes, but as I told you before, I had no choice. The only thing that I could do at the time was go along with it, but make sure that they survived,' Andrew answered.

'It's true; there was nothing that Andrew could do about it.' Stella managed to whisper in Michael's ear.

'So they chose the victims, but it was you who ultimately gave the orders?' Michael asked now looking round at Edmond, whilst still holding Stella up.

'Yes I did,' he replied.

'But you knew who these two were, didn't you?' he asked indicating to Sadie and Ann.

'No, they chose them again,' Edmond lied.

Michael looked at Andrew who shook his head. 'He told us which address to go to,' he replied.

'So you're lying to me again?' Michael said, as he turned back to Stella.

Edmond saw Stella's face change as Michael lowered his head to her neck.

'No!' he yelled, but it was too late. The blood was already running. After a while Michael lifted his head back up and moved so that he could look Stella in the eyes. Then he slowly let her body slide down to the floor. When Michael moved Edmond could see the blood all over her neck and it was now running down her shoulder. The same blood that Michael was now licking from his lips. Richard handed him a cloth to wipe it from his chin and cheeks.

Ann was now crying openly and Sadie was trying to comfort her. All Michael wanted to do was go to her himself, but he couldn't.

Sadie stared at Richard he seemed to tell her something with his eyes. She then turned and held Ann close to her and whispered something into her ear. She looked up and stared at Stella's body then at Michael.

'Do you want to be next, Mr Parr?' he asked.

'No,' he croaked. 'I did know who they were. I had them followed by Martin.'

'And who are they, Edmond? Michael asked. 'I want you to tell me,' he said, glaring at him.

'Sadie Moon and Ann Grayson,' he replied.

'Why have you been doing all of this?' he asked as he came to sit back down.

'To discredit you, I wanted you to suffer for Matilda's death,' Edmond said, nearly in tears.

'I told you, that wasn't us,' Michael said.

'That doesn't matter, you're all just as bad.'

'Richard and I can honestly say that we have never taken a human life,' Michael said.

'Don't you mean that you have never taken a human life until now,' Edmond said, pointing to Stella's body with his cuffed hands.

Michael ignored him. 'Now *you* know what it feels like to be hurt for a change. I've heard that you have hurt a lot of people. Including your own daughter.'

'What! Where did you hear that from?' Edmond said, in disbelief.

'Oh' I have contacts,' he said. 'Well did you?'

'Yes, I did, but I regret it,' Edmond said, sadly.

'Oh, I don't think so, a leopard doesn't change its spots.' Michael said.

Just then the door to the cockpit opened slightly. Richard had his back to it he turned around and listened. Leaving the door open Richard began to walk towards Michael, stepping over Stella as he did so. Michael turned towards his brother, 'It's okay, I heard,' he said.

'Have you heard enough?' Michael shouted back towards the cockpit.

'Yes, I've everything I need,' someone said, as they came out of the cockpit.

Edmond stared at his son in law.

'I do believe that you know detective Tony Peters, your son in law,' Michael said.

'That's how you knew about Clair,' Edmond said, angrily.

'Yes, we've had a good chat,' Michael answered.

Ann stared at Michael- she couldn't believe that he had a detective in the cockpit all this time.

'Edmond Parr, I am arresting you for the kidnapping, unlawful imprisonment and plotting to murder Evie Martin, Sally Knox, Sadie Moon and Ann Grayson. I am also arresting you for the physical and mental abuse of Clair Peters and Stella Bexley.'

'What! Are you blind? Look behind you. There's a body on the floor. Stella's dead!' Edmond yelled. 'He killed her,' indicating towards Michael.

Tony Peters looked towards Stella. Richard had knelt down on the floor behind her with a towel and a bottle of water in his hands. He lifted her head up and began to wipe the blood from her neck and nodded towards Michael.

'Stella, can you hear me,' Michael asked.

'Yes, I can hear you,' she answered.

Edmond then realised that he had been tricked into a confession.

'I'm going to count to three, on three you will wake,' Michael continued.

Ann looked at him with her mouth wide open. She couldn't believe that it was all a stunt to get Edmond to confess. Michael saw her staring at him out of the corner of his eye and turned around to face her. Holding up an empty vial, still slightly stained with blood.

'One, two, three, wake,' he said, whilst smiling at Ann.

Stella woke up and looked up at Richard. 'Are you okay?' he asked her.

'Yes, did we get what we needed?' she asked.

'Yes we did, thank you Stella, you did well,' the detective said. 'You're a good actress. You can watch the recording later if you like.'

Stella couldn't tell him that she had been terrified.

Richard helped her up into the seat next to Andrew. He took a wipe from Richard and began helping her to clean up, and gave her a hug.

'You bit!'

'Now, Now,' Tony said, stopping Edmond before he could say it. 'Ladies present.'

'But none of that will hold up in court,' Edmond said, with a laugh.

'No, but I've enough witnesses anyway and it certainly gave a lot of us the satisfaction of seeing you in pain for a change,' Peters said.

'And you have this,' Andrew said, throwing the bag with the fork in to Tony. 'Edmond had it made by someone especially for the job. You should have another witness there if you can track him down.'

'I have another question though,' Michael said, 'What's with the tattoos?

'I can answer that one,' Andrew interrupted. 'It was all a question of authority. Showing us that he owned us, or so he thought.

'Well he got that one wrong, didn't he,' Richard said.

'Approaching Bembridge airport,' George said, over the intercom.

Michael moved across to Ann and took her by the hand. 'Come with me,' he said to her. Ann stood up and allowed Michael to lead her into the cockpit; he sat her down in the co-pilots seat and fastened her seatbelt. He then knelt down beside her. 'I know that all this isn't easy for you. It's a completely different world, and serious decisions would have to be made. If you want to walk away from me, I'll understand. I love you enough to let you go. Although I hope that you won't,' he said. 'I would never hurt you.' Ann's eyes filled up once more, and she opened her mouth to speak. Michael put a finger to her lips and stopped her.

'If you ever need me, I will always be here for you. But if you were to decide to stay by my side, you must understand that from time to time, you may see things that you don't want to. There are things that Richard and I have to do. Not only to safeguard the nest, but also to keep the humans safe on this Island. Don't always believe what your eyes are seeing. Sadie has gradually learned that one. Stella was in on that, by the way. I wouldn't have done it otherwise.' Ann glanced out of the cockpit window just as they landed back at Bembridge Airport.

'I will gladly tell you anything that you want to know, I won't keep any secrets from you. Now I'll leave you alone, and give you time to think,' he said, standing back up to leave.

'Michael,' Ann said, as she unbuckled her seatbelt and stood up. 'I don't need to think about it,' she continued, as she looked into his eyes. 'I've already made my decision.' She reached up and put her arms around him and kissed him passionately on the lips, Michael responded.

George looked up from his seat and smiled. 'I don't normally allow that behaviour in my cockpit,' he said.

'Sorry George, but I needed to talk to Ann, somewhere fairly private,' Michael answered.

They both left the cockpit hand in hand. 'Are you two alright?' Richard asked.

'Yes, of course we are,' Michael answered.

'Thank goodness for that, because he would have been a grumpy vampire without you,' Richard said, with a smile, looking at Ann. 'Once we've got Andrew's trial out of the way, can we get back to normal?' he said, giving Michael a slap on the back.

'I'm afraid that you can't yet,' Andrew said, as the jet taxied to a stop.

'Why, What is it?' Michael asked, puzzled.

'You know I said that I couldn't stop the kidnappings until I'd found out what else was going on,' Andrew said.

'Yes, but I thought that you meant the family tree,' Michael replied.

'No, I wish it was. This is a bit more serious than that.'

'Go on,' Richard said.

'I discovered that Edmond is being used for smuggling purposes. I also know for a fact that he doesn't know,' Andrew replied, looking at Edmond.

'What sort of smuggling?' Tony asked.

'It's coming in from Varna,' Andrew said, as he looked back towards Michael.

'What?' Michael said, slowly looking round in Richards direction.

'Where's the shipment originating from?' Richard asked.

'Bistrita,' Andrew answered.

'Please tell me that you're joking,' Michael said.

'No, I'm not,' he answered.

'What are you talking about? I'm importing herbs and spices from Varna. What's the panic?' Edmond interrupted.

'I have seen the first shipment Edmond and believe me it's more than herbs and spices,' Andrew answered. 'You don't even bother to check your shipments do you?'

'What's coming in?' Edmond demanded.

'Put it this way, Bistrita is the home of the vampire,' Andrew said. 'It is believed to be the region from where the Count came from.'

'This is ridiculous, are you trying to say that I've been smuggling vampires into the country?' Edmond said, going red with rage.

'I know you have, because I saw the last shipment and set fire to it,' Andrew said.

'That was you? ' Edmond shouted.

'Yes, I traced the shipment to a warehouse that you were renting in Southampton.'

Andrew turned to face Michael. I opened one of the crates; there were herbs and spices on top. But it had a false bottom I lifted it to find a male vampire sleeping underneath.'

'How many did you import, Edmond?' Michael asked, seething.

'Eleven crates,' he answered.

'And you destroyed them?' Richard asked, looking at Andrew.

'There were only eight when I got there,' he answered.

Michael and Richard looked towards detective Peters. 'This is all we need,' Richard said.

The detective got hold of Edmond by the throat, 'Where were those crates heading for?' he demanded.

'The Island,' he replied.

'What! Your own daughter and grandchildren live on the Island. How can you put them into such danger?' The detective shouted at his father in law.

'I didn't know, did I,' Edmond replied.

'Whereabouts?' he asked, still holding him by the neck.

'I have the address of the warehouse here,' Andrew interrupted, getting his notes out of his pocket. 'They are supposed to have been transferred to a warehouse in Newport. We also found three addresses on the Island rented by Mr Weston.'

Tony let go of Edmond's neck.

'Who's Mr Weston?' Michael asked.

'He's the one I've been shipping the herbs and spices for,'

Edmond answered. 'But why would he want to import vampires into the country?' he said, puzzled.

'He's probably being paid for it. Giving vampires sanctuary on the Island,' Richard said.

'Where do we find this Mr Weston?' Tony asked, Edmond.

'Patrick Weston contacts me, he lives somewhere in London,' he answered.

'You mean you don't even know?' Michael asked.

'Wait a minute,' Richard said, 'I know that name. Didn't Matilda Parr have a stepbrother called Patrick Weston?' he said glancing at Michael.

Suddenly the penny dropped. 'It can't be him surely?' Michael said.

'Why not? It's possible that he was turned as well. It may even have been him who killed Matilda,' Richard said, looking at Edmond.

'Oh come on, are you trying to tell me that I spent two days in London entertaining a vampire?' Edmond shouted. 'Not to mention that he may even be the one who killed my ancestor,' he went on.

'Ironic, isn't it,' Michael said, looking at him.

Ann let go of Michael's hand and sat back down again putting her head in her hands. She couldn't believe that all this wasn't over yet.

'I can't believe it. Why did he choose my shipping company to do this?' Edmond said, with his eyes blazing.

'He may be your great, great, uncle,' Joshua replied. 'Maybe he wanted to put a bit of business your way,' he said sarcastically.

'Yes, he wasn't to know that you had a hatred for them,' Tony said.

'How many crates are there altogether?' Michael asked.

'There's another fourteen due in next week,' Edmond answered.

'What's the name of the container ship that's its due in on?' Michael asked.

'Parr's Diamond,' he replied.

'When?'

'Six days,'

'Okay, We'll go and take a look at the warehouse first. If they're not there, we'll split up into three groups and go to each of the houses. See what we can find, use your discretion,' Michael instructed.

Joshua moved towards the computer mounted into the table in front of the TV screen and switched it on.

'Andrew, give me those addresses,' he said, 'I'll look them up.' Joshua's screen saver appeared on the TV.

'That's him!' exclaimed Edmond, pointing towards the screen.

They all looked round to see who he was pointing at.

'Who?' Richard asked.

'Patrick Weston,' he replied.

'This isn't Patrick Weston,' Joshua said, with a slight laugh.

'I spent a full two day's with him and I'm telling you that that is Patrick Weston.'

'This is a copy of an old oil painting that I have hung in the front lounge of the castle.' Joshua said.

'We knew Patrick Weston, this isn't him,' Michael said.

'I'm telling you, that is the guy,' Edmond insisted.

They looked at each other in disbelief.

'Who is it?' Ann asked.

'This is an oil painting of The Prince of Wallachia. More commonly known as Vlad Dracula,' Michael replied, stunned. 'Maybe our Mr Weston, isn't Mr Weston after all?'